FOLKLORIST

The Tommy Histon Story

Andy Bracken

A Morning Brake Book

Copyright © 2020 Andy Bracken

All rights reserved.

ISBN: 9798615107092

First Edition.

All art and design by Steve Hallam.

For C & R. With love.

And Steve Hallam.

x

For more information on Tommy Histon and his music, please visit-

https://chemisetterecords.wixsite.com/mysite

or search 'Chemisette Records'.

Facebook - come join us at 'Tommy Histon Appreciation Society'.

FOLKLORIST: THE TOMMY HISTON STORY

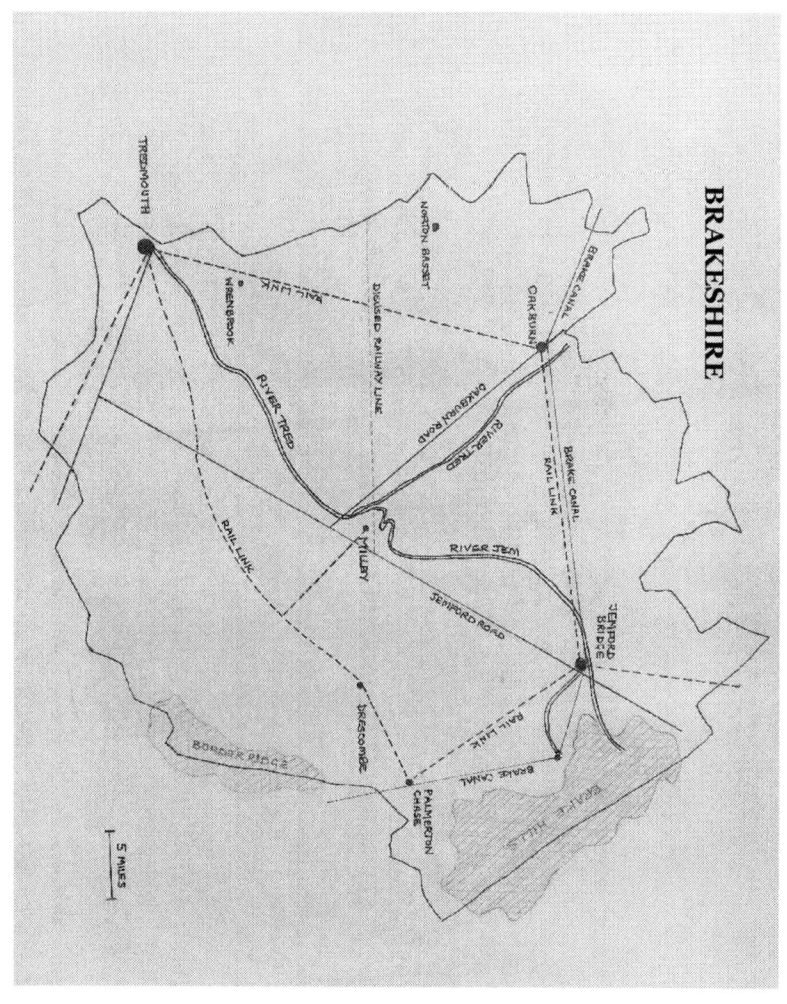

Tommy Histon Discography.

1947 - 6" booth recorded 78rpm acetate - 'Looking Down At The Stars'

1947 - 6" booth recorded 78rpm acetate - 'Slitherin''

1949 - 10" 78rpm - 'Cookin' On Embers/ Wipe Your Chin (Or You Ain't Comin' In)' - Tommy 'The Piston' Histon (Rovertone ROT-10-4)

1949 - LP - 'Three Minute Hero' - Tommy 'The Piston' Histon (Rovertone ROT-12-3)

1953 - LP - 'Track Back And Trail On' (Jury Duty JUD-00001)

1954 - LP - 'Coda' (Jury Duty JUD-00006)

1964 - LP (acetate only, 2 copies known to exist) - 'Kimono For Kip' (Chemisette CH-770001)

1974 - LP - 'Kimono For Kip - Acoustic Demos' (Salvage Yard SALLY14)

1975 - LP - 'Tommy Histon Live In The UK' (Salvage Yard SALLY19) Live performance recorded by Patrick 'Oggy' Ogden at the Baker's Dozen public house, Norton Basset, Saturday April 18th, 1964. Billed as 'Pat & Tom'

1980 - LP - 'Three Minute Hero Plus' - Tommy 'The Piston' Histon (Salvage Yard SALLY40) Contains all of

Histon's Rovertone recordings plus the two booth recorded songs)

1982 - LP - 'Track Back And Trail On' (Salvage Yard SALLY52) Reissue on red vinyl

1982 - LP - 'Coda' (Salvage Yard SALLY53) Reissue on blue vinyl

1984 - 5 X LP - '20th Anniversary Box' (Salvage Yard SALLYB64) Disc one - all Rovertone recordings plus the booth tracks. Disc 2 - 'Track Back And Trail On'. Disc 3 - 'Coda'. Disc 4 - 'Pat & Tom Live Tracks'. Disc 5 - 'Kimono For Kip' Acoustic Demos. This was every known recording by Tommy at the time.

1987 - CD - 'Kimono For Kip - Acoustic Demos' (Salvage Yard SALLYCD72)

1993 - CD - 'The Complete UK Recordings Remastered' (Salvage Yard SALLYCD88) Combines the Acoustic Demos with the Live material on one CD, with improved audio quality. The booklet features sleeve notes by Patrick Ogden, recording engineer and producer at Chemisette Studio, Norton Basset, Brakeshire.

1994 to 2020 - numerous CD reissues

2020 - LP - 'Kimono For Kip' * (Chemisette CH-770001)

* Tommy Histon Appreciation Society (THAS) notes on 'Kimono For Kip'.

'Kimono For Kip' was set to be Histon's fourth studio album. It was recorded in England in March-April of 1964.

For fifty-five years, it was believed destroyed by Histon himself, prior to taking his own life at Cemlyn Bay, Anglesey. Only acoustic demos of the songs remained.

Until, in 2019, Brakeshire native, Danny Goods, discovered two acetate copies of the finished album in his deceased father's record collection.

For his seven week stay in Britain, Tommy arrived with a guitar, a violin, one change of clothes, a sum of cash, two cartons of cigarettes, and a bottle of bourbon.

He didn't bring his medication.

Rather, he brought with him his genius.

Oh, and a bit of trouble.

Prologue.

i.

I'm not sure we choose our heroes. I think, perhaps, they choose us.

Tommy Histon is my hero.

He shouldn't be, because I'm a post-punk kid. Age dictates that, and I was born in 1968. You can do the maths.

They were tribal times, when I was young, and I dipped a toe in all the puddles music rained down on me; whether that be 2-Tone, the enduring punk scene, Quadrophenia inspired modness, the synth based sound that would dominate the early-eighties, and, yes, even ELO lushness and a bit of Heavy Metal.

The truth was, and still is, that I believe a good song to be a good song, irrespective of genre.

Tribes, though. It was important in those days to pick a camp and wear the uniform.

That could take the form of a green parka and a penchant for low-powered motorcycles, or a love of denim and high-powered motorcycles.

I never much cared for motorcycles, and was a firm believer that denim should only be worn on one's lower limbs. Completely over. No shorts.

My niche was narrowing, thanks to my standard of dress.

The thing with it all was, I had a secret!

My father had been buying records since the late-fifties. His taste changed after he settled down with the woman who would become my mother.

As a result, he didn't give much of a toss about anything predating Bob Dylan and Cat Stevens.

He didn't give a toss about anything after Bob and Cat, either. Or even Bob and Cat after 1972.

The point is, dad gave me his old singles when I was a nipper.

I was a closeted hep-cat rockabilly rebel from head to toe!

Indeed, I dared to wear florescent socks with my school shoes, and knew both the melody and harmony to quite a few Everly Brothers' songs.

Staggeringly, I even owned a bootlace tie!

I wore this gear outside of the house once or twice in 1980, and received 'a kicking' for my daring.

Thereafter, my wardrobe was re-closeted, and I'd only acknowledge a liking for Matchbox, Jets and Crazy Cavan & The Rhythm Rockers when completely safe from observation or eavesdropping.

For the outside-my-bedroom-door world, come christmas 1980, I got a pair of ten-hole black DM's. Ten-holes were the most mum could find in Brakeshire. I paired them off with anything utterly nondescript.

But the whole rockabilly thing wouldn't go away. It kept cropping up, and even became quite popular. In the charts popular, through the Stray Cats. I also discovered Cramps, Meteors, Polecats, Restless, and others.

Even Queen's 'Crazy Little Thing Called Love' had a certain appeal.

I knew a bloke called Mick. He lived in Tredmouth, wore a drape jacket in a bright blue hue when he went out at night, matching drainpipe trousers, and proper blue suede brothel creepers. Yes, he had a bootlace tie.

When I say I knew him, I mean that I was conditioned to keep an eye open for him, and run the fuck away if I ever saw him heading in my direction.

Nobody messed with Mick. Well, the skinheads outside the chip shop did, but he got them all after he'd regained full use of his leg.

In Tredmouth, there are now a number of men approaching sixty, with misspelt words clumsily tattooed on their knuckles. They have strange scars on their bodies that resemble a motorbike chain.

One day, when I was fifteen, Mick nodded a greeting at me as I tried to hide from him in the city centre.

"Alright?" he said first.

"Alright?" I replied, because it was okay to do that seeing how he'd said it first.

"What shit you got there?" he asked me, pointing at my record bag.

"A record," I answered, and probably stammered.

"I know that, you thick cunt. You're walking out of a fucking record shop, carrying a fucking record shop bag, containing something the size of a fucking record. What fucking record?"

"Oh, n-n-n-nothing, really."

"N-n-n-nothing? N-n-n-never heard of them."

I showed him what was in the bag.

He looked at me funny. I mean, he looked at me funnier than how he usually looked at me.

To this day, I remember the records in that bag. One was The Meteors 'Wreckin' Crew', and the other was 'The Young Eddie Cochran' on RockStar Records.

"You're not such a cunt, are you?" he asked me.

"I probably am, to be honest."

"Do you know where I live?"

I nodded that I did. Everyone knew where Mick lived. Back when I'd had a paper round, I'd walk a quarter mile out of my way to avoid his house.

"Good. Be round mine on Thursday at eight. Are you allowed out that late?"

Again, I nodded, and twisted my face in a way that implied I was allowed out much later than that. At least nine. Maybe half-nine, while the nights were still light.

"See you then, then," he added, handing back my records with more care than I'd ever witnessed him handle anything. He didn't even handle his girlfriend that carefully.

"Yep, see you Mick," I dared to say, and walked off with a cocky little skip in my step.

"Oi!" I heard him call out.

"Yeah?" I asked, turning and walking backwards.

"You're still a cunt."

That was how Mick and I became friends.

ii.

Mick's house was a shit-hole.

It struck me as strange, as he took such great care with his personal appearance.

He gave me a beer, and I sat on the floor because he only had one chair. He sat in that.

The only other furniture in the room was a side unit with his stereo system on it. All other space was taken up by vinyl records and cassette tapes.

He gave me two cassettes as well as the beer.

"I made you those. Figured you might like some of it," he growled as he gently handed them to me.

"Cheers, Mick. That's very kind of you."

"Alright, don't start fucking crying!"

To occupy my face, I sat reading the track listings, and had heard of next-to-nothing on them.

"Know any of the tracks?" he asked me.

"One or two," I lied, because I wanted him to like and approve of me.

"Which ones?"

Shit.

Thankfully, the door rattled.

It was Mick's girlfriend, Trudy. She had a friend with her. Her name was Debbie. I really liked Debbie, and I knew that within one whole second of vaguely seeing her.

She was female.

She sat down next to me on the floor, as Trudy dropped into Mick's lap. They started snogging.

"Stick one of the tapes on," Mick said to me when he came up for air.

That was the setting of the coolest night of my life up to that point. There aren't many that have eclipsed it in the nigh on forty years since, to be fair.

I drank beers, listened to brilliant music, and, between tracks, listened to Mick and Trudy swapping spit.

It was also the night I fell in love.

"Know this one?" he'd ask me every so often.

"No, who is it?"

"Guana Batz. Brand new, this. Just got it."

"Cool," I informed him, because it bloody well was.

Thirty minutes on, and I got up to turn the tape over.

Debbie had definitely moved a little closer to my spot on the floor by the time I returned.

"Know this one?"

"No, who is it?"

"Ivan. It's The Crickets, really."

"Buddy Holly?"

"See, I told you he wasn't a complete twat," he informed the girls, before going back to Trudy's mouth.

I glanced over and saw that he had his hand up her jumper and was massaging her chest.

Finally, Debbie spoke. "How old are you?"

"Seventeen," I lied. I'd never lied so much in my life.

"Bollocks," Mick called over, "he's only about fucking twelve."

"How old are you?" I asked Debbie, aware that we were really making headway, and that it would quite possibly lead to something.

"Nineteen."

"Wow," I said, because I was wowed. It never occurred to me that she might lie about her age, just as I had.

When I next arose to eject and insert, I became aware that it was probably after nine o'clock. And it was a school night.

On my return, and seeing how Debbie lay down and rested her head on my lap, I also knew that I didn't give a shit.

I can still smell her, all these years on. It wasn't anything specific, but a cocktail of all her aromas - hairspray, make-up, perfume, soap, toothpaste, washing detergent, fabric conditioner, and god only knows what else. Oh, and the mouldy smell from Mick's carpet.

She stretched up to me, and I had to arch my neck over to find her lips. Her tongue filled my mouth. She tasted so fresh.

I had a bit of a cold, and leaning forward blocked my nostrils. I didn't breathe for as long as I could, but in the end had to pull away and snatch a breath. I would have gladly died for her, but thought it a little melodramatic. Besides, I had no desire to lie face down in that carpet, breathing or not.

She sat upright, and snogging was easier like that. As was locating her breasts.

Debbie wasn't so keen on that activity, and pushed my hand away.

"Tape's finished," Mick pointed out.

"I know," I replied, because it was obvious by the lack of music, and a click.

"I'll do it," Debbie volunteered, and I shall adore her for my whole life for that kind and considerate act.

Mick never got to see that I was nursing an erection.

Debbie returned, but I was suddenly not quite so interested.

Something else was grabbing my attention, and it was aural.

It was so compelling, that when Debbie stuck her tongue in my ear, I actually pulled slightly away.

"Who's this, Mick?" I called over.

He cocked his head and listened for about two seconds.

"Tommy Histon," came the answer.

"Tommy who?"

"No, you twat. That was much later!"

"What?"

"'Pinball Wizard' and all that shit."

I was astonished to learn that my erection had almost completely waned. Because I could, I stood up and retrieved the cassette case.

"Tommy Histon - 'Wipe Your Chin (Or You Ain't Comin' In)'," I read aloud.

"Good, innit?" Mick said. He, like I, had momentarily given up on his girl to listen.

We did that thing I've observed many people do since. We both stared at the source of the music, and focused on the spools rotating at different speeds, as tape wound from one to the other.

And we simply listened.

Just as we did for the next track, Tommy's 'Cookin' On Embers'.

"He was the first, by my reckoning," Mick said to me.

"The first what?"

"The first rockabilly artist. 1949, he did this. Elvis was still sucking on his mummy's tit back then." Trudy pouted at that turn of phrase, and tucked herself back in.

Approximately four minutes was the combined run time of those two songs. By the end, I was bitten and smitten. I'd fallen in love. I would never be the same again.

"What else did he do, Mick?"

"Those two tracks are from a 78 he did. Later that year, he did an LP. It's fucking blindingly good."

"I wonder if he's still playing music," I mused.

"I doubt it. He died in '64."

I felt sad learning that. Why? I'd only just heard of him.

"What of?"

"Killed himself. He was here, you know?" Mick said. He seemed sad, too.

"What, in your house?"

"No, you wanker! He was in Brakeshire. He recorded his last album here. What a dippy prick you are."

"Can you do me a tape of all you have by him, Mick, please?"

"I'll lend you the first album, as long as you look after it. I wouldn't bother with the next two."

"Why not?"

"Hippy shit, mate."

"Oh, right. Yeah, fuck them," I concurred.

"Yeah!"

Leaving a gap of about two seconds, I added, "that said, I wouldn't mind giving them a listen."

"Haven't got 'em. Wouldn't waste my money on those," he declared, and went back to Trudy.

Once the tape was finished, Mick dug out his reissue of 'Three Minute Hero', and handed it to me.

He and Trudy went up to his bedroom.

I sat and read the sleeve notes on the album.

Debbie took my hand from the record and placed it inside her blouse. She'd unbuttoned it herself.

"I don't like his music that much," Debbie stated from her position close to my side.

And I knew we'd never be wholly compatible, Debbie and I. It was a shame, because, apart from that, she was pretty bloody perfect.

Still, it didn't stop me having sex with her on Mick's mouldy carpet.

Thus, an obsession was born.

iii.

The next day, I ran out of school as soon as classes ended, and ordered 'Track Back And Trail On' and 'Coda' on reissue coloured vinyl. They'd be there the following week.

I had no idea how I was going to pay for them.

By the grace of god, that weekend was the one my parents chose to announce they were separating. Dad gave me a fiver by way of severance.

Mum matched it by way of buying my vote.

Tommy Histon became synonymous with all of it. He was with me through those turbulent times.

I fell hopelessly for all three of his available albums, in contrast to Mick.

It was the diversity that appealed to me. Just as Mick desired Tommy to stay the same, and repeat the formula of his debut, I was drawn to the changes and shifts in direction.

Only later, once I became more musically astute, did I truly recognise how different to his contemporaries Histon was. And it opened so many doors musically, as I sought out anything to which a comparison was drawn.

He'd spent time right here in Brakeshire, where I was from!

And yes, there was a morbid fascination that came with knowing he was dead at thirty-two, and had taken his own life.

I began drawing parallels between my life and his, so far as I knew it at the time. His mother died when he was fifteen. My parents had split when I was fifteen. Ergo, we were practically related!

Music magazines were purchased and devoured, looking for any reference to Tommy Histon.

Small-ads of records for sale were pored over, to the extent that my eyes became trained in picking out the T and H constituting his initials.

I've hated Tony Hadley ever since.

Record fairs were attended at least once a month. Relatively vast distances would be travelled to enable this. Some would even be in neighbouring counties.

Boxes of shite were thumbed through, in the pathetic and forlorn hope of unearthing a Tommy album that had been overlooked and misfiled in the 'pound each or three for a fiver' section.

On all other weekends, car boot sales were suffered, often in atrocious weather. I saw it as my mission to save that elusive Tommy Histon record from the elements and cow shit peppering a field in rural Brakeshire.

Over time, I amassed a sizable collection of reissued vinyl albums and CDs. They were the same fifty-something known recordings packaged in different ways.

Very occasionally, I'd hear about a copy of an original selling for more money than I could ever imagine having at my disposal. A house was a more realistic ambition for me.

Indeed, as of this year 2020, I have a house. I have no Histon originals.

On a business trip to New York in the late-nineties, I mapped out every record shop within the entire city limits, and hit them all in five days. If I was going to find a Jury Duty original, it would surely be there in the nation of his birth.

It was horrific to learn that most Americans had never heard of Tommy Histon. He was better known in England than his own bloody country!

Still, I consoled myself with the undeniable fact that it increased the likelihood of my finding his releases at a very reasonable price. Christ, I'd get three, flog two, and remove any concern stemming from my non-attendance at the conference I was actually there for.

I flew home empty-handed, and with a lot of reading to do on the flight.

Around the same time, I bumped in to Mick. More accurately, he bumped in to me, having misjudged the kerb as he pulled over in his work van one Friday night just before the new millennium.

"Wanker!" was all I heard, but it was said in a friendly manner.

"Alright, Mick?"

"Want a lift? Get in, you cock!"

Despite him being eight years my senior, we'd remained friends for the intervening sixteen years. His hair was still styled in the same heavily greased duck's arse way, but there was a lot less of it. It meant it had to come a long way forward before it could be swept back. As a result, it flipped up vertically before flopping back down every time the van hit a bump.

The van vividly reminded me of his old house. It was the carpet, I think.

It conjured up Debbie.

I was thirty-one. Still single.

Tommy was dead by thirty-two. It played on my mind a lot at the time, the numbers.

"What are you doing on February 29th?" Mick wanted to know.

"I have absolutely no idea," I replied, "are you going to propose?"

"Well, I do have a fucking proposition, as it happens."

"You might want to rephrase that."

Mick dramatically announced, "it's a Tuesday, and we're going to Cheshire!"

"Why?"

He winked at me, gave his little Elvis-Cliff lip-lift, and said, "to attend the first meeting of the newly formed Tommy Histon Appreciation Society."

"Seriously?" I said, and found myself beaming with joy.

"Uh-huh," he said, and revved the van's engine as we sat at traffic lights.

"Superb!"

"I know. I'm going to wear my studded belt with the heavy Gene Vincent buckle on."

"Why?"

"Be some hippies there. Crack a few skulls!"

And, skull cracking aside, that is precisely what we did.

iv.

It began with a hundred and eleven members, twenty-one of which attended the first meeting. One guy came from Germany with his wife. Another came from France without his.

It was the diversity that struck me. Age ranged from a girl in her teens, to a couple of men in their seventies. One lady looked to be early-sixties. Mick spotted the tattoo on her upper arm. It was Histon's Gretsch guitar, with Tommy's signature spelt out by the cord beneath.

Three-quarters men, one-quarter women. A man of colour. Rockers, hippies, bearded chin-stroking folkies. Importantly, though, music fans one and all.

Well, aside from one gentleman, who left after a few minutes having mistakenly attended in the belief it was The Thomas Hardy Society.

Members, we were informed, were located all over the world. There was already talk of a sister organisation to be based in Japan. It was provisionally titled the International Tommy Histon Appreciation Society (ITHAS).

Plans were presented. Membership drives. Fifteen quid a year. A six-monthly newsletter. Organised trips every spring, to the studio house in Norton Basset where he recorded his final album. A similar pilgrimage to Cemlyn Bay in Anglesey on the anniversary of Histon's death. A proposed trip to America. Coach hire. Visiting known addresses associated with Tommy, as part of a grand tour. A show of hands. Gauge interest levels.

A website on this new internet thing. A chance to interact with other Histon fans all over the planet. A suggestion to raise funds for a permanent memorial on the headland close to where he took his own life.

Mick sat jigging his leg. He was eager to get to the pub. We'd booked a B&B for the night, and he was keen to get on with it. It was a rare night away from Trudy and his two kids. That may have been his motivation for proposing a vote be taken very rapidly on anything discussed, and his voting yes to everything.

Me? I'd found my place in the world, and was in no hurry to leave.

I was meeting all the people I would consider friends in my life. It began with Mick, I suppose, and is ongoing. All because of music. Specifically, Tommy Histon.

They filled the pews on my side, those people, when I finally married in 2003. They saved my parents from having to sit next to each other.

Mick was my best man, because I didn't know a better one. He wore a purple drape jacket.

They were there congratulating me a year later when I became a father. My son is called Thomas. He goes by Thom.

He's not had much to do with me since the divorce. It was the THAS members who helped me through that. And Mick, of course; always Mick.

John Greene, whose idea THAS was, was unanimously voted Chairman. Twenty years on, and he remains such.

A bloke called Phil owned a printing business, and volunteered to produce newsletters as well as membership cards.

The tattooed lady, Angela, was a recently retired accountant, and proposed herself as Treasurer/ Secretary. She was a wonderful, kind woman. Mick and I attended her funeral in 2018.

Most of the proposals put forward in that first meeting were achieved. The coach tour of America never came off, but individual members have visited sites associated with Tommy, and sent pictures and stories of their experiences.

The fight for a memorial on Cemlyn Bay continues, but a commemorative plaque is on display at Norton Basset, funded jointly by the THAS and Brakeshire County Council.

Mick became Angela's minder whenever we attended functions. She was a rock'n'roller like him, and I have so many happy images of them jiving together to Tommy's earlier tracks.

When she died, Mick was as devastated as I've ever seen him. As a result, he's drifted away from THAS a little in the couple of years since.

At that time, THAS had just over three-hundred members globally, though many more people visited the website daily. The number had fallen from a two-thousand-plus highpoint achieved in 2005, and had declined year-on-year since then.

The truth was, people who were drawn to Tommy were getting older.

They were dying.

It proved harder to fill a twice-yearly newsletter, as no new information came out. It became a re-hashing of old stories for the new members. Except that there weren't many new members.

In 2013, it went annual. A year later, it ceased being printed, and became more of a check-in email.

The organised pilgrimages stopped in 2014. Individual members now embark on that trip alone or in small groups.

I'd visited Anglesey with Mick and his family in 1997. I still close my eyes and hear the rain on the caravan roof. We found the headland, but there was no information available as to the exact location at that time.

We'd always planned to return, just the two of us, but life got in the way.

Nobody had the time.

There were simply too many other distractions. Too much other music. Too many things to do.

Fifty-five years after his death, Tommy Histon was finally dying.

v.

In 2019, everything went ballistic.
John Greene sent the email to members.
'Kimono For Kip' had been discovered.
Nobody could believe it, I didn't believe it.
We'd heard rumours of such a thing before, but it usually turned out to be the demos, cover-versions, or, on one occasion, 'Kimono My House' by Sparks.
Mick said, "it's bollocks, you mark my words. Some tosser trying to get famous and make some money."
But no. Someone heard a track, played down the phone. The backstory was plausible - how it came to be in Bill Goods' possession.
The 1964 Grand National explanation tied in to a lot of the lyrical content.
This was different. This wasn't like before.
John Greene posted a picture of the acetate on the THAS website. It looked and felt right.
For the first time since 1985, when I'd been seventeen and had bought the five album set released on Salvage Yard as a christmas present to myself from my dad, I was set to hear music by Tommy Histon that I'd never heard before.
Thirty-five years I'd waited!
I never thought it would happen.
Tommy was back in the news. Interest levels rose. Stories appeared on websites that bore no correlation to anything I'd ever read about Histon's life.
Then came the notebook!
John Greene emailed the members again. Tommy's handwritten notebook had been discovered in Anglesey.

Some bloke called Ivan Roberts had found it at Cemlyn Bay on the morning of May 2nd, 1964.

The day Tommy Histon died.

It was coming up for auction.

I donated. We all did, the remaining members of THAS. The notebook was purchased for far too much money.

Mick said, "it's all bollocks. Any cunt could have written it." Still, he donated to the cause.

John Greene contacted me. He knew I'd written a couple of novels. He was one of the few people who had read them.

He'd photocopy the notebook carefully, and send me the facsimile. How would I feel about writing a book?

"What book?" I asked.

"The Tommy Histon Story. You're the most qualified person I know."

Less than a second later, I was on-board.

If this is to be the only other book I write in my life, it shall be enough. I shall be sated.

We chatted about what form the book should take. John suggested it be Tommy's story lifted directly from his notebook, as well as any interviews and other material that I could find corroborating his account.

In addition, John thought it might be of interest to add my own story pertaining to Tommy.

There wouldn't be many pictures in it, as Tommy had a habit of sending other people's images rather than his own. There's a lot of confusion about all of that.

I called round Mick's to tell him the news.

Trudy was just leaving the house. She looked a mess.

Mick had suffered a stroke.

"How bad?"

"Very."

Fuck it.

Introduction.

i.

**An Introduction To Tommy Histon.
By Mark Baird, Arts Correspondent.
First published in the Brakeshire Gazette, April 1964.**

It's an imposing property, standing on several acres a mile or so west of Norton Basset. All about is vibrantly green, as I drive along the gravel road.

Winding down the window, I draw in the fresh clean air on this perky April day. It's cold, but at least the rain has abated, and the sun seems brighter than ever as it laps up the beads of moisture sitting on every blade of grass.

Prior to last week, I confess that I'd never heard the name Tommy Histon.

Since then, I've heard stories about him. He has a unique way of greeting people, I'm told, and can be an awkward character.

Some of what he might have to say, I was further warned, may not make total sense.

I'm nervous, and I don't mind admitting it.

Local businessman, Barry Baxter, set up the interview. He dropped two long-playing albums into the office so that I could be somewhat prepared.

They are astonishing records, both. Only after the second play did I learn they were recorded ten years ago. That knowledge made them even more remarkable.

A man comes out to greet me as I park up. He's Tommy, I know. The long hair speaks of musician.

He's not a big chap, but, even so, he appears to tread so lightly. He's knotted and wiry; svelte and graceful; to an extent that he almost floats over the ground.

Up close, a scar on his face is arresting. It runs from beside his right eye and arcs down to the point of his chin. I get a sense his wavy dark hair is grown long to cast a shadow and somewhat mask it.

Tanned of face, with dark eyes that never settle but never stop looking at me, he is, I must state, a handsome man.

"Hey, buddy," he greets me with a broad smile, "you must be Mark from the paper."

"That's me," I reply, and shake the strong hand he proffers.

The greeting is not at all unique.

He keeps moving, never letting his feet remain still. Wheeling, he invites me to follow him inside the house.

"Whiskey?" he offers.

It's half past nine in the morning.

"No, thank you."

"Coffee?" he adds. His voice is soft and breathy. The calmness of his speech is at odds with his quite jittery mannerisms.

"Please, if it's no trouble."

"No trouble at all."

He goes off to make it.

I'm in the ante-room. The control room, I will learn, is through the wooden door on my left. A heavy white door then leads to the recording studio.

Baxter owns the property. He owns a lot of property around west Brakeshire. His business partner, Alistair McIntyre, or Ally Mac, is from the east of the county.

They are the two men instrumental in bringing Theodore Thomas Marshall Histon over to Britain from America.

He's here to record the debut release for their new label, Chemisette Records.

Chemisette is the logical next move for both. Ally Mac is in the jukebox business in Brakeshire, and Baxter owns the county's premier nightspots, regularly putting on live musical performances.

McIntyre heard something in the two albums Baxter left with me. He hopes Histon's sound will translate well into Britain's burgeoning music scene. I can report that I think it will.

The recording facility I stand in was recently constructed, the house adapted to accommodate musicians, recording staff, et al, and an outbuilding was turned into a vinyl pressing plant.

The idea is, a recording can be laid down, pressed to record, and in the shops and jukeboxes of Brakeshire in the space of a few hours.

Histon returns with two large mugs of coffee.

"Instant granules," he informs me, "that's why I was so quick."

Through another door, to what I imagine was once an office or library, I'm invited to take a seat at a small round glass table.

I decline a cigarette. Tommy has one, sliding it up from the packet with his thumb before drawing it clear with his lips. A match is removed and drawn along the box one-handed. He didn't even need to put his coffee down.

As I sit here typing this up the day after all I describe, I can inform you that I've spent quite a lot of time attempting and failing to light a cigarette one-handed. And I don't actually smoke.

"What's a basset, Mark?" he asks me brightly.

"Oh, as in Norton Basset?"

"Yeah. Other than a dog, I'm not familiar with the word."

"It's a low-lying rocky outcrop. It's up at the lake."

"I was there this very morning!" he beams. "I go there for a walk once we finish recording."

"A basset sits on the edge of a stratum of rock layers."

"I saw the rock layers up there. So that rise on the east side is the basset?"

"That's right."

"That's one weird looking lake, I gotta tell you. Ain't never seen anything like that on this planet before. And I've travelled a bit around the States and elsewhere, you know?"

"It's man-made. They used to quarry the quartzy stone."

"It was made by man! Well, that's good. Figured it wasn't anything natural to this earth," he says, and stares through his smoke at me.

I have a sense he's attempting to read me. I'm unsure why.

"So, I'm familiar with your two long-playing records," I begin.

He ignores me, and asks, "what did they use the quartz for?"

"Erm, I'm not sure. It was merely decorative, I think. You see it around the county. It gets polished and used for tabletops and coasters and things. Some people have it on their floors."

"Three," he says.

"Sorry?"

"Why, what have you done?"

"You said three. Three what?" I clarify.

"I made three long-playing records. I'm working on my fourth."

"Oh. I only had access to two of them."

"What do you mean, you only had access to two? Because the other one wasn't broadcast over the airwaves, so you couldn't pick it up?"

He seems more wired all of a sudden.

"No. Not at all. It's just that Mr Baxter only brought two to the office. I think that was all Mr McIntyre owned."

"Ally gave you the records?"

"That's right."

"Well, why didn't you say? If Ally knows you, then you're all good by me, Mark!"

I feel as though I'm the one being interviewed.

"Where were you born?" I ask, trying to get some control.

"Virginia."

"When was that?"

"1932, I think."

"You think?"

"My momma wasn't exactly sure. See, we lived in the hills in a very remote way. Dates weren't too precise in that environment."

"I see. Were you always musical?"

"I've been hearing tunes in my head for as long as I can remember. I recorded my first record when I was sixteen."

"That's the one I wasn't aware of. What was it like?"

"Well, people said later on that it was rock'n'roll, but I just recorded tunes I wrote. They were folk songs that I played fast, you know? They called me The Piston on account of it!"

"Who taught you to play guitar?"

"Have you ever been bitten by a snake?"

"Erm, no. Why?"

"I could always play guitar, once I shown the beginnings of it. I see things like that in my head, and my hands contain the patterns, I guess. A lot of things are like that in life."

"You asked about a snake. Why?"

"I was just curious."

"Okay. Erm, so, you're self-taught, would you say?"

"I guess."

"I was listening to your two albums on Jury Duty. They were released in 1953 and 1954, I read, but they sound like more modern records."

"What are you writing?"

"Your answers."

"Where are you from?"

"Erm, Tredmouth. I was born there."

Histon then snatches my notebook and uses swear words I'm not permitted to quote in the Brakeshire Gazette. The gist of it being that he wishes to know what language I'm using.

"It's shorthand," I plead.

Tommy Histon thinks my hands look a normal length.

What follows is written purely from memory. He refused to let me have my pencil back.

"What guitar do you play?" I ask, keen to move on.

"A Gretsch archtop. I bought it in '53. You wanna see it?"

"Yes, if you don't mind."

"Come on through to the studio. I'll show you around."

Following him, I ask about his albums. "Why didn't more copies sell, do you think?"

"One day I believe they will," he states amiably, "when the world's ready."

I recall the slogan on the sleeve: 'The sounds of tomorrow available today! You be the judge - it's the Jury Duty way!'

"How do you like England?" I ask, as he hands me his guitar.

"It's swell. I like the people very much. Do you play?"

"A little, but I'm left-handed."

"You didn't write with your left hand." The atmosphere becomes tense again.

"No, I was forced to write with my right at school."

I'm not convinced he entirely believes what I just said.

"Did humans do that to you?"

"Erm, yes. It was the teachers at school. They were kind of human."

"Why'd they do that?"

I'm supposed to be interviewing him.

"Because thirty years ago, that's what they did. It wasn't acceptable to write left-handed."

"Did they put anything in your brain?"

"Erm, no. They tied my hand behind my back."

Tommy Histon uses an expletive, and ruefully shakes his head.

I wonder if it's all diversionary.

Handing his guitar back to him, he sits on a stool and begins to play.

This is the moment I truly meet Tommy Histon.

Instantly, he settles and is completely focused and reasoned. All of the twitchiness is gone, and an easygoing fluidity enters his body and mind.

It is, I must report, a privilege to sit in this intimate setting and listen to the man play his music. As it takes place, I'm acutely aware that it shall remain with me for the rest of my life.

Indeed, a few minutes ago, I wished to conclude and leave. Now, I desire to stay for days.

His first Jury Duty album is titled 'Track Back And Trail On'.

Histon explains it to me as he picks and jangles on his guitar, effortlessly switching to a folk song on which the tune he plays is based. He shows me how he skewed and stretched it, and took it into the future, before adding his own lyrics that paint beautiful landscapes.

His second, 'Coda', is more humanised. If the first is landscapes, the follow-up is portraits.

All of the tunes are original, he informs me, and is a concept album with strange classical overtures courtesy of a lone violin. On it, Histon delivers vignettes of characters based on people he'd known during his life. He was just twenty-two when he recorded it.

Tommy thought he was finished with the recording business after 'Coda'. He is immensely grateful to Chemisette for offering him another chance.

Just as I am immensely grateful to have had the honour of meeting and listening to a true craftsman; a master of his art.

We all laud Vincent Van Gogh these days. Yet, he was criticised and ridiculed during most of his thirty-seven years of life. That was when he wasn't being resoundingly ignored.

I wonder if Tommy is correct: Perhaps the world isn't ready for him. Yet.

Well, this writer can't help but think that his time isn't far away.

For the perfect introduction to Tommy Histon, simply listen to his music. Because, I believe, that is the essence of the man.

"How would you describe your new album?" I ask him as he concludes a beautiful acoustic performance of one of the tracks from it.

"Well, whereas 'Coda' was a concept of sorts, each track remained individual and stand-alone. It was a dozen different stories. My new record is going to have more of a concept running throughout, if that makes any sense. I desire for it to tell a story from beginning to end."

"What is the story?"

"Well, that's for people to work out. My hope is that everyone who listens will take something different away from it."

When the time arrives for me to depart, Tommy accompanies me to my car. The jitteriness is back as he bids me farewell.

He is a man who has to keep moving. Only his music absorbs him to such an extent, that it physically settles him.

Well, it absorbed and settled me, too.

I tell him, "it's been a pleasure," because it has.

I never did get my pencil back.

ii.

Ivan Roberts' 2019 statement sent to John Greene, THAS Chairman.
Note: Ivan was born on the day Histon released his first record in 1949.

I was fifteen, and I took the dog for a walk on the island of Anglesey, North Wales, where I've lived all my life. So far!

It was a bright but blustery morning, and I recall it clearly. It was Saturday May 2nd, 1964.

The sun was just up. I hadn't slept much. Perhaps a couple of hours, like.

My girlfriend had broken up with me the evening before, so I walked for longer than usual. I ended up following the north coast eastwards to Cemlyn Bay.

As I stood on the tip of the headland, I looked over at the construction work taking place a mile or two away. It was where the Wylfa nuclear power station was to be. In the spring of 1964, work had just begun. It wouldn't be up and running for years.

It would bring work, the power station, I thought to myself.

In that moment, I decided to leave school. See, now, my girlfriend had left me for an older lad - a young man with a car, a job, and money in his pocket.

The sodden dog ran towards me from the pebbly shoreline. It held something in its mouth. A bird, I thought. Perhaps a fish, as I saw silver glint in the morning sun.

She was a spaniel - made to retrieve. A water dog - always in the sea, she was.

An adder, came my next notion. They nested on the headland. One had to be careful. As the dog came closer, I relaxed when I saw it was too square to be a snake.

Treasure!

Treasure would be good. I'd get her back then, my girlfriend. She'd want me if I had a few quid in my pocket. And I could stay on at school. I'd get a flashy car, and have a driver until I passed my test. A chauffeur! That was my daft dream.

No. It wasn't precious metal, I saw, as I bent and took the package from the dog's soft mouth - a mouth that could carry a raw egg and not break the shell.

It was something wrapped in tinfoil. Was it somebody's lunch? I brushed the sand from it, squatted on a large grey rock, and opened it up.

A thick book was all it contained. Not a printed book, but an exercise book. My thumb flicked along the edge of the leaves, and I saw that each page was filled with blue handwriting.

The hand was neat and uniform, the lines level and unslanting despite it not being ruled. It wasn't joined-up, the writing, each letter meticulously printed as a separate character. Like type.

There were no corrections, I observed, knowing that my own such work would be littered with crossings-out and alterations. Afterthoughts and regrets, I suppose.

Turning to the front and last pages, I saw no name. There was no hint as to the author, beyond that day's date, and the initials TTMH.

After one final glance out to sea, I drew a long breath, tucked the book and foil into my pocket, and headed off towards home.

The dog wouldn't come. She barked and stood her ground.

She was a good dog, and required no lead. A whistle would bring her to heel. My father had trained her for the gun.

'Swut,' I whistled, and she ran along the faintly worn path in the grass on the higher ground.

Well now, had I heeded the dog, she would have led me down on to the beach. There I would have discovered a guitar case and crash helmet also wrapped in foil.

Somebody else would stumble across those later that day.

Had I just hopped down, I might have saved a man's life. That's the thought that's haunted me for all these years.

Because a day after that, on May 3rd, a body was found in the water off the north coast.

Well, that was a bloody shock to learn. I asked everyone I knew what they could tell me about it. Most knew even less than I did.

It was all very hush-hush, as I recall. The nuclear people didn't want any bad publicity, or anything that might hold up the construction, like.

I knew I should come forward and hand in the book. It would have been simple enough, to tell what happened, and explain how I came to have it in my possession.

But I was afraid. That's the reality of it.

I heard that the body had been stabbed through the ear before slipping into the water. I didn't want to get mixed up in that.

I read bits of the book over the years. I saw the name in the text. Sometimes Tommy. Other times Histon. Still, I kept quiet about it. After all, the man was dead, so there was nothing could change that simple fact.

Time passed, as it has to, and people forgot. That's what they do. At least, most forgot. Occasionally, I'd hear about it - 'the fellow who stabbed himself through the ear up at Cemlyn Bay. A musician. An American. Wonder what brought him here?'

Now, see, a few weeks back, two chaps from Somerset came to the bay to pay their respects. Loads used to come. Busloads at one time. But not so many in recent years, mind.

Anyway, they stayed in a lovely, friendly, clean and respectable guest house near Tregele, called 'G&Ts', and got chatting to their landlady one evening. Her name is Gwenda. Her maiden name was Roberts. She's my daughter, see.

On mentioning Tommy Histon as the reason for their visit, Gwenda told them that she, 'knew a bit about all that business.'

Now, I'd recently moved from the home I inherited from my parents - the house where Gwenda, and myself before her, were born and had grown up. It was down the road a bit, over towards Carmel Head.

See, I'm seventy now, and can't manage the old place any more, not with my arthritis. So I agreed to move to a nice little flat with a smashing view over in Red Wharf Bay. More sheltered there, and a bit of a social life since my wife died. Cancer. She was only sixty-eight. Never smoked in her life, I tell you! Nor a drink. Never touched a drop of anything, except tea and water. And perhaps an orange juice on a special occasion. I blame the power station, I do!

Anyway, once I was out, Gwenda set about clearing the house ready for sale.

That was a bloody job, that was! A hundred years of junk, mostly. Some bits were worth a few quid. She found a nice clock, she did, with a mouse carved on to it. Oak, I think it was. From Yorkshire, the man at the auction house said. My father got it because of Middle Mouse being just off the coast. It's an island, you know? As are West and East Mouse. Middle Mouse sits between them.

The clock was packed for shipping, the auctioneer keen not to damage it during transit. As a result, according to Gwenda, she wrapped it in an old blanket that wasn't even fit for charity, there were so many bloody holes in it!

So, to stop it sliding around in the wooden box, she suggested he wedge some books all around it, this auctioneer chap. They were only old paperbacks, gone yellow and falling apart, half of them were. The damp got into everything in that old house, see. Including me!

Anyway, as it turned out, one of the books was the one the dog found on the beach that day in '64.

So, my Gwenda told the gentlemen from Somerset about it coming up for auction. In Llandudno, of all places. Very excited, they were!

They took off like a bloody shot, according to my Gwenda! They didn't even stay for the night they'd paid for, and Gwenda had the bacon in, and whatnot, for their breakfasts.

Well, that's it, really. Nothing more to tell.

Funny, I suppose. They reckon this book will sell for a lot more than the clock it was protecting!

Gwenda's very happy about it.

This is Tommy Histon's story:

PART ONE: Three Minute Hero

1.

My mother was a teacher. My father was unknown to me. If this was another person's story, that may well be how it would begin.

In my case, my mother was 'the' teacher. Singular. That was her role in the hill-dwelling community into which I was born. One member of the collective was my father, but I was unaware of which one for my formative years.

Money played little part in that society. Even so, it didn't stop greed.

Greed will manifest itself in many different ways, I have come to learn.

A contributing part was played by every individual member of the community, whether that be carpentry, hunting, fishing, cooking, medicine, washing, tool making, or whatever. Oh, and preaching. There was a lot of fuckin' preaching.

My role was to gather wood and build the fires. That began when I was probably five or six.

The rest of my memory is filled with learning from my teacher mother.

I owe her everything.

She taught me to read and write, having learned from her mother, and so on. That was how everything came to be known. But, because our home was the only one with books in other than the bible, I guess you could say I had a broader education than my peers.

She also taught me to play the guitar. The basics, I mean. The rest of it I taught myself, by watching the men strum and sing around the fire, or by playing around until something sounded right to me.

As a rule, children were done with education by the time they hit twelve or so, but Momma made me carry on for all the time I was with her.

I wish it had been longer.

Through her, my life was shaped. The guitar tutoring and her singing led to my love of music. And I am capable, sitting here on an airplane en route to England, of writing my story because of her lessons.

Why am I writing my story? Because I have a feeling my life is about to change, and I have a desire to capture and remember it.

Snow was on the ground when I was born. That was all Momma knew of the day. But, up in the hills in the mid-eastern States, that could have been any time from November through March. Even earlier and later in certain years.

That said, she calculated that I probably made an appearance in February time.

To fly to England, I required a passport with a date of birth on it. I opted for February 29th, so I wouldn't have to think about where and how I was born too often.

Initially, she was too ill to care for me. I never tasted her milk.

She was laid up through much of the summer of '31. Around July time, she'd been bitten by a copperhead snake. She hadn't spotted it lurking beneath a fallen tree trunk as she'd walked to the stream.

It was an old snake that bit her, so he held back somewhat on his venom. A young one will give you all he's got, and make himself vulnerable. She was lucky in that regard, I guess.

I always think of a 'he' when I depict that reptile in my mind. A short, fat male striking out and injecting where he shouldn't.

Momma told me it hurt like hell, and the Medical Man made a poultice of something green and leafy. She was laid up for a long time, because lying down is best when a snake bites you. How long, she couldn't say, as that venom worked its way through and out of her body.

I've hated snakes since the day I was born, I reckon.

But I'm not afraid of the fuckers. They know to stay away from me.

Perhaps they smell the lingering poison in me. As a result, do they know that I've built up an immunity to their venom? Shit, I could probably bite them and they'd be the ones to die. The fuckers.

Because it is in me, that poison. It coursed through me as I lay forming in Momma's belly that summer of '31.

The Medical Man thought that was why I am the way I am. Well, that, and because I was born premature. But he was wrong. All the doctors were wrong over the years.

As I tried to explain many times - how can it be wrong to know things other people don't? How can it be wrong to see further than other people can?

That's the only difference between me and anyone else. I'm simply more able to see what's going to happen.

That, I reckon, is my legacy from that snake juice.

But that ability of mine led to a lot of my problems.

And, of course, it was what attracted the attention of the aliens.

The fuckers.

2.

Collecting firewood became my job because the snakes would slither away whenever I approached.

It suited me. It was something I could do alone. It wasn't a group activity. I didn't have to be part of a team.

I've always been a loner, I guess. A one-on-one is about as much of a crowd as I can stomach for any length of time.

When I was eight or nine or so, I was sat round the fire one evening. It was cold, the days not far off as short as they ever get.

Stories were being told, as was the way of things. They were the old stories that were told and retold over and over, so that they might live on.

For the first time, I was asked to tell a tale to the gathered souls. I felt so proud. It made me feel akin to the men of the group.

I closed my eyes, and began to speak about what I saw there on the insides of my eyelids and in my mind's eye.

It was fantastical, the rich-green island in the ocean and the people in their spotless white clothing!

Had I opened my eyes, I might have seen concerned expressions. It wasn't one of the stories we told. It must be one I got from those damned books!

The truth is, I was too self-conscious to open my eyes, so I carried on, describing all that I could see. I chanted it, almost singing it.

The planes came from out of the sun, fire-spitting from their noses, and bombs dropping from their bellies that blew the white-clothed folk to chunks of bloody raw meat.

I told them of the man I saw losing his head, but taking half a stride before falling to the ground. Dead. And of the ships in the harbour, holes being blasted into their decks, smoke billowing and fire...

They stopped me telling my story. The little ones were getting upset.

I opened my eyes and saw Momma looking at me curiously. It wasn't bad, that look she gave me. She was smiling all the while in a knowing way.

A short time on, and three of the brethren went away to fight in the Second World War following the attack on Pearl Harbor.

A newspaper came by the camp somehow or other. That was how we knew about America joining the war. Momma would read it to folk who wanted to know anything of the outside world.

A week or so later, after the news became old, it was given to me to start fires with.

My eyes took in the front page, and the picture thereon. And I knew it was part of the story I'd seen on the insides of my eyelids.

Until then, I reasoned that I'd read about that in one of the books in our home. Or in a magazine I'd flicked through on one of my rare trips to a town to trade a little for supplies.

Well, things dawned on me at that moment. I understood that I could see into the future a long way off.

Other folk could see a little way. They could anticipate the weather and which path a rabbit might take, and know where to set a snare.

Something also told me that it was dangerous, having that gift of mine. So I went off by myself one night. I climbed up to the highest point on the neighbouring hill, just as the sun was setting.

There was a shelf of rock up there, where one could sit comfortably and watch the stars and the moon on a clear night - nothing above, and seemingly nothing below on that overhanging ledge.

Each star was a sun, I knew, much like our own sun. And try as I might, I could never count them all. And each sun, as with ours, had planets spinning and rotating around it.

I understood, as I looked up - I was certain that there had to be life up there somewhere. It was the law of averages.

The more I stared up, lying on the cold stone, so I saw things differently. What if each star was a hole in the sky that allowed light to shine through? And if that were true, how many millions of times must the sky have been breached to produce so many pricks of light?

Or perhaps each sun was, in fact, our sun, at different times, both past and future. A million depictions of our habitat, and all of the places in which it has settled. Did it start afresh every time, and get to begin again?

I drew in a breath, as deep as I could, and held it. I willed myself to know. I wanted to understand how it all worked.

Because everything exists for a reason. Nothing is random. There is a pattern and a purpose to every seemingly arbitrary act.

One thing leads to another, to another, and to another. Endlessly.

Soon enough, I knew, I would have nowhere to call home, as the life I was born to would dissolve, and the people in our community would go off to settle in towns elsewhere.

A storm of change was coming!

I saw it all in the time it takes to hold one single breath. For, as that breath was exhausted, and I sought another, everything disappeared.

A darkness came over me. I was slithering off the rock on my belly, and wriggling my way through the grasses and ferns that covered the ground up on the hill.

Coldness filled me - my blood running chill - my body kinking and flexing as it propelled me along that bitter earth, my tongue tasting the air...

Awaking, I found myself in my bedding in our home. It was light, a dull flat light, the sun not quite peering over the edge of the planet to fire up the cabin.

In my head was a song that I didn't know before that morning.

And Momma whimpered in her sleep across the room, as I struggled to recall what was real, and what was a dream.

3.

As soon as I picked up a guitar, I could play the song I woke up knowing. My fingers went straight to where they should go without need of practice. The muscles in my hands already contained the memory of it.

It was within me.

A guitar came to me from one of the men who went away to fight. It was a loan. But I wound up keeping it, because he wound up dead.

It wasn't a very good guitar, being home-made. The wood was too thick, so the vibrations got lost in it. The strings were worn and harsh metal, picked up years before somehow or other.

It required re-tuning every couple of minutes. That's half the reason my early songs never lasted too long.

The neck was too wide and the wood too soft, so that the strings cut grooves into the frets.

But, after learning to play on that guitar, I could always play any other.

On account of all the things in my head, I kept all of my thoughts and songs to myself.

Whenever I played and sang my own compositions, I'd do it far away from the settlement where I couldn't be overheard.

Most times, that led me back to the rocky outcrop atop the next hill in the range.

As a result, I learned to sing softly so my voice blended in with the wind playing on the foliage and shrubbery about.

I am a good mimic, I consider, and not necessarily a good singer. I could impersonate all the men around the fire, and all of nature pretty well.

My voice broke early, when I was around thirteen. I sang myself hoarse one night, and when I woke up the next day, it was broken and deeper.

My voice breaking didn't much affect my singing.

If I ever sang in a group around the fire, I'd stick to the familiar songs everyone knew. There was one thing I did notice. When others sang, people would join in, either to bolster the melody or harmonise around it. When I sang, everybody listened attentively.

Momma told me I had the voice of an angel.

Girls began paying me attention. I'd matured earlier than the other boys of my age, but girls were a year or two ahead in that regard.

Janie was my first girlfriend. I was thirteen - she a year older. Her father was one of the ones that went away to fight in the war. He never came back. Momma helped them out as best she could, by looking after her little brothers and sisters. That was how Janie and I got to know one another in 1945.

She'd like me to sing and play guitar for her. As I'd do so, Janie would squirm on the rock or ground, massaging her legs together tight. Her face would flush, her breathing deepen, and little squelches would emit from her crotch. I was naive, and didn't understand that she was pleasuring herself right there in front of me. I just figured it was her way of dancing with herself.

During the summertime, she led me out into the woods.

Janie asked to see my snake.

I didn't know what that meant, and wondered how much she knew about Momma and I.

"It's okay," she told me tersely, making me feel stupid, "the Medical Man told me that it's a perfectly natural thing. In fact, he told me that it's vital to use what we have down there. If we don't, it'll be of no use. The Medical Man said that my hole would heal up. In boys, your snake will come away, and go off into the grass never to return!"

Now, Momma had told me certain things as part of my education, and I knew that wasn't right. The books tended to agree with my mother. But, Janie was older than me, and more worldly-wise, I suppose you might say.

I didn't resist her as she picked at the buttons on my dungarees, and let them fall to the floor.

Being summertime, I had nothing on beneath.

Thinking back on it, I suppose she was very selfish in her desires. Her own gratification was all that mattered, until, as she termed it, "it was time for the snake to spit."

Being my first time, I didn't last long, and ejaculated on to the ground. I hadn't meant to, but couldn't contain myself.

Janie was angry at me for that. She began to frantically comb the earth, scooping my semen into her hand.

Once she had it all, she deposited it in her mouth and swallowed it, along with bits of dirt and leaf.

She instructed me, "it's vital all of it goes in me. Never spill a drop, or the tiny little baby snakes will take over the world.

"Tommy, are you listening? You must never make the snake spit when you are alone. Do you understand? There are too many snakes in the world already. Look at what happened to your momma!"

I asked her, "how do you know all of this?"

"It's a secret," she whispered.

"I won't tell," I assured her.

"Well, okay then. The Medical Man showed me. He has a device which magnifies things thousands of times bigger than they are to the eye," she reported with wide-eyed awe.

"He showed you the snakes?"

She nodded her head emphatically.

"He made his snake spit, and showed me what it looked like through the device. I saw the snakes wriggling, trying to escape."

I looked at her dubiously, but she was oblivious to it.

She added, "the only other places it's safe to put the snakes is in my lady-hole or in my behind."

When we got back to her cabin, her mother instructed her to "wipe your chin, or you ain't coming in!"

Later, I wrote a song about that. It would be one side of my first proper release on record.

Over the next few weeks, I suppose she was my girlfriend. We'd head off somewhere quiet of her choosing, or snatch time in her cabin or mine when everyone was out.

She was stick-thin, with spindly legs and sharp hip bones. Her cheek bones were like edges of flint rock, her nose narrow and precise, and her clavicles very pronounced. I suppose she was a bit skeletal in appearance, with her dark sunken eye-sockets and long toes.

I'd play guitar and sing while she pleasured herself in various ways. When she was ready, she'd order me to put the guitar down and make the snake spit.

Janie never once enjoyed our activities. It was as though she were doing a job. If my role in the society was to collect wood, hers was to collect snakes.

One day, in the fall time, I asked her why she liked me to play guitar and sing while she readied herself.

An expression which spoke of my dumbness accompanied, "because the music charms the snakes, you retard. It summons them forth from within you! And I have to be sopping wet down there, so my poison can kill the nasty little bastards!"

"And the Medical Man told you all of that?" I asked.

"Oh, yeah, boy. He explained it all to me! I killed millions of his snakes, I reckon, when I was sick in his cabin. He was very pleased with me. Said I was one of the best he'd ever seen at it."

I understood, then.

"Janie," I asked, "do you know how babies are made?"

She laughed at me, her head thrown back, her mouth wide open. She banged the floor with her fists, my question was so hilarious to her.

"You ain't right in the head!" she managed to convey to me.

"I want to understand, Janie. Tell me, please?"

"Almighty God in Heaven takes care of that, dummy! He either sends a baby to a woman when she's in love, or He sends a baby when one is needed to serve His purpose!"

I nodded and smiled at her.

4.

Momma told me I was the only worthwhile thing she ever did with her life.

Going on the things she said to me, I had a sense that she didn't want children. She certainly never desired a man. But she loved me. Of that I have no doubt.

Looking back, I believe she suffered from depression.

From an early age, she made it clear that she was educating me so I might one day be free. Momma always wished for me to go out into the world and make her proud.

"Why didn't you ever leave, Momma?" I asked her one afternoon after lessons.

"Because I was afraid," she answered sadly, "and because I'm a woman. It isn't so easy when you're a woman."

I was set to walk away, but she continued. "I went once. It wasn't long before you came into my life. I had a job lined up in a town a-ways away. It was in a store down there selling clothing and farming supplies.

"I got to know the proprietor and his wife over a few visits, and they offered me a position. They even said I could live rent-free in a room above the premises. Any time I was ready, they said. All I had to do was show up, and it was mine for the taking.

"So, one morning - early, before the sun rose - I packed a few books and personals into a bag and set off. It was a two day walk, and I spent a night sleeping in a field along a lane someplace.

"It had been six months since I'd last visited. When I got there, the store was boarded up. There was no sign of life.

The Great Depression had hit, and taken them down with it."

Momma stopped talking. I waited to see if she was going to add anything. But, after a few minutes, I knew she wasn't. That was the end.

I wanted to ask her why she returned? Why didn't she keep going? Did she look elsewhere for work? Did she turn on her heel and walk the two days back? Did she sleep in a field along the roadside again? Was it the same field?

"It'll be time for you to go soon," she said suddenly, just as I reached the doorway.

Silence seemed like the best option on my part. I didn't understand the context of her comment. Was she throwing me out?

"Never go back in life, Tommy. Keep going forward. Keep heading to your future."

A storm blew through a few nights later. I knew one was coming. The animals told me by their behaviour.

Birds stood motionless on branches, staring off at the sky to the northwest, reading the wind as it played on their feathers. I figured they were calculating whether their nests would survive it all.

Ground creatures were agitated, the horse tossing back its head and whinnying, as it stamped its feet on the ground. Dogs became excited, yapping at nothing, and running around in figures of eight.

Yes, there was a big storm coming our way.

Tempestuous black clouds rolled over one another as night came a lick early that evening. Lightning scarred my vision, as I counted the seconds before the thunder came. The flashes and crashes were so rapid they merged into one, and were impossible to decipher.

The wind started to howl through any and every crevice, and I began extinguishing all fires out in the open, lest embers should be whipped up.

That was my job. Not only did I build the fires, I had to manage them, too.

Momma lay in our home - as safe a place as any. Her mood, I knew, matched the sky that evening. A blackness hung over her, an angry energy contained within. Thoughts, like black dogs, barked in her ears and ran figures of eight around her mind.

The community began to ready itself. Nobody spoke. Words were unnecessary.

My concern ratcheted up when the wind began to swirl. It whipped around from the direct north before shifting to the northeast. The hill, as a consequence, wouldn't offer us much protection.

In addition, it had been a wet winter in those parts. The ground had been sodden, or at least moist, for months, even on a hill where gravity would usually take care of such things.

I scanned the tree line to see where potential danger stood.

The rain stung my skin. It hit with such velocity that I had to turn my back before I could fully open my eyes - eyes that were open to danger from fire and debris and projectiles, and the towering hulks of trees surrounding the community.

I wanted to watch that storm. I knew what a storm such as she could do.

It was, it dawned on me, the storm I'd been waiting for.

Sheltering in a crater where once an oak had stood, I saw movement, as I peered through a rotting root.

The bent shape fighting its way across open ground was Momma.

I shouted, but any sound was snatched up by the wind and rushed away.

No hesitation. I was out of my hole, running hard but making slow progress. Bent almost to the ground to minimise the impact of the wind on my body, my shoulders higher than my head to take any impact from above, I ran towards her.

Momma disappeared into the Medical Man's cabin.

A crack. Thunder?

No.

A tree ripped from earth; a taproot snapping; an umbilical tether severed.

Down it came, that magnificent tree.

Smack onto the cabin with all its almighty form!

Neither stood a chance, Momma nor the Medical Man.

It broke her neck. A quick death, at least. She wouldn't have known much about it.

He was pinned beneath it, his body twisted and snapped.

The generator had been overturned, and fuel ran from it into the cabin.

The smoke from the stove was choking by the time I reached them, the oxygen in that storm firing it up, the wood catching aflame; first the twiggy tips, then larger limbs.

I went to her. Mostly to say goodbye while her body still contained her final breath.

As for him, I was content to let him burn.

He screamed as the fire supplanted the pain of his broken bones.

Nothing hurts like fire.

His eyes met mine.

I saw then. I'd long since suspected. Janie was the line that connected the dots.
The light went out in him. My father.
I was just around fifteen.
And it was time to head to my future and never go back.

5.

Interview with Mary Brown from 1984, as part of a feature on Histon. First published in the 'Old Music Expression' on May 3rd, to mark the twentieth anniversary of Tommy's death.

You knew Tommy Histon when he was young, is that correct?
Sure, I knew Tommy Histon. I knew his mother, too. She was a kindly young woman, as I recollect her.

They were peculiar, though, I must say that. They never really fitted in, and were seen as un-Godly by the rest of the community.

That said, I never had no problem with her. Sarah, her name was, and she was a pretty thing. I guess she was about twenty-five or so when she fell with child. That was a shock, 'cause nobody had ever seen her with a man.

How old were you at the time?
Oh, I was a couple of years older than her. I turned eighty this very year.

Sarah would read to people, and teach the children. I myself was taught by her mother when I was a child. It was the way of things in that place at that time.

What else can you tell us about Tommy and his early life?
Tommy came out of nowhere. Sarah had been bit by a snake, and spent some time in recovery. That was when we seen she was with child.

There was daft talk about it. About how it all came to be, I suppose I'm meaning. I heard people talking about the boy being half-snake. I guess that sounds pretty crazy now, in this day and age, but there was a lot of superstition in the hills back then.

I was there at his birth, being a helper on matters such as that. In fact, Sarah wouldn't have the Medical Man there. She hollered and screamed for him to get away from her!

On account of him being born small and pre-mature, the Medical Man had to see him, but we made sure Sarah wasn't aware of that.

The Medical Man said Tommy wouldn't see the new growth arrive that spring, not with him being so undeveloped and all.

But he did. And he grew up to be of normal size, I would say.

Hexed was the word people used for that family. Sarah's mother had died of something when Sarah was around fourteen, and her daddy hanged himself not long after.

It was a very closed community, I might term it. We were very protective of our heritage and way of life. So, when Tommy came out, he didn't look right on the eye.

How do you mean?

Sarah was fair, and very typical of our kind in her appearance.

Tommy was what I would describe as somewhat swarthy. Others said he had a touch of the tar brush. Just a touch, mind, and his features looked fine enough.

So, he was a good looking boy?

Yes, I suppose he was. And he was kind of naturally lithe, if that's the right word to use. He had a way of moving that put you in mind of an animal. Yes, a snake, I might say. But also a wolf or a fox. His eyes were always looking and seeing.

They were different certainly, the Histons, and they thought themselves better than the rest of us. That was my impression.

Was he always musical?

Music? No, I don't really recall Tommy being too musical. He could sing sweet enough, around the fire, and did possess a pleasant way of delivering a tune.

But you have to remember, I was looking after five children, the first one coming along when I was seventeen.

It must have been a hard life?

Oh yes, it was a hard life. I never shed a tear for the hills when we upped and left before winter of '47. And thank God in Heaven we did, because that was a bad winter.

Well, we went to West Virginia, and my husband-as-was worked in the mines that-a-ways. From high up in the hills to low down in the ground, was how he described it.

Until he died of the drinking, and stayed under ground.

Did you hear about Tommy's death in 1964?

Yes, I heard about his death, but that was a couple of years after. I forget how. It may have reached my ears through someone from the community. I'd see a few of the members in Church or in the town from time to time.

Was it a shock?

No, I wasn't surprised to hear the news. Hex will follow a family, in my experience. It will wipe out an entire line. That's the only way to break a hex. It dies with its hosts.

What do you think of his music and legacy?
I ain't never heard a single song he wrote or re-corded. In fact, I didn't know he made records until fairly recent times.

I'm also aware that he has a following, and is high regarded. Still, I ain't too keen on music, and never have been. Heard too much of it when I was in them hills, I reckon.

What else can you tell us about him?
Well, I do remember Sarah disappearing for a time before Tommy came to the world. She came back and seemed different after that. My guess is that something happened to her when she was gone, but I don't know what.

Talk was of her having lined up a job in a town, but when she got there it wasn't what she thought it would be. Some people said it was a whoring profession she took up for a while. Some such thing, anyways.

She wasn't gone long, I do know that, because she was teaching three of my children by then, and they didn't miss much learning through it.

What is your last memory of Tommy Histon?
Well now, that I do recall. Some images stay in your mind just as they were, and all. It was the day he left the hills.

Sarah had died two nights before, along with the Medical Man. A storm brought down a tree, and a fire was stoked up in the cabins as a result.

Tommy was supposed to have been in charge of the fires. That was his job. Talk was, he was off doing un-Godly things to himself and neglecting his duties.

Well, his own momma was killed because of it, some people said.

I didn't believe it, because I'd seen him out in that storm when it had first hit. There was no fire burning in the open.

Truth of it was, another man was supposed to have cut down the tree that fell on them, but had been neglectful. I can tell you that now, because the man was my husband-as-was.

Tommy got the blame for something that was not his fault.

Because they blamed him, the leaders and elders, they forbade anyone from helping him bury his own momma. That was to be his penance, it was decided.

I don't mind telling you that I wept as I watched him. He was just a boy, really. Barely fourteen or fifteen.

He pulled what was left of her body free from beneath the burnt tree, and bits of her were coming away, you know, in his hands, she was so charred.

It quite sickens me to depict it, even all these years on.

Well, that boy got his momma out, carried her to the burial site, and interred her in a hole he'd dug.

He sat on the mound, and stared at each of us when he was finished.

Real loathing was in those eyes of his. A most un-Holy look, if ever I seen one.

Even so, I took him a glass of water.

"Thank you, Mrs Brown," he said to me in his soft spoken courteous way.

The following morning, on account of his momma being cooked, and because he hadn't dug a deep enough hole, two dogs were eating bits of her hand that they'd pulled free of the ground.

That boy had to dig her up, make the hole deeper, and rebury her.

And still, none of the menfolk helped him.

It split the community, the way they treated him. I think that was the day we knew it was all over.

Tommy said to them, "if this is your God, I want no part of it."

Well, a few people agreed with that. I myself became a Catholic as soon as I got away and could think for myself.

Once Tommy was done with his momma, he walked back to the cabin.

Well, that was the only time I saw him cry.

And that is my last image of Tommy Histon, God rest his soul.

6.

There wasn't a great deal left of Momma after the fire was extinguished. There wasn't a whole lot to him to begin with.

Her blackened bones were buried in a hole I dug down the hill that morning after.

The talk told me that the community was set to break up. People were keen to go into the bright new world that had emerged after the war. Most such hill-dwellings had done similarly over the past half a century. We were a dying breed.

Before leaving, I burned all of Momma's books and personal possessions.

I stood by the spot she was buried and turned a circle, so that I might remember the location and find it again.

My way of mourning was to further isolate myself. So I hit the open road with a guitar in my hand, and a bag containing not much of any use slung over my shoulder. I had no money.

No sadness for the place and way of life accompanied me as I set off on my journey. Without Momma, it meant nothing to me.

She was, and always will be, my only kin.

It bothered me as to why she went to his cabin that evening. I considered that she'd been down of late, and went for medicinal purposes. But why venture out in that storm?

Years later, I reckoned on her being able to see events in the way I can. After all, I must have got that gift from somewhere. And if it came from the snake, well, she was the one bitten.

I recalled as a child, that people - women, mostly - would come to her to have her read them. In my ignorance, I presumed she was reading to them. Anyway, I was always sent away when the women came.

Naturally, that led me to a dreadful conclusion. If she could see that tree falling, and knew what devastation it would wreak, did she go there to end her own life?

Had she been watching and waiting for that storm just as I had?

One foot in front of the other was my way of blocking everything out, composing tunes in my head as I did. Only when I stopped and rested, did I dwell on circumstances and events. So, I kept moving along and didn't sleep much.

At some point, I crossed the state line into North Carolina, and encountered the ocean for the first time. The sound of it was orchestral to my ears.

How I loved the smell of life and death contained within it. Death was pretty stingless, I thought, as I gazed down at the minuscule pieces of shell that made up the sand that slipped through my fingers.

I stripped and bathed. The water was cold, it being spring, but I didn't care. I walked the shore in my bare feet, studying how the water came and went up the beach as I advanced, lost in my dreamy world. There was a pattern to it all that I couldn't quite grasp.

Only hunger forced me back inland.

Now, I'd worked a little on my trip south, to earn a few nickels and dimes for food and footwear.

Cleaned up, and with my spare set of clothing on, I entered a fruit farm and asked for work. There wasn't much at that time of year, but some jobs were found for me. I must have proved my use, because I was asked to stick around for the summer season, and the peach harvest.

It suited me to do that, so I readily accepted. The wages were miserly, but I could eat all the fruit I wanted, so I saved on that. Plus, accommodation was for free in one of the barns converted for the influx of seasonal staff.

That was how I met Juice Cartwright, and he showed me how to pick the blues as well as the fruit.

He got his name from being able to squeeze all the moisture from any piece of fruit you cared to toss him, no matter how firm. I'm pretty sure he could have got a couple of drops out of a beach pebble.

Juice was the first black person I ever spoke with in my life. It quite took me aback when I came to learn that he spoke words pretty much the same as me!

I guess old Juice was my first real friend.

He knew a lot of the blues musicians from being on the road in the Delta. He was surprised how cleanly I picked my notes on that old homemade guitar of mine, and he reckoned I was half way to being a bluesman first time he ever heard me play. To me, it was all just folk music coming from alternate angles and different places.

Juice helped me in obtaining some new strings, and fitted new winders so they'd hold tuning better and not slip all the while. And he lowered my action a little by making me a shaped bridge.

It was through him I learned to play my guitar like a percussion instrument, deadening the strings through my laid-on forearm, and slapping down a little higher up.

"Make it buzz and whine a little, boy!" he'd tell me, "blues is supposed to have a dose o' hurt and pain in it!"

Between us, we made a pretty good sound, as Juice blew his harmonica and feathered his hand, or blasted out a staccato beat.

Come, I guess, August, we were sent off with a truck to a big market away down on the coast. We'd stay there for the weekend.

Juice could only work behind the scenes, because the posh white folk wouldn't buy any produce if they saw him handling it. The fact that three-quarters of it had been picked by men and women of colour was, seemingly, fine. What the eye doesn't see...

Me? I was front and centre on that stand, dealing with customers and taking their money in exchange for goods. I could do the numbers and write out receipts, if need be. Oh yeah, they loved me on that stand.

I was so good, at the end of the day I earned myself a dollar bonus! And the promise of another, if I repeated it on the Sunday.

"How'd you get to be so smart?" my boss asked me, and smiled his bright white teeth at me.

"My Momma," I replied, "she was a teacher."

It was the first time I'd thought of her in a while, and it made me sad.

Juice saw that melancholy in me when the work was done, and we'd packed up for the night.

It explains why we ended up heading into town.

Most places had a 'No Coloreds' sign on the door. So, I'd go in, buy a couple of beers, and we'd slope off somewhere to drink them and enjoy the sun setting on the sound side of that strip of land.

It was the most beautiful place I'd ever seen up to that point in my life.

I told Juice Cartwright that very thing.

He laughed gently and shook his old grey head. "Well," he finally said, "you ain't barely ripe enough for picking yet, so I ain't surprised. But you will see a lot of places, Tommy, so long as you make old bones like me here. And many will be more beautiful than right here right now."

"You see my future, Juice?" I asked him.

"Oh, I do, boy! I do indeed. And it's bright, I tell you. You just gotta get ripe, and all the goodness will come flooding out! Like fruit, you see? People's just like fruit."

"How far in my future do you see?" I pushed him.

"Oh, now, not that far. My eyesight ain't what it once was!"

And we laughed, the pair of us, sat on the sand with our beers in our hands.

7.

There was a booth near the boardwalk. It enabled a person to make their own record.

If it hadn't been for those beers I'd supped, I never would have had the courage to go in. Well, it was down to that and Juice's encouragement.

"Never be afraid of your own talent, Tommy," Juice said as he pushed me through the door. "Leave that to others," he added before it swung shut.

It was hot and cramped in there, and I had to hold my guitar almost upright to fit in. As a result, my playing wasn't so good.

There was a time limit - a minute to a minute and a half, as I recall - and I seem to remember it costing thirty-five cents.

So, I set the machine running, and played a little song I'd written called 'Looking Down At The Stars'.

It was a simple strum, a brush of my fingernail, and some clumsy lyrics about being up on the slab of rock on the next hill. The second verse was a recent addition, as it had a reference to Momma, and flowers growing where her eyes had been. It was a folk kind of a song.

I didn't quite get it finished before the machine stopped recording.

Probably because of that, I stumped up some more nickels and dimes, and decided to make another, putting the first down as a practice run. It was the last of my money, until I could earn another dollar on the Sunday.

'Slitherin" was a recent addition to my canon, and was partly influenced by the blues Juice had injected in me.

The simple fact of the matter is, I played it with short stabbing jolts of my right hand because of the cramped space. That was all it was. And I sped it up to speed-and-a-half so that it would fit in the time limit. It was all fluke, really, as much as I'd love to tell you that I was inventing this rock'n'roll thing as we now know it.

That increased speed forced me to sing it differently and force the words out breathily, with an increased urgency as a result. I was, without exaggeration, struggling to breathe.

I will admit, there was a certain energy to that song, as I described the world rushing by me as I slithered through the grass like a snake.

With my two 6" 78rpm records in my hand, Juice and I carried on along the main boulevard skirting the shoreline.

"Them's precious," Juice informed me, as I swung them proudly by my side.

I looked at him to see if he was laughing at me. He wasn't.

"Thirty-five cents a piece ain't much," I replied.

"Already worth more than that."

"Ha! You reckon?"

"I do," he said sincerely.

Now, I was fifteen, cocky, and with a few drinks in me.

"Want to buy my record?" I asked a couple of girls walking towards us. They were approximately my age. Perhaps a little older.

"How much?" one of them enquired.

"Half a dollar," I beat out.

"What's your name?" the other asked, smiling at me. They were both pretty, and middle-class, in their best summer dresses.

"Tommy. Tommy Histon."

"Never heard of you."

"Is that important?"

"Sure! I wouldn't buy a record by someone I've never heard of," the fairer-haired one of the two said matter-of-factly.

"Then remember my name. Tommy Histon. And when you see that in the store, be sure to buy my record. Promise?"

"We will."

With that, they went on their way, giggling, arm in arm, and looking back over their shoulders every few paces.

"If you want to follow, I'll make my own way back," Juice said to me.

"Why would I want to do that?" I asked him earnestly.

"You got a lot to learn, boy."

Before we left the seafront, Juice pushed me into another booth. That one took photographs.

Juice insisted on paying, as I had no money left. It was a few cents, but it was the first time anybody had given me anything, except for Momma. My guitar didn't count. It was a loan from a dead man.

"You gotta promote yourself, boy. Ain't nobody gonna do it for ya."

As I stared at myself in that black and white photograph, a few things registered with me.

That was the very first time I'd seen my own image, other than by way of a reflection; whether that be in Momma's mirror, or in a pool of water.

In those photographs, I barely recognised myself. Perhaps it was because my face was the way round that other people see it. At first sight, I wondered if it was me, though I kind of knew it was. I was smiling, but not fully, just the beginnings of it. But my eyes had anticipated it coming, and had glintingly changed shape accordingly.

In those eyes, and general countenance, I saw a meanness that jarred me. There was a little hint of evil and devilment in the face looking back at me from the grainy grey image.

"Never seen yourself before?" Juice astutely asked.

"Nope."

"Now you sees what them girls seen, boy."

I looked at him askance.

"You got all you need now," he informed me.

"What's that?"

"You got them records, and you got some pictures. You can go to one of them recording labels, and present yourself."

I laughed.

My long weekend of firsts was completed when, on the Monday, we got back to the barn we slept in, and played my record on the old wind-up gramophone. Juice wouldn't let me play them more than twice.

"They deteriorate with every play," he said, "and you need to keep 'em good and clean for them recording label people! And them's fragile, as well as precious. So take good care of 'em, you hear me?"

"Sure, Juice."

I played 'Slitherin'' three times, because I kind of liked that one.

As for the other, it was for my Momma.

On my bedroll that night, a straw-stuffed mattress for support and comfort, I tried to think about the two girls in their best summer dresses.

As much as I desired it, my mind wouldn't settle on them. It veered off to my mother.

My dearest wish was that I could send her that 'Looking Down At The Stars' record. I'd put the dollar I earned in with it, so that she could treat herself to something or other of her choosing.

And she could tell me that I had the voice of an angel.

8.

Work dried up on the farm as the weather changed. The tourists disappeared along with the fruit harvest.

Juice was tramping inland and south for warmer climes, and to check in on family. He suggested I go with him, but I had a desire to stick to the coast. I was most drawn to the thing I'd never known.

Besides, people told me that it snowed a lot less on the eastern seaboard. As a result, I hugged the shoreline and drifted north, back to Virginia and up to Maryland.

I should have gone south.

The snow began on christmas day. It was a silent snow, with no wind accompanying it. It simply fell straight down from the heavy smoky clouds overhead. All the while, as I trudged through it, I kept telling myself that it wouldn't accumulate too much.

I began to get damp, and any exposed skin grew numb. Yet, I was sweating in my clothing. I had to raise my feet higher and higher to advance on. It was like walking on the sandy beach in that regard.

Finding shelter under a bridge, I managed to grab a few fitful minutes of sleep that christmas night. I'd doze for ten minutes or so, and snap awake to an eery silence that accompanied a heavy blanket of white.

A branch I'd driven into the ground was covered completely by the morning. It was close to a yard long.

On the 26th, it continued, that steady padding down of flakes. It hypnotised me, as each fragment fell to find a perfect place in the great puzzle building all around me.

Momma once said that every snow flake was unique in shape and size, yet here they were slotting together to make a perfect mass and crust.

It forced me to consider myself, and that one day I would find a place where I could fit perfectly.

There was no option but to sit tight all of that day. I had seen no lights the night before to show where salvation, by way of a town or farm, may lie. I had no food, but scavenged enough damp wood to get a fire going. I was back to collecting wood!

Melting snow in a can I carried, I drank hot water for sustenance. It warmed and cheered me, as it penetrated my aching body.

All through the 26th, I watched the gap at the top of each arch become narrower. Seeing how I couldn't fully stand up in there, I'm figuring that bridge was about five feet high at the centre point.

And as those gaps closed, I became warmer in my cave.

It broke my heart to break up my guitar and use it to add to my measly pile of firewood. Shelter and warmth were my priorities, though, and that guitar perhaps saved my life.

I knew, no matter what, I'd have to move the next day in search of food. A town was my best bet. I'd seen a signpost on the road, but hadn't paid enough attention to what it indicated. As a result, I wasn't sure if the next town was a mile away, or ten miles distant.

Cold does strange things to a person. As does fear.

All of my years building and tending fires, and I neglected to ensure ventilation. There was no chimney for the smoke to escape through.

My mind was heavy, incapable of holding a thought, when I snapped to wakefulness.

I called out for Momma.

Instinct alone told me that I needed oxygen desperately. But I dared not draw a breath in there.

Standing, I cracked my head on the stone bridge. My hands reached up and traced the structure.

I stumbled and fell, my lungs screaming for air, my eyes closed and stinging, my head throbbing and extremities numb and tingling.

My hands scrabbled and clawed at cold dense snow, as I swam through a frozen wall in search of air.

Finally, and not a moment too soon, I was sucking avariciously on the glorious and beautiful air, before spewing up grey water and hacking forth the poisoned lining of my lungs. Smoke blasted out from the sealed tomb behind me, it being as keen to escape as I.

It took an hour or so for me to recover; for the dizziness to abate.

Warm water heated on the last of the embers flushed me further. I had diarrhea - a vile liquid jettisoned from my body. Cleaning myself with snow as the ashen light of a new day barely dawned, it occurred to me that it was no longer snowing.

It was time to move.

Stashing the winders in my bag, I tied the guitar strings around my feet to offer some traction, and headed out.

The town, and salvation, lay two miles away. No light had been visible in the blizzard. It took me a long time to cover that ground. A fair amount of it I traversed on my belly, so as to spread and distribute my weight.

The snake in me helped with that.

On arrival, I was glad of the dollar I'd kept from that Sunday selling fruit to tourists.

Eating a hot meal, I wondered how many of those dollars I'd need to earn to get myself a new guitar.

9.

My singing was less angelic after that night of the smoke. In a way, it helped me, as it made me sound older and more mature.

Within half a day of arrival, I had myself a job clearing snow. By the time all the snow was cleared, and 1948 arrived, I was employed on the railroad as a coal man.

It was shovel work, all of it, but I was young and fit. I rode out six months in that town in Maryland before moving on. I turned sixteen at some point, but paid the fact no heed.

My goal was to head back to the fruit farm in North Carolina, and hook up with Juice once more.

As spring's freshness waned, I was back in Virginia, having hitched a ride to Washington DC with one of the guy's from the railroad. His name was Zachary, but I forget his family name.

Anyway, he was a good man, and he let me have a Gibson J-45 acoustic guitar he inherited from someone, but had no need for. All it cost me was a day assisting him in digging a drainage ditch on his property. I'd have done it for nought, for old Zachary.

That Gibson was a huge step up from the homemade guitar I'd had previously. I vowed to myself that I wouldn't burn it, no matter how desperate I became!

As I tramped my way south, the heat and humidity kicked in, but I never bitched about it following my experience in the blizzard. In fact, much like a snake, I basked in it every chance I got. I happily slept out in it during the day, my guitar stowed in the shade. I'd then travel through the night.

I'd busk in every town I encountered and liked the look of. Not once did I have to dip into my savings, as I lived off my wits and talent. Just as Juice had told me, "never be afraid of your own talent!"

Mostly I played crowd-pleasers, because that's what people would toss you a coin for. I'd read the people, and play something befitting.

In a more rural town, they liked their country music, but I didn't. I'd stick to my folk roots, and it went down well enough.

More cosmopolitan places had a liking for popular hits and music from the movies, I learned. It was simple enough, to work out an arrangement for, say, 'Am I Blue?', and entertain them with that.

The blues numbers Juice had shown me were well received in the black neighbourhoods, but I never got much money from those places. I understood why, but I'd go there regularly anyway, to keep my blues hand in.

For students, I'd play my own compositions, such as 'Slitherin'' and 'Looking Down At The Stars'. I had some twenty to twenty-five of my own songs by that time.

They usually began with a melody in my head, to which I'd add some lyrics, and then work out a guitar accompaniment. Oftentimes, I'd change the words almost completely once I had the rest of it, simply because they fitted better. The sound of the words was, even back then, important to me. Whether they made total sense to anyone listening or not, less so.

"Too fast," a gentleman called out after I played a standard down in Richmond, Virginia, "you're playing it too fast."

"Shhh!" the girl with him hissed, her embarrassment evident via the flush on her cheeks.

"Sounds right to me," I replied.

"No, the version released was quite a bit slower," he insisted, "I have it on an album."

"An album?" I asked.

"Yes, a 33.3 rpm vinyl disc. They're the new thing."

"Well, that's what it sounds like at 78 rpm," I shot back at him and grinned.

That man, I discovered from the card he handed me, was named Roberto Vertoni.

Half an hour on, I decided to call it a day, and stood to leave.

Vertoni was sat at a table outside an Italian restaurant, and beckoned for me to go over.

"What's your name, son?" he said.

"Tommy Histon."

"I'm Roberto. This is my daughter, Clarissa. She likes the music you make. She says you might have something with the faster pace. She says that young people will like to dance to it. What do you think?"

I shrugged.

"Some of those songs weren't known to us. Are they your own?" Clarissa asked me.

"Sure are!" I answered proudly.

"They're very interesting," she added.

"Thank you."

"Will you join us for a glass of wine, Mr Histon?" her father invited.

"I'd like that. But call me Tommy, please," I suggested, and took the hand he offered.

His handshake belied the man. He oozed confidence and power. But that handshake was like a limp leaf in a drought.

I nodded a greeting to his daughter, and took a seat.

It was the first time I'd ever tasted wine. It was red and sour, but I didn't let on that I didn't like it. My heart sank as Vertoni ordered another bottle.

"Chianti," he said to me, raising his glass.

"Chianti," I rejoined, and raised mine similarly.

He laughed. "No, Tommy. The wine is a chianti. From Italy. Like me. Cin-cin!"

"Chin-chin," I echoed.

"Or salute!" Clarissa added.

"Salute!"

Wine, I began to understand, got better the more you had of it.

As did Clarissa. Had it not been for her, I probably would have made an excuse and left. She had the blackest hair I'd ever seen in my life, but her skin was paper-white. Her eyes were large and brown, catching every bit of light and splitting it myriad like a crystal. Her lips were full and red, and she twisted her mouth to demonstrate every emotion she wanted others to see.

That mouth smiled benignly as her father outlined his desire to start up a record label. "Would you be interested in working with me, Tommy?"

"Doing what?" I asked, imagining I'd be employed in some manual, and probably menial, capacity.

"Making a record, of course! What do you think I've been talking to you about?"

"Oh, I'd like that very much, sir," I replied instantly, "thank you, Roberto."

My mind hadn't been on his words. Clarissa had sat smiling passively, whilst all the while massaging my genitals with her foot beneath the long white tablecloth.

Leaning over, I reached down by my feet and retrieved the two records I'd made the summer before in North Carolina. "I did make these," I said, as I handed them over.

"Mind if I borrow them?" Roberto asked.

"Not at all."

Within a month, Vertoni would have formed a new company called Rovertone Records. And I'd be signed to it.

10.

"Luca, the boy needs new clothes!" Vertoni snapped at the tailor.

"I quite like what I have," I tried to protest.

Both men shook their heads at me.

"Look, I have a meeting," Vertoni said, "Clarissa, make sure he gets a suit. Smart. Modern. Italian. He cannot go to the radio station looking like that!"

Following further instructions delivered in his native tongue, he was gone.

Clarissa was twenty-two and working with her father in the family firm.

The suit, I would learn some time later on, was invoiced at over seven hundred dollars. It didn't matter, as it would be deducted as an expense from anything I would earn from record sales.

"Which way do you dress, sir?" Luca asked me in his thick Italian accent.

I looked at him blankly. I usually began with my shirt.

"To the right," Clarissa answered for me.

The tailor smiled amiably, and ran his tape up the inside of my left leg.

His smirk broadened as he made contact with my penis. Clarissa twisted her mouth mischievously.

"Sorry, I meant the left. I was talking about from my perspective," she said with a straight face.

Once I was measured, Luca pulled out half a dozen suits of varying styles and left us to "see which one suits the best. Perhaps, in this case, a woman is the better judge."

Now, to tell the truth, my only sexual experience had been with Janie, so that was what I was basing everything on. I was naive, I guess. It didn't once occur to me that Luca was a homosexual. Moreover, I didn't know that word until Clarissa used it later, and I processed it until I understood.

Once we were alone, she flicked through the garments, settling on a light grey, thin material that she thought would be better in the hot summer weather.

Now, I was naked beneath my slacks on account of the dense, sticky August heat, so I shuffled off to the curtained cubicle to get changed.

As soon as my pants hit the floor and I stepped from them, she drew the curtain back. My arms were engaged in tugging my shirt over my head. I couldn't undo the front, as I'd lost buttons and sewn it together. Anyway, it resulted in me not being able to cover up. Also, I was somewhat incapacitated, as the shirt played a kind of straightjacket role.

She stood there regarding me, her mouth pursed appraisingly.

"You appear to be mildly aroused, Tommy. Is everything okay?" she asked of me, with a tone of concern.

I nodded that it was.

Clarissa took a hold of me, gauging my degree of arousal. Of course, her doing that only added to the level.

"Is this because of Luca touching you?"

"Not really," I answered her. But the truth was, that had caused a stirring as he'd gently dragged his manicured fingernail over me. I'd felt myself flinch at the contact, before he rested the weight of my balls on the backs of his fingers.

"Then really, Tommy, what is the cause?"

"You," I told her, because that was the truth. I'd cast her in Luca's place.

"Don't move!" she ordered, and I wondered if she was angry at me as she walked briskly away.

I obeyed her, my arms still caught up in the shirt, and resting on the back of my neck.

She plucked up a pair of scissors, and I began to get concerned. To my relief, Clarissa hoisted up her mid-calf length skirt, and cut clean through the gusset of her fancy underwear garment.

Thereafter, she returned, and positioned herself, kneeling on the bench inside the cubicle. She was tall, about five-ten, and a little widening of my feet had us lined up.

She reached back, and guided me in.

I barely lasted a minute, so inviting was she, and so long had it been.

A warm jet shot from me.

"No!" she cried, but it was too late.

Jerking forward, she dislodged me, and I watched the next wave stream through the air before landing stringily on her buttock.

I clenched and held back as best I could, conscious of my experience with Janie.

Clarissa was angry. I was confused.

"Jesus, Tommy!"

"Sorry. Look, I can still get it all in you..."

"In me? If you get me pregnant, you'll ruin my fucking life! Anywhere but in me, Tommy!"

Shit.

So, I was cocooned in my shirt, my arms pinned to the back of my head, and my throbbing, half-drained penis on full show. A line of pearly fluid extended from the tip towards the floor of the changing-room.

Clarissa was shouting at me, flushed in the face, semen spattered on her exposed cheek, and a creamy dribble threatening to leak from her.

Luca entered at that moment. Wordlessly, he turned and locked the door, and with fluid movements grabbed a towel and strode towards us.

I wondered if he'd been in this situation before, as unlikely as it seemed.

He tended to Clarissa first, mopping up spillage and dribble, as I finally got to completely remove my shirt. Once done, she set about tidying her skirt and rearranging herself generally.

Luca took great care in cleaning me up before wiping the tiled floor.

He handed me the grey suit and a plain white shirt, left the cubicle, and tugged the curtain back across before unlocking the door.

Fifteen minutes later, as Roberto Vertoni arrived to collect us, the scene was one of efficient calmness.

Pins had been applied to the grey suit I stood in. Clarissa sat looking bored but immaculate, as she thumbed nonchalantly through a magazine.

"Did you get the boy sorted out?" Vertoni asked.

"Yes," Luca answered, "I think we found something he can fit inside very comfortably!"

"Good!"

"Talking of which, Mr Vertoni, sir - your future son-in-law is due for a fitting for his suit next week. Your wedding is less than two months away now, if I'm not mistaken, Miss Vertoni?"

"That's right," she answered coolly.

"Now, slip it off carefully so everything remains in place," he instructed me.

11.

I must admit, I looked a million bucks in that suit. Momma would not have recognised me.

The shirt I wore cost a hundred dollars, according to the receipt I caught sight of. I was allowed to wear it open-neck. A tie was something I drew a line at.

We arrived at the radio station, Vertoni and myself, one day in early-September. It was the public launch of Rovertone Records.

"Don't speak unless you're spoken to," Vertoni instructed me, "and only answer 'yes, sir' or 'no, sir'. Understand?"

"Yes, sir," I thought to be the correct response.

Quite why I needed a suit for radio made no sense to me. Until a photo was taken at the end.

Prior to that, I was introduced as a signing to Rovertone Records, a hot new imprint, and I had to physically sign a contract on-air. It meant that I had no opportunity to read it.

It didn't make any difference to me, as I'd have signed it anyway, no matter what, just to get a record made and in the stores. Hell, I'd have signed anything to hear my record played on that very radio station.

"Where are you from, son?" the presenter asked me.

"Right here in Richmond, sir," I answered, because that's what I'd been told to say.

"And how old are you?"

"Eighteen." It was a fib, but Vertoni assured me it was for the best.

"Wow! Just eighteen. Your parents must be real proud of you, son, having a recording deal at eighteen?"

"Yes, sir. They sure are!"

"And what kind of music do you make?"

"Oh, I don't really know how to describe it."

"Well, we like a good ballad on this station. Will you be doing ballads?"

"No, sir."

"Sure you will, Tommy," Vertoni jumped in, "he'll be playing all kinds of styles on Rovertone Records!"

"Ballads are old hat," I said confidently.

"Old hat!" the presenter screeched.

"Tommy doesn't really know what a ballad is, Dan..." Vertoni started to say.

"My music's about the future, not the past," I said in an even voice.

"Well, we like a ballad here on WKGG, where the music runs free, sponsored by Dale's Soda Fountain right here in Richmond! But, just like at Dale's, there are a lot of different flavors you can sample. It would be a boring old-hat world if we all liked the same thing, hey, Tommy, son?"

"Yes, sir."

"Coming from dear old Virginia, I'm betting you like a bit of country in your music. That's another popular style in these parts."

"Well, that's not..." I began.

"You know, we have a four hour show hosted by my good friend Howlin' Jake on a Saturday evening from seven. The younger listeners love to tune in to that one, I can tell you..."

"Country music isn't..."

"...and it's sponsored by our very dear friends at E&E Steak House in the heart of downtown! So, I look forward to hearing your music on Jake's show, and wish you all the very best, son!"

"Yes, sir."

Two blasts of a camera flash later, and we were heading out the door.

12.

With the contract signed, I was put on a wage of fifteen dollars a week, and got to reside in a tidy little trailer parked out on Vertoni's property on the fringe of the city. It cost me nothing in rent.

Later, I would discover that the trailer accommodation was being charged at a hundred dollars a week. It would all be off-set against earnings.

It gave me freedom and time to play guitar and write my songs. Vertoni was looking at a new format vinyl LP, and it was slotted for the middle of '49.

Clarissa snuck over to me a week or so before her wedding.

We had sex, and I have to say that it was very pleasant. It was far and away better than any I'd had previously.

She held me inside her at the finale, as I went to pull away.

Reading my confused expression, she said, "it doesn't matter now, Tommy. The timing is right for a honeymoon baby."

I figured I'd never understand women as long as I lived.

It surprised me to discover her silently crying, as we lay in the first bed I'd ever called my own that was raised off the ground.

"What's wrong?" I asked her.

"I'll be married by this time next week."

"Isn't that a good thing?"

Rather than answer me, she stretched out to her purse, and rummaged around until she found a bottle. Unscrewing the top, she took three or four of the pills, and slapped them into her mouth.

"A little pick-me-up," she explained, and offered me the bottle.

Following her lead, I swallowed a few of the tablets and lay back down.

Not long after, she was full of beans, and keen to have intercourse again. As was I.

They were amphetamines, and it became a regular thing for her and I to take a few every time I saw her. They gave me a nice little buzz, and made the world seem like a better place, so where was the harm?

She began taking lithium around that time, as I recall, but I never took any of it. That said, I probably would have done, had she offered.

The truth is, I got pretty reliant on those uppers in time.

But back in 1948, music was all I truly cared about. I wasn't wasting my days lying around that trailer. I was honing my skills, and polishing my songs.

Vertoni wanted me to go to a recording studio before the year was out, and cut a minimum of fourteen tracks from which an album would be constituted. Two of those tracks would be released as a 10" 78 by way of launching me and testing the market.

Following Clarissa's wedding, to which I wasn't invited, she moved away to live with her husband. It was just a few blocks away, and she still swung by to see me as often as she could. Her husband worked in local government in some capacity.

Amphetamines, which I got easily via the doctor, fuelled my industry. In fact, sleeping was my problem rather than working. Until I'd run out. Then I had no energy for anything until I could replenish my supply.

As with my body, my mind was also alive like never before on those pills. By the time I hit the studio a week before christmas, I had fifteen songs ready to go, and another twenty worked out that I imagined would be my follow-up record.

Vertoni wanted a couple of ballads, but I was having none of that. If anything, my playing was faster than ever on those pills. It was the studio engineer who, in reference to the speed of my strumming arm, dubbed me 'The Piston'.

Thus, Tommy 'The Piston' Histon is what I became.

'Three Minute Hero' contained twelve tracks, and had a total run-time of just under twenty-three minutes. No song on it lasted for three minutes! That said, they may have done, had I been inclined to play at the speed anyone else would have played at.

Later on, people said it was one of the first rock'n'roll records ever made.

The Jitterbug and Lindy Hop had been around for years, and were pretty frantic, but I didn't know of them. All I knew was, what I was doing wasn't like anything I'd heard before.

It was folk music, for sure, because that was what I knew best. But it was rapid and kind of skewed. It wasn't far removed from the 'Slitherin'' track I did in the booth a year before. I kept the short stabbing strum patterns, or quick-fire finger picking, and sang, spat or wailed words over that.

That's all I can say about it, really.

The studio was a two-track facility. It was just myself, the engineer and an assistant, so I played everything on that record save for some handclaps and other sounds the assistant helped me out with.

Most of it was nailed down in one take, with a microphone on my vocal, and another on the guitar. Any additional percussion came from my habit of tapping a foot as I played.

On a few tracks, such as 'Cookin' On Embers', I'd lay down a noise, such as 'tsah-tsah-tsah' I made with my mouth, which people later commented sounded like a muted cymbal being tapped. Truth is, I was keeping time with that spat sound, and I figured it sounded a little like meat spitting in a pan over a fire.

There were other things I tried in the moment, most of which, fortunately, worked out. For 'Fruit Of My Labour' I spotted a banjo standing in a corner. Now, I wasn't having banjo on my record, as it was too country sounding. Instead, I sang through the open back, the banjo propped between my mouth and the mic, and it picked up a little resonance on its way through.

Everything was very basic and raw.

It was my nature to improvise. I like to use what I find, and in a way different to the intended purpose.

I reason it was garnered from my childhood. Games were invented in a similar way, as there were very few toys to play with. As a result, any plaything was improvised from what was lying around, and any games dictated by what was available. All it took was a little creative thought.

Books were limited, and once I'd read them all, it was down to my imagination to conjure up stories as a means of entertaining myself.

Music was no different. Momma and I had no radio, and, even if we had owned one, no clear signal would have reached us in the hills. Thus, if I wished to hear new songs, it was down to me to come up with something.

Whatever is popular in the moment is of no consequence to me, and it never has been. I like what I like, whether that be from the past, present or future.

Nobody was ready for that record, I guess, as I look back at the grand old age of thirty-two.

Vertoni hated it, I knew. But he still released it.

There were reasons for that, I would discover. And those reasons had nothing to do with my music or me.

If I could go back, perhaps I'd do an album full of fuckin' country ballads.

The aliens wouldn't have paid me any heed, had I done that.

The fuckers.

But I couldn't. I could never do that. I could never compromise.

So, everything that's happened, had to happen.

13.

Just after New Year, Clarissa showed up at my trailer early one morning. Her parents were away in Boston or some place, visiting family and tending to business.

She insisted I accompany her to the house. Being in possession of a key, she dragged me up the stairs and out through French doors in the master bedroom to a balcony.

It was bitterly cold, but she seemed not to notice it.

There, in a reenactment of our first time in the tailor's, we had sex, but without the mess of that encounter.

The property was a few acres in size, with plenty of trees skirting the back lawn. Even so, anybody glancing up from the roads framing the corner plot would have seen us cojoined.

I noticed that she felt different. Her breasts were a little heavier, and a very slight swelling of her tummy was evident.

"That's better," she breathed at the end, "I wonder which one of you is the father?"

"Father?"

"Honeymoon baby."

"Ah."

"It was either that week before my wedding, or the week of it. I don't suppose it makes any difference."

"Of course it does!" I replied, a little sharply.

"No, it really doesn't," she snapped back, standing and letting her skirt fall back into place.

A handful of amphetamines were deposited down her throat, chased down with lithium.

For the first time, I saw the greed in her, as I declined anything else she had to offer that morning.

14.

My first record release, 'Cookin' On Embers/ Wipe Your Chin (Or You Ain't Comin' In)', credited to Tommy 'The Piston' Histon, was released on February 4th, 1949.

It was the debut release on Rovertone Records, despite having the catalogue number ROT-10-4. The missing numbers in the sequence should have told me something. But I was blinded by having an actual, real, tangible record out.

Any buzz quickly vanished as the record sank without trace.

One highlight was listening to the radio, and WKGG gave the lead side a spin, at the culmination of which came, "a new one there from Tommy 'The Piston' Histon, on Rovertone based right here in Richmond. And right here in Richmond is where you can get a new Ford at Green Lake Automotives, guaranteed cheaper than anywhere else in the state - find it cheaper, and they'll match that tag!"

I'd spend several hours each week walking around every record store in the city, and surreptitiously move my 78 to the front of the rack, or drop one in the featured stand near the counter when nobody was looking.

My worry was, if the 78 did nothing, would Vertoni still be game when it came to releasing my album? To help it along, I'd buy a copy in most places I visited, until I had a fair old stack of them back at the trailer I called home.

To my surprise, he was keener than ever. It was slotted for a May release. Friday the 13th. That should have been a warning to me.

Vertoni's accounts showed that my 78 sold some seven thousand copies, and was a local 'minor hit' in a suburb of Boston.

It was broadcast over the airwaves three times in all; once in Richmond as described, and twice in Massachusetts.

Seven thousand seemed like a fair few to me, and Vertoni was happy enough. Though, as he showed me on the reports, it was very little in terms of income, once manufacturing and distribution had been factored in.

Then there were the other overheads, as detailed as part of my contract. It boiled down to me being twelve thousand dollars in arrears.

I began to panic, worried that I'd have to pay it back.

"Relax, Tommy," Vertoni assured me, "studio time and promotion don't come cheap, but this is an investment. Yes, we seem to have lost money, but the 78 was just a teaser - what we call a loss-leader. The album is where the money is, and that's already recorded, so no more studio-time costs!"

That was okay, then.

Later, I'd learn that the record was never distributed outside of Richmond, aside from two dozen copies sent to a family connection in Boston, which also led to the radio play up there. The truth was, just a couple of hundred copies sold, and the rest were never even manufactured.

Saddest of all, was that I bought about ten percent of them.

I was oblivious to all of that in 1949. Yes, I can make the excuse that I was barely seventeen years of age, and, on the surface, uneducated. But I know, looking back, that I should have been more astute.

March came and went, and nothing happened. I stayed in my trailer, got handed fifteen bucks a week in cash, and wandered around Richmond all day waiting for something to come along.

I paced away my time amongst the students that frequented the parks and other open spaces. Despite them being my age, I never felt like a part of that scene, and was never invited into it.

In cafes, I'd sit alone, often with my guitar propped against the table, and crave interaction that would never chance to catch my eye.

I wore my suit and shirt on a lot of those jaunts, in a bid to be more acceptable. It made no difference. I wasn't like them. They could see it in me, just as easily as I could see the chasm between me and them.

I was lonely, it dawned on me.

I'd spent so much time alone, even when with Momma in the hills, but had never felt loneliness before.

A depression accompanied the realisation, so I furtively took a handful of pills and washed them down with milky, frothy coffee.

With more clarity of thought, I vowed to myself that I would get the album out, and if nothing altered, I'd head on down to North Carolina and the fruit farm for the summer season. Juice Cartwright would set me right! I'd take him a copy of both of my records, and he'd be pretty pleased for me.

It was on one such day in mid-April that I headed back to the trailer. On arrival, I found Clarissa lying on the bed clutching her lower belly. I'd not seen her in a few weeks, and there had been nothing intimate since that day on the balcony.

Her hand reached out to me, and I saw that it was covered in blood.

Running to the house, I banged on the door. Nobody was home.

Clarissa's screams compelled me to return to the trailer, rather than run into the street to raise the alarm and summon assistance.

I arrived just in time to see her give birth. She was approximately twenty-four weeks into her pregnancy.

She'd sought no medical help in that time, having told her parents that her husband had made arrangements, and her husband that her parents had. To her regular doctor, she'd told a tale of a private facility specialising in such matters.

The tiny body that came from her was motionless and cold. No breaths did it take, and no blood pumped independently through its blue form.

Instinctively, I knew it to be dead.

There was so much blood.

How to stop it? It was coming from within.

To this day, I maintain that I did the only thing I could. I padded her with a towel, and ran to the public telephone, where I rang for an ambulance.

Yes, I should have done that when I first found her, but I didn't know. How could I possibly have known?

I went back to her and waited for the ambulance.

She survived. Just.

One thing remains starkly vivid in my mind. Hauntingly so.

That baby. A boy.

It was grotesque. Deformed.

They said it was because of the drugs she took.

But I recognised myself in those blue monstrous features.

I knew it was mine, and that it was its father's son.

15.

'Three Minute Hero' came out four weeks later. It may as well not have done.

It received a review in the local free newspaper that read: 'The kids, I'm told, like their music a little raucous and frenetic these days. Well, if this is the kind of thing they respond to, I suggest they put more energy into their studies and sporting endeavors, negating the need for this type of recording.

'I'd like to tell you about the lyrics, but they're delivered too quickly to be made sense of. The guitar is strummed and picked so fast, that whether it's competently played or not, is beyond this humble reviewer's aural capacity to tell. I would presume the pace is there to mask the fact that it isn't.

'Slow down, Mr Histon, is my advice. Do so, and you may find a decent tune somewhere within your canon. The vocal, after all, is not unpleasant.

'In a world where everyone is in such a hurry to get to nowhere, this record is perfect, as it hurries and goes nowhere.

'In summary - let this one pass you by.'

Vertoni said there was no such thing as bad publicity.

I was crestfallen, and hit the pills hard to raise my spirits. In fact, I was spending more money on uppers and drink each week than I was on food or anything else. My fifteen bucks wasn't sufficient.

No new songs came from me as the summer drifted pointlessly by. I'd lost the will, along with my confidence.

The only bright moment came when, one evening in the trailer, I was lying on my bed listening to WKGG. It was a roasting hot Sunday, and they played requests sent in by listeners at home.

I swung my legs down and sat bolt upright when I heard my name. "...Tommy Histon, a local boy, and Brenda and Jeannie want to hear a track from his current album titled, 'Pick Me Up'. Well, this one's for you gals, and don't forget to stop by Dale's Soda Fountain whenever you need to pick up a refreshing pick-me-up!"

There is no better feeling than hearing your own song played on the radio when you weren't expecting it.

I stared at the wireless and smiled for the first time in weeks; the first time since before Clarissa in that very trailer.

As I stared, it was as though I could see the waves entering the radio in pulses that distorted the warm air as they carried my own music to me. And potentially millions of others!

Those waves, I reasoned, were an energy like any other. They could never be destroyed, simply reclaimed and converted to something else.

It's no different to throwing a ball. It is friction that saps its energy. Give it a completely smooth ride, with no elements or terrain to negotiate, and it will continue on ad infinitum.

It was friction, I knew, that was slowing me down. I was grinding to a halt.

Looking up, those radio waves were everywhere, passing through me and the walls of my home. But every barrier they passed through diminished them.

The ones going upwards caught my eye, as they carried my song up to the clouds and beyond, fighting against gravity and the earth's very atmosphere.

Perhaps one - just one - would make it through the ceiling of our world and escape out into space, where there would be no resistance. Once there, it could continue on for ever and ever!

And that, I would come to learn, is precisely what happened.

But it was Brenda and Jeannie who were foremost in my mind at that moment, as I wondered if they were pretty, and how I might go about meeting them. At seventeen, that's how we are.

Were they, perhaps, the two girls I'd encountered at the beach that night with Juice?

If only I could ride on those waves! I could pass through matter, and see Brenda and Jeannie grinning at their names being mentioned on the radio, before leaping up and dancing around their bedroom to my music!

To make them happy for a couple of minutes was enough, wasn't it? If enough people did that for everyone else, there would be a lifetime of happiness available to everyone.

Well, it brightened my mood no end, that thought.

A rap on the door snapped me out of my mind-wanderings. It was Vertoni.

"Did you hear it?" he beamed.

"I did," I said, matching his expression.

"Ha! I thought it would cheer you up. They fell for it."

"Fell for it?" I echoed, making it sound like a question.

"Brenda and Jeannie. I picked the names from an article in the newspaper, and wrote the letter myself."

And with an inaudible bump, I fell back down to earth.

16.

One morning, I walked over to Luca the tailor to get my suit altered. I'd slimmed down, perhaps because of the pills and their affect on my appetite. Plus, I was still growing at seventeen, so had gained an inch in height.

"Such a shame about Miss Clarissa and the baby," Luca said as he worked around me, unpicking and re-pinning the hems.

I nodded in agreement.

It had been the best part of a year since I'd last stood in the fitting room.

"Still, perhaps it was for the best," he added, in his clearly-enunciated but heavily-accented way.

"How do you mean?"

"Oh, you know. Perhaps this baby is not from the husband, and so better to happen the way it did. Imagine if it were to become known that the child belonged to someone else."

I looked down at him, and he smiled lasciviously up at me.

"It is difficult for me," he continued, going back to his pinning, "with Mr Vertoni being an old friend and valued customer. I feel I should have told him what I know. It is disloyal, and I worry about what would happen if he found out that I had kept what I know from him."

"What is it you know?" I asked calmly.

"I know that you were screwing his daughter, Tommy. You don't mind me calling you Tommy, no?"

"No."

"Good, because we, too, are becoming friends, I think. Do you agree?" he asked, and began kneading the front of my groin.

I didn't reply, but neither did I stop him doing what he was doing.

Continuing, he added, "but Vertoni is a dangerous man, so I am a little worried. Perhaps, if I knew I could trust you, it would make me less anxious."

"What do you want?" I asked him.

"I think you know what I want, Tommy, my friend."

At that, he stood and exposed himself to me.

Luca only had one testicle. He claimed he lost one to shrapnel in the war.

"It is very dangerous for me, Tommy, to be the way I am. I am an alien here, and if I am discovered, I will be sent away, or locked up. So, now we both know a secret about one another. It makes us allies, I think."

"You got me all wrong," I notified him, "and you can trust me."

"I need to be sure."

"You can be sure," I assured him, and began changing into my regular clothes.

A few days later, I went to pick up my suit. Luca's appearance shocked me. His face was a mess of bruising and cuts.

"What happened?" I asked him.

"I think you know," he slurred through swollen lips.

"I don't know what you're talking about," I informed him honestly.

"Well, Vertoni found out somehow."

"Found out what?"

"He found out that I made alterations and didn't supply you with a new suit."

"Why would I need a new suit?" I asked, confused.
"You don't. That is the point!"
I was flummoxed. "Luca, I have no idea what's going on here."
He looked at me with his sad eyes, half closed with swelling and fatigue.
"Get away from him, Tommy. He's using you. He doesn't care about you or your music."
"What?"
"This suit of yours - I have to invoice at nearly a thousand dollars. It is a fifty dollar suit! I get paid sixty, so am making money. I was supposed to make you take another suit at the same price."
"Why?"
"Oh, Tommy, you have so much to learn in life. It is hiding money. And it is about not paying tax. If he can claim it as a business expense, and you are contracted to his Rovertone company, he can offset it on his accounts. Everything is like that!"
My blank expression told Luca that I didn't really understand.
"Look, Tommy, he does not want you to be a success with your records! It is all a trick. He is pressing hardly any number, and claiming thousands to lose the money."
"Why would he want to lose money?" I asked, still not grasping the reality.
"No, not lose money in that way. He wants to... What is the phrase? Launder! He is laundering the money through a legitimate business."
"No, it doesn't make any sense. He wrote to the radio station, and we did the interview..."
"He has to make it look real! And, if you have a massive hit, so what?"

"You lost me."

"If, by luck, your record sells a million copies, he still makes a load of money, Tommy, all of which will be deducted from your expenses. He wins every way. People like Vertoni always win."

A wave of anger and crushing embarrassment flowed through me as I suddenly understood Vertoni's agenda.

It was only much later, when I thought back on all that had occurred in my life, that I began to make some sense of it all.

The best lies are based on truth.

When Luca told me he was an alien, he wasn't talking about being an immigrant. When he spoke of being sent back, he didn't mean Italy.

The way I figure it, 'Pick Me Up' being played on the radio did break through the earth's atmosphere. It was heard by something far away in the sky, and identified as something futuristic.

Now, I would come to learn that those aliens want the power that comes from my insightfulness. They don't have that. They are in the moment only.

So, Luca - whose single testicle proved he was an alien - was tasked with obtaining my semen. To that end, he tried to seduce me, but failed. I guess he had some from that day in the changing-room.

Through that sample, they would discover the snake venom coursing through me.

They would understand that I am unlike any other person on this planet. I am unique in my flaws and talents.

All of which was very interesting to those fuckers.

17.

Roberto Vertoni interview with journalist Walt Young. First published in 1975 in 'Centre Hole Magazine'.

WY "How well did you know Tommy Histon, and how did you meet him?"

RV "I thought I knew him well. I thought I could trust him. But he turned out to be a snake in the grass. He showed up at my door having heard I was starting a record label. That would have been in 1948. To be honest with you, I wouldn't have touched him, but my daughter was a fan, so I did it for her."

WY "You didn't like his music?"

RV "Not much."

"WY "Your daughter had heard him play?"

RV "I guess so. In the street, I think she said."

WY "He would help your daughter at one time, wouldn't he?"

RV "Help her? If it hadn't been for him, she would never have required help."

WY "What do you mean?"

RV "He introduced her to the drugs that led to her problems. I wish I had never tried to help that man. I should never have let him into her life!"

WY "You went ahead and released a 78 and an LP by Histon?"

RV "What's your question?"

WY "Well, I suppose, why did you do that?"

RV "Because I said I would, and I'm a man of my word."

WY "Do you regret doing that?"

RV "Yes I do. I believe that man took advantage of my generous nature, as well as that of my family. We opened our door to him, housed him, treated him as one of our own, and he betrayed us."

WY "In what way?"

RV "He... I firmly believe that he used narcotics to control my daughter. To take advantage of her! He caused her to miscarry her child through the drugs that he made her take. It all led to her problems.

"He was a bum when I met him. And despite my showing him nothing but kindness, he sabotaged his own record by screwing up every interview, and recording music that was pretty much unlistenable! He..."

WY "If I may interrupt, that music is now seen as being a precursor to rock'n'roll and all that followed."

RV "And what's your point?"

WY "Do you not admit that Tommy Histon was years ahead with that album?"

RV "Fluke. He got lucky with that."

WY "And with his other records?"

RV "I wouldn't know about his other records."

WY "You lost the publishing rights to 'Three Minute Hero' when you were arrested, correct?"

RV refuses to respond.

WY "Isn't it true that you had all assets seized after being convicted of tax fraud?"

RV "That does not mean that I was guilty."

WY "What are you saying?"

RV "I served fifteen years for that piece of shit."

WY "You're saying it was Tommy Histon's fault?"

RV "I am simply stating facts. He came into our life, and within a year, my daughter is a mess, I am arrested and he is a free man."

WY "I don't understand."
RV "Then you are not listening to what I am telling you."
WY "I'm trying. How did Histon play any part in your arrest?"
RV "Like I said; a snake in the grass."
WY "Do you think he grassed on you?"
RV "I never said that. But, I think, now you are listening."
WY "Did you see Tommy again after your arrest in 1949?"
RV "No."
WY "Can we get back to your musical involvement with him?"
RV "Why?"
WY "Because it's why I'm here."
RV "I paid for him to record his music. It was a pile of shit. I released it to please my daughter. It did nothing. I am then arrested for trying to help him. He disappeared. I heard he came into a lot of money. End of story.

"Make of it what you will. You have ears and eyes, after all. You are capable of thought, and can follow a simple idea, can you not?"
WY "Are you saying Histon sold you out?"
RV "I think you just said that. Ask about my tailor. Ask about his friendship with Histon. Ask the real questions, and you might get answers worth knowing."
WY "Your tailor?"
RV "It is sick, what I heard about them. Perverse! They had plenty of opportunity to talk and plot."
WY "Do you believe you were wrongly imprisoned, and that Tommy Histon played a part in that?"
RV "You are the journalist. What do you think? Let me tell you one thing, and listen very carefully to what I am telling you. When they searched, the only stockpile of

Histon's records they found were in his possession. So, you tell me."

WY "Why did you agree to meet me?"

RV "Because I keep hearing about Histon this and Histon that. It's all bullshit. All of it. I tell you now, and listen to this very carefully. Anything good on that album came from me. Half of those tunes were mine, and he butchered them. And what do I have to show for it? Eh, answer me that?"

WY "But you weren't involved in his other records..."

RV "So what? Dig around. He did to others what he did to me, no doubt. Snakes may shed their skins, but they are the same snakes, are they not?"

WY "Would it be possible to speak with your daughter?"

RV "Sure. If you can find her."

WY "You're not in contact?"

RV ignores the question. "I tell you this now. It's a good thing Histon died. That's all I'm saying."

WY "What do you mean by that?"

RV goes to leave the room.

WY "You were released from prison in 1964, Mr Vertoni. Tommy Histon died that year, just a month after you were released..."

RV leaves the room.

PART TWO: Track Back And Trail On

Tommy in Richmond, Virginia, 1949.

18.

By October of '49, I was back on the road. Vertoni had been arrested for tax evasion, along with other charges, and Rovertone was no more.

None of it made any difference to me, as I'd had enough of it all anyway.

I was done with the music business.

There are times in life when we don't know where to go. It was too late to head down to the fruit farm, and I didn't want another winter north of Virginia.

My low confidence pushed me towards what I knew. So I turned my face west, and headed for the hills. Once back on familiar ground, I planned to move south and stay ahead of the weather creeping down.

I carried my guitar, a pack containing clothing and one copy each of my 78 and album. I made sure I took that fuckin' fifty dollar suit!

The records I'd recorded with Juice Cartwright had been taken as part of the investigation into Vertoni. All of his assets had been seized or frozen.

They questioned me, but I told the truth and was released without charge. After all, I didn't actually know anything beyond what Luca had intimated.

There is no worse feeling in life than knowing one has nobody they can go to and no place to call home.

By rationing my amphetamines, I was attempting to ween myself off them. Constant movement helped with that. It was only when I stopped that I got the cravings.

I covered at least twenty miles a day, skirting any towns I encountered, and sleeping wherever I could improvise or take advantage of shelter. An old abandoned mill served me well one wet night, and bridges chanced along conveniently.

Offers of rides came my way on the roads, but I declined them. I didn't wish to arrive too early. It felt like failure, heading back there, and I was keen to delay my arrival.

Also, I was worried about what I might encounter when I got there, and how I might react. But I had an urge to pay Momma a visit.

On reaching the settlement I once called home, I was shocked to see how nature had reclaimed it in such a short space of time.

There was no sign of human occupation, and, judging by the look of it, there hadn't been for a while. I'd only been gone for two and a half years or so. The others must have left not long after I had.

One cabin had most of its roof left on it, so I dropped my guitar and bag there, and set off to find Momma's grave.

A damned copperhead lay atop her mound. They were more aggressive that time of year, as they sought food to see them through hibernation. But he soon slithered off when he sensed me coming. The fucker.

Gathering wood for a fire, I felt like a child again. It depressed me, that thought, and the notion that I'd been away for so long and had achieved nothing. It was added to by the fact I'd let Momma down.

I recalled her words: "Never go back in life, Tommy. Keep going forward. Keep heading to your future."

An hour before sunset, I hiked over to the rocky outcrop on the neighbouring hill, and sat there picking on my guitar. My fingers were clumsy, having not played it in weeks, and I had to bite off my extended nails and file them down on the rocks to stop the strings buzzing.

Heading back to the cabin in the dark, I snagged my foot on a vine and fell headlong down the steep bank. I landed on the neck of my guitar, and knew it was snapped before my hands set about inspecting it.

Come the following day, I carried it to Momma's grave. That fuckin' snake was back, just as I'd hoped. So, I used the guitar like an axe, and brought it down on the fucker's skull. I took the broken head of my instrument, and drove it into the brains of that bastard.

"Got the fucker, Momma!" I announced, "you can rest easy now."

Flinging my remaining five amphetamines into the undergrowth, I retrieved my bag and walked away, safe in the knowledge that I would never return.

19.

I rode out the winter months in Charleston, South Carolina. There was something positive to be found in a new decade, as 1950 arrived. It felt like a fresh start.

Nothing much happened over the next two years, which I didn't see as a bad thing.

Come the back end of '51, an offer came from Lance, a guy I was working with. We were in one of the Carolinas cleaning swimming pools, and he was heading over to the west coast for the winter. He asked me if I wanted to tag along.

Despite me not having a licence, we shared the driving. Lance said, "if you get pulled over, and we can't switch seats, tell them you're from South Dakota."

"Why?"

"'Cause you don't need a fuckin' licence there, boy!"

Lance claimed to have served in Europe during the war, and parachuted behind enemy lines just before D-Day. But I caught sight of his ID, and he only turned twenty-three in 1951, though he did appear older.

He added, "that's why I move around the coast, boy, 'cause I don't ever wanna be ahead of the landing again!"

Women loved him for his tanned skin, muscular build, and tousled blonde hair. He had a cheeky, clenched-teeth grin that best showed off his perfectly straight, white choppers. You could almost picture them pulling the pin from a grenade.

He was as shallow as a puddle in a drought, and any brains he had were fully occupied with knowing facts such as which states didn't require driving licences, or getting women to adore him.

But, to his credit, he had an uncanny knack of getting whatever he desired, and an ability to talk himself in or out of just about anything.

"Where are you from, Lance?" I asked him.

"I was born in Vienna, boy, where my father was a diplomat before the war. Course, we had to hightail it out of there when Hitler came along. My dad knew him, you know?"

"Hitler?"

"Oh, yeah! He was set to be my godfather, but mom wouldn't let that happen. That was why they parachuted me in ahead of the invasion, boy!"

"Why?"

"Because I could get to him. I was the only one who could get close. I'd just walk right up through his security, say, 'hey uncle Addy!' and slit his fuckin' throat, man!"

Lance's ID said he was born in Cleveland, Ohio.

It was he who first told me Hitler only had one testicle. It may have been the only true thing he ever told me.

Still, I liked hanging out with him. There was never any angle, and he had a way of simply shrugging off anything he encountered. In short, nothing ever bothered Lance.

We'd drive for fifteen hours a day, splitting the shift, and grabbing a few hours sleep in the passenger seat. At around seven every evening, Lance insisted on stopping at the next place we came to that offered food and drink. Sometimes that would be ten minutes on, and other times, maybe two hours.

Once or twice, it got so late, and we were in the wide open spaces of the south, that we'd keep driving till the morning, when the next place selling food and drink might be a diner which we'd hit for breakfast. There were always cookies in the car to keep us going.

It was during that trip across country that I got back on the pills. They overcame fatigue and sharpened my senses.

Lance's lies were so convincing because they weren't told for personal gain. There was no real point to any of his bullshitting, beyond, I suppose, making himself appear more interesting.

For me, lying had always been associated with other forms of deceit. Meet a liar, and I'll show you a thief.

However, Lance was otherwise completely honest. All food and money were shared equally, and I never once felt taken advantage of.

I'll go even further, and state that I trusted him above anyone else I'd met up to that point in my life. Along with Juice Cartwright and Momma, I should say.

On the road, I spotted a sign for New Orleans, and recalled Juice Cartwright talking of it. He told me about the music scene there, and the French Quarter.

"Why don't we hit New Orleans?" I suggested to Lance.

"Ain't never been there!" he announced gleefully.

So that was what we did.

20.

New Orleans was my kind of place.

I knew it as soon as I entered a bar, and was greeted by a man playing piano, and singing 'Boogie Woogie Baby'. I believe that man was Fats Domino, but I didn't know it at the time. He was certainly a large man.

Everywhere we went was the same. Or similar. They were doing something not dissimilar to what I'd done on 'Three Minute Hero'. It was more the feel, than the music itself. There was pace and energy in it all.

Piano was the accompaniment in New Orleans, rather than guitar. And there was definitely a groove that came from race, as I heard the blues Juice had introduced me to.

Blues or folk? It's the same, I guess - the only difference being skin colour. And skin colour never bothered me none.

They gave us some looks in those bars, us two white boys walking in. But we never had any trouble. As soon as they realised we were there to drink a beer and enjoy the music, they treated us just fine.

It helped that Lance told them he was "paid to keep an ear open for new sounds."

"These ears," he continued to the bartender, as he pulled on his earlobes, "can spot a million-seller from a hundred yards away on a busy street, let me tell you."

A few locals turned to us and listened intently, nodding their heads approvingly as Lance waxed lyrical.

"You know, I spotted one of the biggest stars in the business in just those circumstances. It was in Holland in '44, and there was a group of us pinned down in a trench. Three German machine guns had us covered on three sides

- front, left and right. Only one way we could go. Know which way it was?"

"Back, I should think!" a man called over.

"That's what them Germans expected us to do. So, I got half the men to act like that's what they were doing - pulling out. As soon as the machine guns were swivelled in that direction, me and the rest of the company ran straight forward, took that middle gun, and turned it on the two flanks. They never saw it coming!"

"What about the singer you spotted? Who was he?" a different man asked eagerly. Lance really did have a gift.

"I can't tell you who he was," Lance countered, "it wouldn't be right after what we went through in that war. But I can tell you that you've heard of him, and I'd wager a hefty sum on you having seen him in the movies."

There was a lot of speculative muttering in the crowd as Lance nodded knowingly.

He cut over it with, "as we ran over the top of the trench, we all let out a blood-curdling scream. Nyaaaaaarrrrrhhh!

"See, now we did that to disarm the enemy. Not 'cause we were afraid. That barbaric scream made them hesitate for a second, and a second can make all the difference in a situation like that."

Heads bobbed up and down in agreement.

"When it was all over with, I turned to the man I mentioned, and said, 'when we get home victorious from this war, I'm gonna make you a star!'

"He said to me, 'so, how you gonna do that, sir?' To which I replied, "cause I heard you scream when we charged that gun, and I heard perfect pitch and melody in that voice. That's a million-dollar voice right there, and I'll set you up with the right people when we get back Stateside.' "

Lance drained his beer. Another was placed in front of him. Nobody asked him to pay for it.

"New York is where all my contacts are. That's where the money is," Lance informed them, "and I was true to my word for Albert. Oops, I shouldn't have said his name. Still, that ain't his showbiz name, so I guess it won't matter none."

"What are you? Some kind of A&R man?" the bartender asked.

"I ain't nothing. I just keep my eyes and ears open, and give people a helping hand."

"Is this boy a singer?" someone asked, pointing at me.

"I had a record out a couple of years back," I answered, wishing I hadn't as soon as I had.

"What's your name?"

"Tommy Histon."

"Ain't never heard of you," came a call, but not nastily.

Lance was looking at me peculiarly.

"You never told me that," he whispered.

"You never asked," I hissed back, and smiled.

"You're getting the hang of this," he mumbled.

"Of what?"

"You know, working a situation."

Before I could answer, I was invited to take a seat at the piano.

"Oh, no, I don't play. Just the guitar."

Lance breathed a sigh of relief. "Nearly caught you out there, Tommy boy. Always make sure you can back it up."

A guitar appeared from somewhere, and was handed to me.

It had been a long time since I'd broken my Gibson back on the hills of my birth.

Still, it felt good to have my fingers press down on the strings. I went for something safe, an old song I'd known since childhood. It was a simple thumb pick for the bass, and an up-drawn index finger thereafter.

Given where we were, 'Black Is The Colour' seemed apt.

My voice still worked, and the hush in the bar told me I held the attention of the gathered.

Applause greeted the end, so I pushed straight on with a bluesy number I'd written.

Lance sat staring at me, his mouth slightly ajar, as a million thoughts peppered his brain. Each one had a dollar bill pinned to it, I reckon.

"A white man who can actually play and sing the blues!" I heard from over my shoulder at the finale. In that environment, it didn't get much better as far as praise went.

"A man called Juice Cartwright taught me the blues," I announced generally.

"Ah, Juice. You knew him?" the same voice asked.

"Sure. I'm hoping to see him again this coming summer in North Carolina. Picking fruit is what we do."

"Then you really did know him. I'm sorry to tell you, son, but Juice was killed up in Tennessee a few months back. Hit by an automobile, he was, as he made his way home to see his family."

"Oh no," I breathed, and handed back the guitar.

"You okay, son?" the same old man asked, laying a hand on my shoulder.

I nodded, too afraid to speak lest something should come pouring out of me.

'Never be afraid of your own talent, Tommy. Leave that to others,' I heard his voice tell me, as he pushed me into a recording booth.

The man's hand resting on my shoulder made contact in the exact same spot as Juice's had.

21.

"I'll be your manager!" Lance enthused, as we headed back to the car.

"There's nothing to manage," I shrugged.

"Sure there is. You really had a record out?"

"Yes," I admitted absently, Juice Cartwright occupying the majority of my thoughts.

"When was this?"

"Two years ago. Just over. Nearer three, now I add it up. Two records, actually. A 78 and an album."

"I hope you got the publishing rights."

"The what?"

"The publishing rights. Jeez, man, you ain't got a fuckin' clue!"

"Ah, no, I think they went to the record label, Rovertone."

"You ever see any money from those records?"

"No. I was paid a wage for a while, and given a place to live, so I guess that off-set it."

Lance went quiet.

"Happy new year!" he cried suddenly, punching me on my arm.

"Is it?"

"Sure is, Tommy! This is going to be a good year for us. I can feel it. Sense it! Log this moment in that skull of yours, boy! Two minutes into 1952, and remember where we are and what we're doing. A year from now, I'll remind you of this."

I just smiled and shook my head.

We remained in Louisiana for January and February, the weather being mild. I worked in a bar off Bourbon Street. It was a jazz joint, and I got into that sound through exposure.

I guess I stopped being a teenager, and turned twenty at some point while we were there.

Spring came earlier to the south, so we stuck to it, and left to head east as soon as March arrived.

I believe we were in Mississippi when Lance spotted the sign out front of a run-down shack by the roadside, but we may have still been in Louisiana. It advertised the fortune-telling service within.

"Come on man, it'll be fun," Lance entreated.

"You go. I don't need to see any prediction," I resisted.

I left the car to stretch my legs and smoke a cigarette, and watched him enter through the door.

The old woman turned back and looked at me before sealing them both inside. I was pretty sure I saw a tug around her mouth that flushed a little of the colour out of her complexion when she did that. She followed it with a small bow of her head, before she shuffled away.

Lance emerged a few minutes later, and a few cents lighter. His clenched-teeth grinned at me, forcing his jaw squarer than it usually was.

"My future's bright, man! You know how many children I'm going to have?"

"No," I replied.

"Seven! Lucky fuckin' seven, Tommy."

He added, "I'd better get started soon, I guess!"

Over his shoulder, the woman... Was she a woman? She may have been a man. There was a whole mix of all things. It was as though everything I'd seen in people was contained in that one form.

Thin and brittle, yet strong; tall but not, her bowed legs lessening her height; black and white; Cajun; American Indian; Asian; blue-eyed; black-haired; kind; evil.

The blue eyes turned black, as her pupils filled her irises. It was as though she was looking into complete darkness.

A finger jutted out and pointed directly at me, as fluid ran from somewhere beneath the smock he or she wore, and muddied the sandy earth.

"Only listen to your dreams when you know it's safe to do so! And only tell your life story when you're ready to let it go!" she wailed, before snapping back to the here and now.

"She pissed herself!" Lance felt the need to point out.

The woman, for she was a woman again, looked down at her feet.

"Hubba! My waters just broke!"

A man appeared from the rear of the shack, and led her inside.

"No harm in it!" she called back over her shoulder as she shambled away. "No harm in telling of a future people want to hear, rather than what is! Let the boy be, I tell you. Little white lies never hurt nobody if well intentioned! Enough bad in the world! More bad coming outta me, I'd say. Who knows? Tell 'em a little story 'bout kiddies and happy living, and maybe things turn out different! Maybe change the course!"

"Fuckin' crazy, man," Lance whispered in my ear, "let's get out of here. We'll be drinking fresh orange juice in Florida before you know it, boy!"

22.

It was in Miami that Lance discovered LSD, though we didn't know it was called that back then.

I only ever tried it three times, and regretted every occasion. Lance took to it in a big way.

Whereas I was somewhat nervous of exploring my own mind through heightened senses, Lance was a different character. His shallowness made him unafraid of diving in.

I don't mean that in a bragging way. Lance was a good friend to me, and he was as straightforward as they come. I think he knew that about himself.

When he saw the fortune-teller, he thought it funny and dismissed it, aside from the bits it suited him to retain. I thought it both terrifying and fascinating.

Somewhere in that is why LSD didn't suit me.

My plan altered after hearing of Juice's death. Returning to North Carolina in May no longer appealed. Instead, we remained in Miami until the heat kicked in, and Lance and I began driving north to New York, where "I'll work my contacts to get a deal you ain't capable of imagining. You'll be on the television and in the movies in no time."

Smiling, I nodded along, not believing a word of it.

"That face," he said, stabbing a finger in my cheek, "will be on billboards all over the country. No! Fuck that! All over the world, boy. All through the music! Think Frank Sinatra. Or Dean Martin. That'll be you."

"Shouldn't we have a contract, Lance, if you're going to be my manager?" I asked him, as we drove north through my native Virginia.

"Why, you planning on ripping me off?"

"No."

"Then why the fuck do we need a contract, boy? Mister Twenty Percent, that's me. That's my slice of the pie. Shake on it now," he said, taking his hand off the wheel, spitting in it, and offering it to me.

I shook his hand and knew that he'd never see twenty percent of anything.

"As soon as I get the deal done, I'm gonna find me a nice wife and start having them seven kiddies. Time for me to settle down, Tommy boy. I've seen enough of this world. I fought my way through Europe all the way to Berlin, and then went over to the Pacific to make sure them nukes went where they were supposed to go. I've been to every state in the union, and plenty places besides. All I seen is blood and carnage, boy, and I'm done with it."

I nodded my understanding, and blew smoke out the window as we snaked up Route 1.

"By the way," he continued, "when we get up to The Big Apple, best you call me Rick. Hey, do me a favour, will you?"

"Sure."

"Dig through my bag in the back there, and slide your hand under the gap at the side of the bottom. Feel it? That's it. Find me the ID for Richard Doyle. No, not that one. That's it. Here, stick Lance away in there for a while. It's time for me to become Rick again."

"But I thought your name was Lance," I stammered.

"Perhaps it is, perhaps it ain't!" he winked at me. "Plenty of men died in the war, boy, so there are a lot of boots waiting to be filled! Now, what's my fuckin' name?"

"Rick."

"Rick what?"

"Rick Doyle."

"Who do you wanna be?"

"Tommy."

"Bullshit. Everyone wants to be someone else."

"Nope. Tommy Histon is who I am."

"Fair enough," Rick said sceptically.

"What?" I asked after a period of silence during which he glanced at me every few seconds.

"Why don't you be Lance?" he suggested.

"I don't want to be Lance."

"But Tommy Histon..."

"What about it?"

He paused, before saying, "you had a record out under that name."

"Yeah, so what?"

"Well, how did it do?"

I hung my head before answering, "not great."

"No, and the name Tommy Histon will always be associated with it. Look, if you don't like Lance, make up a name for yourself. Who do you want to be?"

"I like Tommy. I like my name."

"What about Maximus?"

"Tommy Histon," I reiterated.

"It don't sound like a star name to me, boy, I gotta say. No showbiz in that name!"

"Well, it's the name my Momma gave me. So what's your real name?"

"My real name was left in Berlin. That's all I'll tell you."

So, Lance became Rick and I stayed as Tommy.

Every few miles, he'd ask me, "what's my name?"

"Rick."

"Rick what?"

"Rick Doyle."

And he became the person who he wanted to be.

23.

"I'll need a suit. Gotta look the part, boy," Rick decided.

"I have one in my bag. All it needs is an ironing and an airing."

"How tall am I?"

"Six-two?" I ventured.

"Six-three. How tall are you?"

"Okay, not that tall, but the hems could be dropped."

"You're about five-seven. If that."

I was slightly taller than that, but the difference was negligible, so I let it slide.

"What do you weigh?" he asked next.

"Not sure."

"You don't weigh fuckin' two-thirds what I weigh. How will I ever fit in a suit made for a fuckin' midget?" he wailed at me, but in jest.

Feeling the need to recover some ground, I noticed the sign for Richmond. "I know a tailor in Richmond."

"No shit?"

"Yep."

"How much cash we got, boy?"

"Not enough. But the guy might do me a favour."

That was how I came to end up back in Richmond, Virginia.

Luca the tailor was gone, his store and upstairs fitting room taken over by something I don't recall and had no use for.

We wound up sitting in a bar in Carytown sipping cheap beer and watching the world pass by.

"That suit of yours?" Rick asked eventually.

"Yep."

"How much hem is there to play with?"

"Not enough."

"We need a blag, boy!" he announced brightly.

"A what?"

"A blag. It's a term we used over in Europe. We need a play!"

"A con, you mean?"

He nodded his big blonde head and grinned with all his considerable teeth. As we sat there thinking of a blag, it was the first time I'd really noticed that his neck was broader than any part of his skull.

"Here's the plan!" he relayed with gusto. "You go into a department store, locate the men's clothing area, and ask for your suit to be cleaned and pressed.

"Tell 'em you require it in a hurry, and I'll bet a dollar to a cent they'll have it ready by this very afternoon. Tomorrow morning at the latest. Besides, with you being a midget and all, it ain't like they got a lot of material to get through!

"Take a sharp blade in with you, and when inspecting it, slash the pants and jacket in a clean line somewhere not obvious.

"You then notice the cuts in the material, and make a hell of a scene, boy! When they offer to replace it, you just gotta make sure you get one that'll fit me."

"I think they may check the size," I pointed out.

"You just tell 'em you still got growing to do! Trust me, they'll believe you."

"I'm five-nine, nearly five-ten. And I'm not doing that, Lance, it's not right."

"What's my name?"

"Rick. I mean Rick Doyle."

"Aw heck, I ain't gonna ask you to do something you ain't comfortable with. Besides, if you can't even get my name right, you'll probably fuck up the rest of it."

He drifted into another spell of deep thought, as he stared through his beer at the window.

"Got it!" he declared, slamming his glass down. "I'll take your suit in, and ask for a chemical cleaning. When they give it back to me, I'll insist on trying it on. Well, I'll look like a sack of shit in a dwarf suit. And I shall insist on them replacing it after their chemical cleaning process shrank it to such a midget size, boy!"

Saying nothing, I simply shook my head and smiled at him.

"Well, do you have a better fuckin' idea?"

"How much money do we need?" I asked.

"A couple of hundred bucks should see us okay. I need a suit for the meetings. Fuel, food and drink, a haircut each, some new leather shoes to go with the smart rags. We can sleep as we have been while the weather's nice, so no need for accommodation. And we need a PO Box, so's we can get mail."

"What can we sell or pawn?" I asked.

"I thought of that. The car is the thing, but we need that to get around. Besides, it's what we sleep in. If I hocked off everything I own, I can maybe get a third of that. You?"

I shook my head. I'd be lucky to raise thirty dollars. My suit was worth fifty new, according to Luca, so maybe fifteen second-hand. Still, I'd do what I could.

My biggest disappointment came when I offered the pawnbroker my 78 and album. He looked at them, shook his head, and offered me a quarter each for them.

I took it.

My life value at that point was worth eighteen dollars and fifty cents.

Aside from the clothes I wore, a set to change in to, and a bag I carried them in, I owned nothing on this earth.

I've never forgotten what Rick did for us that day.

I like to think that he did it primarily for me, because he believed in my music. But, yes, he did it for his twenty percent, too.

He sold everything he had. It wasn't much, but it was his entire life in material terms.

The medals broke his heart.

His teeth clenched inside his closed mouth, the pain at letting them go sending jolts of anguish along his chiselled cheekbones.

I didn't see what they were, those medals, but I saw what they meant to him.

Between us, we had our two hundred dollars.

Rick was the quietest I'd ever known him that evening and the following day.

I even began to wish we'd tried the suit blag.

"Those medals..." I ventured, as he drove north towards New York the next afternoon.

"Just fuckin' metal and ribbon, boy. That's all they were. Let it go."

"We'll get the money and buy them back," I told him.

"Sure we will. Sure we fuckin' will, boy. You know it! Or I'll earn me some fresh ones! Shit, I earned more medals in that war than any soldier anywhere, I reckon. I had a fuckin' drawer full of the bastards once. As well as the ones I took from the fallen, both friend and foe, boy. I ain't proud of taking them gongs, but you do that in wartime.

"Your head ain't right when the shells are falling, and the bullets are whizzing by you, and the planes are screaming above, the ground shaking below!

"If I didn't take 'em, some other piece of shit would have done, and who knows what he'd have done with them? Me, I took 'em to stop that. To preserve them, and keep them sacred. Because, no matter what side you're on, boy, them medals were earned by suffering hell!

"That's why it felt wrong letting them go. It was like I was letting down the fuckin' dead, you know?"

And just like that, Rick Doyle, or Lance, or whoever he really was, was back.

24.

"No, ma'am, I don't have an appointment, as I explained already. Thing is, I have a hot new talent, and I know Jimmy will want to hear him!"

Rick Doyle pointed at me when he said that.

The lady gave me a quick look, and replied, very pointedly, "Mr James Ardanian will hear him if you send in a recording and a biography."

"Oh, I know, and I also know that he'll take a fu... What I mean to say is, that he'll take a firm grip of my hand, and shake on the deal there and then. Thing is, and this is the thing, between us," Rick said, and leaned in low to the lady behind the desk, "I know a lot of top brass in this business from the war, you know? And I already have three fu... Three, maybe four, people interested in Mr Histon here, and I'd hate for Jimmy to miss out. That's the thing. You hear what I'm saying?"

She looked dubiously at Rick, as he gave her his best grenade pin smile.

He then added, "I'd also hate for you to get into any trouble for being the reason Tommy Histon here fu... fell through the cracks, so to speak."

With that, Rick slipped her twenty dollars to, "pick up something nice to wear for the big launch party! Hey, you don't happen to sing, do you, 'cause you certainly do look right for the business?"

Much to my surprise, Mr James Ardanian would meet us in his office at eleven the following day.

Rick then used that appointment to secure two more, all for the next day.

"I don't even have a guitar," I pointed out, as we strolled aimlessly around New York that late-evening.

Whatever Rick's reply was, I didn't hear it.

Even in the dim light from the streetlight, there was something familiar in the way she held herself, just as there was in the blackness of her hair and the whiteness of her skin.

"Clarissa?" I asked, as I veered across the road towards her.

Her once shining brown eyes were dull; her mouth slack where before it had playfully portrayed her every emotion.

"I know you," she slurred, but it was clear she couldn't quite recall where from.

"Tommy," I reminded her, "Tommy Histon."

"Still singing songs, Tommy?" she garbled.

"Yes. Well, just about to start again."

"Give me some money, Tommy. I just need a few dollars, baby."

"I don't have any money, Clarissa."

"Sure you do! Just a few bucks. Don't worry, there'll be something in it for you. And your friend here. A few dollars, and you can both fuck me at the same time."

"What happened, Clarissa? Where's your family, your husband?"

"Prison. Italy. Fuck knows. How about three bucks between you, and we can go up to the room?"

"No," I said firmly, "come on, you're coming with us."

"Two, as old friends. Two bucks..."

Taking her arm, I began to walk her down the street. Rick said something about not getting involved, but I wasn't listening.

"What the fuck do you think you're doing?" a voice asked me, as I became vaguely aware of two men who had emerged from the doorway near where she'd been standing.

Cold metal pressed against my temple.

Still I tried to walk Clarissa away.

Rick, or Lance, or whoever he was, was talking, "hey, guys, calm fuckin' down, we don't want any trouble, okay? We were just walking along, and he thought he recognised the lady, that's all. Mistaken identity, that's what it was. A mix up, I suppose you might call it. No harm done. Look, I'm happy to pay a little for any inconvenience. How much will make this right, eh?

"Here's a twenty bill, to cover any time lost and trouble..."

Clarissa was trying to pull away from me. Why?

"Let me go, let me go, let the fuck go of me!" she wailed.

The gun was pressing into my skull, making it ache. Rick was talking, talking, talking, the two men talking, talking, talking.

Everyone was fuckin' talking!

I moved like a snake. One fluid strike. It felt and appeared pre-determined, but all of it was instinctive; present from my past, yet dormant till required.

It was something inherent in me over which I had no control.

"Shut the fuck up!" It took a moment to work out the words were said by me.

Somehow, I was the one holding a pistol to the temple of a man who cowered before me.

Clarissa stood still, no longer wishing to return, staring at me with her dead-eyes and slack mouth.

I said her name, but it didn't sound right. It came from way down within me, the 'sssss' hissing asp-like in my ears.

Everyone was trying to get away.

Why was Rick lying on the ground?

His new suit would get dirty, and we had meetings the next day. Important meetings.

Meetings that would set us both up. No need to sleep in the car for much longer. He'd get his twenty percent. Settle down with a good woman. Have his seven children.

We'd buy his medals back from the pawnbroker.

But none of it was ever going to happen.

The fortune-teller knew it.

Just as I did.

25.

I don't remember much. The detail, I mean.

My mind has an ability to go into hibernation. That's the best way I can describe it. Something else I inherited.

I didn't pull the trigger. They knew that, the police. From the ballistics.

And Clarissa Vertoni's statement. That corroborated the evidence.

They let me go, despite me telling them that I did it.

It made no difference to me, whether I went to prison for it or not.

For six months, I remained in New York awaiting the trial. I sold the car and lived off the proceeds, eking out the money. I sat in parks a lot, and survived on very little. Any sleep I got was on a bench with the sun on me.

I never did make those meetings Rick and I had scheduled.

In court, as a witness, I wasn't much use to anyone - prosecution or defence. And least of all myself.

Thankfully, Clarissa Vertoni turned herself around. She looked as she once looked - the spark of life back in her eyes; a playfulness twisting her mouth.

She told the court that I saved her life. She called me a hero.

"Had it not been for Mr Histon, I'm fairly sure I'd be dead right now."

They destroyed her as a witness, playing up her drug addiction, prostitution and time in a clinic rehabilitating. Her family history also came up, as did her father being in prison.

Still, she spoke well, and told the truth.

The defence hinged on it being accidental, the killing of Cecil Morrison, for that was his real name. He was thirty-two in that year of 1952.

He was born in Vienna, just as he'd told me. The only thing was, it was Vienna in Northern Virginia.

Still, it was good to hear that he served with distinction in the war, albeit without ever leaving the USA. His father, I heard, had served in Europe during the First World War, and his brother, a paratrooper, had been killed around D-Day in the Second.

My job title was given as musician, and my address as a shelter in Brooklyn. It's where I'd been since winter had arrived.

I'd seen the christmas decorations around the city, and had a vague recollection of eating a christmas dinner, but it came as a shock to learn it was 1953.

They went to prison, the two pimps. One for nine months, and the other - the one from who I took the gun that killed Cecil - for five years. I forget the term used, but the sentence was light due to the circumstances.

For reasons I didn't understand, I was then awarded two thousand dollars in damages. My legal rep wanted to refuse it, and fight for more, but I wanted out of the place, so took it.

Cecil's parents, who had sat ashen-faced through it all, received a lot more than that.

They thanked me.

"Why?" I asked them.

"For being his friend," they said.

I told them about the medals in a pawn place in Richmond.

"If you give me an address, I'll collect them, and send them on," I offered.

They told me that "the Lord Jesus Christ didn't approve of such trinkets, particularly those that glorified the horror of war."

They added that their compensation would go to the church, and its charitable causes. "It's what Cecil would have wanted."

Two men approached me as I left the court. They were two of the twelve jurors. Their names were Marcus and Johnny Anderson, but weren't related to one another.

"We're setting up a record label, Mr Histon," they happily informed me, "down in Delaware, where business rates are less and Marcus has family."

"Best of luck with that," I told them. I was keen to get to a hotel, after a stop off at a store for some new clothes and shoes. I wanted to start spending my fortune.

"How'd you like to get involved?"

"Sure, I'll look you up. What's the name of it, this record label of yours?"

"Jury Duty!" they announced in unison.

"Jury Duty in Delaware," I reiterated so it went in my memory, "I'll be sure to look you up. Now, if you'll excuse me."

"Swing by next week," they urged.

"You don't even know what kind of music I make," I pointed out.

Marcus shuffled awkwardly. "That's true," he said, "but as part of your statement, you did say there were meetings scheduled for the day after the shooting. With major labels in the city."

"Yeah, and the girl there, Vertoni," Johnny chipped in, "she said you made a record for her father down in Richmond as part of her testimony."

Yeah, thought I, and I have two grand burning a fuckin' hole in my fuckin' pocket.

"Okay, I'll see if I can swing by next week."

With that, I strolled off to have the best three nights sleep, and the best food, I'd ever enjoyed in my life.

26.

For the first time in my twenty-one years, I rode a train. When I say that, I mean that I rode a train from the comfort of a seat in a carriage, having purchased a ticket.

And I didn't have to shovel the coal.

Having lived off a hundred and twenty dollars in six months, I made sure I blew through at least twice that in a week.

In addition, I picked up a '52 Gretsch archtop guitar in a music store in Washington DC, as I passed through on my way to Delaware.

A hundred and fifty bucks in a hard case, I think it was, with some strings, a strap and other things thrown in to sweeten the deal.

So, I arrived in Delaware four-hundred greenbacks lighter. Money never mattered too much to me. And that applied whether I had it or didn't.

To my surprise, the Anderson boys didn't want me to hand over the remainder.

I played them a couple of my old songs, and a cover of something from the movies, right there in their office, and I was signed up. Simple as that. A two album deal.

They offered to fund a recording studio for twelve hours, split into three four hour sessions during the cheap rate hours. Would that be long enough to make an album?

"If I go in prepared, it should be a breeze," I told them.

Twelve hours! I'd nailed 'Three Minute Hero' in about a third of that.

Unlike with Vertoni, I wasn't salaried or offered accommodation.

I saw the pros and cons in that. If they invested more, they would be keener to recoup the cost, and promote me better. However, because there was very little outlay, not much required clawing back. Thus, I was on a higher percentage of each record sale as a result.

The way I figured things, they were starting out. They were correct to play it safe, and not blow a stack right from the get-go, or commit to having to pay me any salary. It was what I'd have done.

Besides, the whole relaxed approach suited me better, and I was more than happy to find cheap digs and re-learn my trade for a few weeks. I had the money to support myself in idleness.

Not that I was idle, but I didn't need to go out and work every day.

'Track Back And Trail On' was the title I came up with for my second long-playing record. It borrowed from many of the folk songs I'd known since childhood, but distorted and stretched them somewhat, and I added my own lyrics in the main part.

Also, I played them slower than on 'Three Minute Hero'. I wasn't in such a hurry.

Over here in England a decade on, people tell me it was folk-rock, folk-jazz or folk-blues that I did on that record.

To me it's all just music. I don't hear much of a difference between what I did then, and what these Beatles boys are doing now. My only advice to them, is to write more of their own songs, because that's the stuff of theirs that I think has legs on it.

All I did, as far as my conscious mind knew, was put into it all of the things I'd absorbed over recent years. Any jazzy or swing presence came from my time in New Orleans. The rock part from my blues training with Juice, and the R&B I'd picked up all over the States.

In addition, the Gretsch archtop had a kind of jazzy flavour to the sound.

I modified that guitar, adding a new pick-up, fitting an unwound string on the third, and sanding down the reverse of the neck lightly for smoothness. I like to feel the grain of the wood on my skin.

My strings were as light as I could get them, for speed, even though they tended not to last as long as the heavier gauge.

The big body suited me, and I found it a very apt guitar for my style, even if it was a little quieter than I would have liked when played acoustically.

I didn't bother vowing to not break that one, given what had become of my previous two instruments. But I am delighted to report, as I sit writing these notes, that the guitar is in its original case by my side.

It is the longest relationship I've had with anything since my mother died.

Momma was always my motivation. Her energy - her life force - lived on in me, and gave me impetus to keep going, even when I hit a seemingly impenetrable wall.

For three weeks, I squirreled myself away in my room, only venturing outdoors for sustenance. It was cold that February, and my fingers would cramp after a short time of playing guitar.

That was why I began writing down my ideas.

There was no means of recording available to me outside of a studio, so I used a simple numerical system, such as 1-7, 1-4, to show the first two notes of the melody were to be played on the first string, at the seventh and fourth frets.

At that time, I didn't know any of the note characters, and still can't read music. It was when I looked at the code, I came up with the alternative guitar tunings people now rave about.

The truth is, I came up with them for no other reason than to make it easier to play.

27.

At midnight on February 27th, 1953, I entered a studio in a beach town in the south of the state.

By six in the morning, we were so close to finishing the tracks, that we stayed an extra hour to do precisely that.

Present were myself, Marcus Anderson and an engineer / producer named Hank.

Every sound on the record was made by me, except for some hand-clapping and other percussion Marcus contributed.

Without question, Marcus fully supported what I was laying down that night, despite what he might have later claimed.

Johnny Anderson hated the record. He'd managed, somehow, to pick up a copy of 'Three Minute Hero', and was expecting something along those lines. Also, the audition I'd done in the office utilised my earlier material.

Yes, I understood that the faster paced music was getting popular at the time, but, for me, it was something I'd moved on from.

"This is the fuckin' record I want to make!" I growled at him.

"How the fuck are we going to sell it?" Johnny snarled back, "there's nothing else out there like it!"

"That's the fuckin' point!"

Marcus sat by and said nothing. If he'd chipped in, weight of numbers may have swung it.

"We need something like 'Three Minute Hero', Tommy. That's what we thought you'd bring to us. Every indicator is that this 'rock' sound is the future. Flash in the pan, I grant you, but it's gonna be huge for a while. You should have seen the kids in California! They were wild for this Western Swing music down there. That's what we need from you!" Johnny bawled at me in his whiney voice.

"Western Swing? What the fuck is that?"

"Look," Marcus chipped in, in a conciliatory tone, "we have plenty of studio time left. Why don't we go back in, lay down some more tracks, and I know a couple of guys locally. One plays the fiddle, and the other an accordion. We aren't that far away from the sound we want."

"Hillbilly rock music," Johnny screeched in enthusiasm, "that's what we need! That's the future right there! Bob Wills is where you should be aiming!"

I was on my way out the door at the word fiddle.

Seething, I went over to the studio that night at twelve. I didn't tell the label I was going. Hank and I wasted the remaining hours on tidying up one or two bits on the tracks I already had, overdubbing, and setting levels in the control booth.

It was valuable time for me, as, thanks to Hank, I quickly picked up the nuances of the two-track facility and the studio desk. I also saw the potential in multi-tracking, by using tape to record two tracks, playing them back as one track, and playing along with the earlier two. Hank wasn't keen on the idea, but assured me I could make a four-track recording that way.

Not that I planned on adding fiddle or accordion.

Hank was a quiet man who only seemed to speak if asked a question. Even then, his answers would be succinct and precise. He gave off an air of being bored by all that he did.

He was born in Europe, and had a certain cold efficiency about him, as well as an accent.

However, that second night I spent with him, he warmed up a little. My showing interest in the other side of the desk, I think, injected some enthusiasm. In addition, he seemed to get a little kick out of me digging my heels in against the record label.

In time, I'd learn that there was something of the rebel in old Hank.

"Know what you want, set your values, and stick to them no matter what," he once said to me.

He retained something youthful inside of him. It resided alongside a darkness that, he gave the impression, was constantly having to be contained.

Johnny was real pissed at me burning the studio time, and it meant Marcus had to choose a side. He went with Johnny.

Still, they put the album out, mainly because they didn't have a choice. I was adamant I would not alter my music.

Johnny was never civil to me thereafter. He told me, "well, we're going to make mistakes on the first record, so it may as well be a record nobody gives a shit about. Imagine if we made those mistakes on something with commercial appeal!"

I believe that was the only reason it saw light of day as the debut release on Jury Duty Records. It was merely a learning curve for them.

It hit the stores in late-April, 1953, and did better than the Andersons expected. It didn't do anywhere near as well as I'd hoped.

That said, a few thousand copies sold, sufficient to net me a small payment. It was the first money I'd earned from my music since my busking days four or five years before. I didn't really count what Vertoni gave me.

All in all, I was pretty pleased with that.

28.

Interview with Johnny Anderson, first published in 'Rooty-Tooty Magazine' as part of a feature on Histon, April 1988.

Where and when did you first meet Tommy Histon?

I met Tommy Histon in January of 1953, and by the February he was signed on to Jury Duty, a label I co-founded with Marcus Anderson, who is no relation.

Marcus and I were on jury duty service together, and Histon was a witness in that case. During the trial, Marcus and I began talking about an idea to form a record label.

Well, when we discovered Histon had released an album, and was a musician, it seemed too good to be true. And so it would prove.

Did either of you have experience of the music industry?

First and foremost, I am a businessman with an interest in music. Marcus, I know he won't mind me saying, is a music fan who wished to enter into a business based around his passion for recorded music.

Fundamentally, that was the difference between us. I probably should never have entered into a professional relationship with Marcus. I saw that early on. He wasn't right for the role, as he allowed his heart to inform his head.

As evidenced by the fact that Jury Duty went under just months after I departed, and I went on to own and run a very successful company.

You worked in septic tank maintenance, correct, as part of an established family business?

It was a little more than that! My father started the company after the war, as a one-man operation. By the time I joined, we had one member of staff, and my mother running the books. Within a decade of my joining, we employed twelve people, and had contracts for the upkeep of many domestic septic waste systems in California.

Am I correct in thinking you weren't keen on signing Histon to Jury Duty?

Oh, I invited him down to Delaware for an audition. I suppose I felt sorry for him. His friend had been killed, which was why he was a witness in court, and he looked as though he could use a break.

I intended it as a kind act. A charitable act, I suppose.

That audition led to a recording contract for two albums?

It did. Marcus kind of screwed that up, signing him up for two. To help Histon out, I figured we could do an album, and use it as a dummy run. I knew we had no experience of getting a record out, and wished to learn lessons on something low-risk.

I made the decision to not put Histon on a salary, thank goodness! He would get a percentage of sales. Even that tells you how little confidence I had in him.

The label's first release was Histon's 'Track Back And Trail On': Did you like the record?

As I've said elsewhere, no I did not.

I tried to help him on that record - to steer him. If he'd listened to me, he may have fared better in terms of sales.

Shucks, I even stumped up for more studio time to get it somewhere closer to what it needed to be.

The son of a b wasted the extra hours without telling us, and, if anything, made the album worse as a result!

That's what I was dealing with.

How did you think the record should have been?

Histon misrepresented himself at the audition, in my opinion. He played us tracks that had a country feel to them, and were more like rock'n'roll in delivery.

That was what I was expecting.

So, you don't think his album was visionary, and hold it in any kind of reverence, as many do?

No. Look, I myself could record an album today in 1988, and go way out there with it. In time, I guarantee you someone will do something similar, and look back on my record with all you describe.

In essence, it was folk-rock. Well, folk and rock already existed. It was obvious someone would combine the two.

But Histon was the first?

I wouldn't know. There were probably a lot of people doing something along those lines at the time. Histon was merely the one who got to release an album. He even stole half of the tunes from traditional songs!

He got lucky, I guess, in being the first to release a record in that style.

But there was no market for it. As evidenced by sales.

Before you go there, yes, I make the same argument for 'Coda'. It wasn't a very good record. It was, in actuality, a joke, I believe.

Histon recorded that album to **** me off. None of it made much sense lyrically, and the songs were very strange.

Well, yeah! Come the late-sixties, and drug culture, there were a lot of strange people around! Of course they'd associate with it, and read into it all manner of things that aren't even close to being based in reality!

I was glad I was out of the business, I'll tell you that.

I truly believe he would be as surprised as anyone that it is regarded so highly. In fact, I bet he'd be sat laughing at all the people holding it in such esteem.

As I say, it was a joke record, made for no other reason than to take a swipe at me personally.

Why did you release it?

Because Marcus screwed up the contract.

Look, in the septic business, if I took on a client for three years, and they proved to be a pain in my rear, there's very little I can do about it. I have to deal with them for three years. You have to take the **** with the smooth in life.

Histon released three albums, each of which preempted music trends - are you saying he got lucky three times?

People hear what they want to hear, and make connections that don't exist. That's all I'm saying.

But think of it like this: In business, it's all about turnover and cash-flow. Whether he was ahead musically or not, is an irrelevance. The truth is - how many records did he sell?

I'd go as far as to say, Histon ruined every label he was associated with.

Rovertone went under after releasing a poorly-received album by him. Jury Duty never recovered from its Histon involvement. And my leaving didn't exactly help with that, of course, because Marcus didn't have the necessary acumen.

And his fourth record, I believe, never saw light of day because he destroyed it!

Histon, in all cases, was a drain on resources and cashflow. No business can afford to sit around and wait for years for somebody to do something like Tommy Histon did before there's any demand for it.

You made money out of Histon, though, didn't you?

No. Not when you really work the numbers. Sure, he sold a few units, but it didn't allow for our time and effort spent. We were having to pay Histon his percentage before we could pay ourselves! Before we could invest in the company!

It was that lack of budget that ultimately cost Marcus.

We had a singer, Greengrass, and he could have been huge. A fine vocalist, he was, with a good range of commercially appealing songs.

Well, if we could have properly backed him, I believe he may have gone on to be as big as, say, Bob Wills. Or even Glen Campbell.

However, because we felt obligated to honour our commitment to Histon, we let Marty Greengrass drift, and the rest is history. The worst of it was, Marty was salaried, so we were having to pay him all the while our time was being wasted.

I still feel gutted for that young man. Now, there was a talent. And he was primed to be a star. He was the kind of boy you could take home to meet your mother.

Coming back to Tommy, do you have anything you'd like to add?

On his music? No.

As a person? Yes. He was a nasty, unappreciative, manipulative son of a b.

He once threatened me with a knife, did you know that?

Why?

Oh, it was over nothing, really. I struggle to recollect. I think he wanted to borrow some money, or some such thing, probably for his drugs and drink.

Well, I refused, and he got very aggressive. He pulled a knife on me. Now, I controlled the situation, and nobody got hurt. That was the important thing.

But how could I deal with someone like that?

Truth is, Marcus was too soft on him. He should have backed me in getting shot of Histon early on.

Look, if a septic system is backing up, it's because there's too much **** in the tank.

When that's the case, you bring in a tanker and pump it out of there!

Well, that's what we should have done with Histon.

Were you sorry to hear about what befell Tommy after 1954?

I wasn't surprised. It was very clear to me that he had mental issues. He was wired wrong, and it was always going to result in something bad.

I'll be honest with you. The tragedy wasn't that he wound up in an asylum. It was the fact that they let him out.

Why did you agree to this interview on Tommy Histon?
I'm sick and tired of hearing about Histon. Whenever someone approaches me regarding Jury Duty, Histon is all they wish to talk about.

What about all the good music I released? Nobody wants to talk about that.

It's wrong, I tell you. Plain wrong.

PART THREE: Coda

Delaware, 1953.

29.

Despite that modest income, my money was dwindling, so I set off on the last day of June, and rode a freight train down as far as Williamsburg, Virginia.

I was twenty-one, and already felt as though I'd lived two lifetimes.

For no other reason than I couldn't think of anywhere to go, I settled there in Williamsburg for some nine months.

Life was fairly routine, as I worked for a gardening company during the day, and busked for extra money in the evening. The tourists were always plentiful, even when the weather cooled off.

Sometimes, I'd earn as much in the evening as I did in the day time.

After a few weeks moving around places, I found digs in a log cabin out the back of a house a mile or so outside the city. I worked a deal whereby my rent was reduced in exchange for tending the grounds of the property and cutting the grass.

Between all the work, there was no time for me to get into any trouble. I met a couple of girls, and had some fun with them, but they went away once the colleges returned.

Come christmastime, the outdoor work dried up. I was let go by the gardening company, but my cabin was kept at the low rent despite there being no mowing to do.

I think the owners liked having me around to keep an eye on the place, as the husband was often away on business.

His wife was a whimsical woman, who hummed or trilled melodies to herself as she pottered about the place.

Leonard and Dotty were their names, and I guess they were in their late-forties to early-fifties.

They were the perfect happy couple, who appeared to live in a picture book, where fairies occupied the bottom of the garden, and rainbows arced over their twee and blessed life every single day.

"Mercy me, it sure is grand having a youngster around!" Dotty cooed one spring day, having come out to enjoy the weather and sit on the porch swing.

Her southern accent made everything sound like a rhyme, her childish lilt adding a layer of purity.

I smiled, as I painted another truss on the porch, taking advantage of the mild dry weather to get a couple of jobs checked off.

"Surely does smell like spring, Tommy dear, and when the birds a-sing, it sounds it to my ear!"

"Sure does," I agreed, and began composing a little guitar piece in my head to match her lyrics.

"Do you have any children?" I asked her as she rocked gently back and forth, smiling up at the sky.

"Oh, as we always say, we weren't blessed in that-a way!"

"I'm sorry," I said, because I could well imagine her being a wonderful mother. She had an air of patience and tolerance; so caring and gentle.

She was also the plainest looking woman I'd ever seen in my life. She had no features that you might describe as attractive, and her figure was utterly characterless. Yet, so much beauty existed within her by way of compensation, it seemed.

It was why it was such a shock when she said, "yes, spring brings the doe, followed by the buck, and once that happens, there's going to be a fuck."

My face blushed furiously, as my mind wondered if she knew what the word meant.

I figured I must have misheard, as she seamlessly added, "won't you come to church tomorrow? Leonard has a jacket you can borrow."

"No, thank you. I want to get a second coat on this porch while the weather holds."

"Ah, mercy me, such a shame," she beamed, as she clapped her hands lightly, "all work and no play, sends Honey's cunny astray!"

"Sorry?" I found myself saying, as I tried hard not to laugh.

"You don't know that expression, dear?"

I shook my head.

"It's a southern thing, I guess."

With that, she rose from the swing, and went into the house humming a happy little tune.

I was left with a very clear enduring snapshot of her briefly exposed vagina.

"Tea for two, and two for tea," she chirped from inside the house.

Glancing up, I saw her standing on the other side of the screen door fanning her skirt in what can only be described as an immodest way.

Leonard walked up to the house at that moment, back from his nights away on business.

"Lenny, sweetheart! Is it already three? You're just in time for tea!"

"Now, come on, Dotty, let's get back inside and I'll help you with pouring it," he said to her, casting a glance at me, which could have conveyed either apology or disappointment.

30.

Len came over to the cabin that evening.

I began to plead my innocence, but he stopped me with a tired smile and shake of his head.

He toted a bottle of bourbon and two glasses.

We sat and drank.

"She's what they call a sex addict. Nymphomania is the term they use. I knew that when we met. Truth is, I fell for the gentle woman beneath all that."

"How did you meet?" I asked him.

"It was down in Georgia, where we were both born and bred. Our families were acquainted through the church, and I'd see her there every Sunday with her folks.

"I was nineteen, and pretty innocent, I guess, looking back. Who wouldn't want a wife who was a sex addict at that age?

"Little did I know the problems it would cause us. Her family couldn't wait to offload her, so it was all very rushed.

"Her sex addiction began when puberty came. And puberty came early to Dot.

"At sixteen, she was so out of control, her family doctor decided to seek a physical solution. She had a hysterectomy, and all. You know what that is, son?"

"No," I confessed.

"Well, it's when a surgeon takes away a woman's insides. Her ladies parts, I suppose I might term it. She could never have children as a result. And she was just a girl, in many ways."

I nodded my understanding.

"But it didn't fix anything, beyond ensuring she didn't get pregnant again. She'd fallen with child three times before the operation, but her family had taken care of that. They were moneyed and saw her as an embarrassment.

"Over time, and after we met and married, the doctors treated her in other ways. At first, they did things to her brain, but that was quack-work, if you ask me.

"Then they tried chemicals, and that somewhat did the trick. But the medicinals don't work now like they did. She builds up a resistance, they tell me. You saw the result of that this afternoon.

"Trouble is, that darned medication takes away other parts of her, too. She's only ever half the person she really is when she's on it. It kills her passion in every sense.

"I hoped she'd come around as she got older, and she is better than she was. But it's still a worry. Truth is, as far as physical make-up goes, there isn't much woman left inside of her."

I had no idea what to say.

"You know," he added, as he poured us both another half-tumbler of whiskey, "I look for reasons to get away on business. I feel guilty, Tommy, but I sometimes just need to stay in a hotel and have a night without all the pressure."

"It's understandable," I assured him.

"No, son, it isn't. For better, for worse. In sickness and in health. I made those vows with God Almighty as my witness. And now I run and hide when it gets too much.

"We had to leave Georgia because of it all. And then we had to leave Alabama, and then South Carolina. We up sticks and move on every few years, because people don't understand."

"Nobody will hear anything from me," I assured him.

"Well now, thank you. That's good to hear. I knew I could trust you. And it sure has been swell having you here these last few months, and all."

We drank in silence for a while.

"What is all this?" he asked, stretching his arm towards the tape I'd lined up all over the walls.

"That's my next record," I informed him.

"Say now! A record? I didn't have a clue you were a working musician."

"Oh, I've released a couple of long-playing records. One last year. This year, I plan on making another. And this is what I have in mind for it."

"I hear you sometimes, playing away on that guitar of yours. She comes and watches you, you know?"

"Dotty?"

"Sure! She comes over and spies on you through the window there. Guess you can't see her with all the light being inside."

"Guess not."

"You know, she'll be going away on Monday morning."

"Where?" I asked, "a little break someplace?"

"You could call it that. That's how I like to think of it."

He pours another drink for us both. Smaller than before.

"Now, see, she's going to go away to a place where they can take better care of her. It's a nice place, out in the countryside north of here a-ways."

"How long for?"

"Well, that rather depends now. On whether she gets well or not."

"Will you go with her?"

"That isn't how the place works, son. Besides, the doctors there reckon it'll be better for her if I keep a distance. Space and time is what she needs."

"Where will you go?" I asked.

"Oh, I plan to sell this big old place. Too much for just me to upkeep. Figured I'd go over to Charlottesville way. My work is mainly there anyways. Fact is, and you said I could trust you, son, correct?"

"Of course, sir."

"Well, I met a widow lady over there. She has a couple of children. I say children, but they're in their late-teens now. Nearly your age, I'll wager!

"So, I'm going to go and start again, Tommy. A new life."

It made me sad to hear that. Not for myself, I realised, as I was planning to head back to Delaware soon enough.

It made me so terribly sad for Dotty.

"What about your god?" I asked, the merest hint of disapproval in my voice.

If he detected my mood, he ignored it.

"I'm fifty next month, son. I've done this for some thirty years. I'm tired. I have to look after myself. God, I believe, would understand that. God helps those who help themselves, after all.

"He knows that I love Dot in my way. Always have. Guess I always will be fond of my Honey."

"I think it's sad," I admitted.

"Me and you both, son, me and you both."

I stared down into my drink.

"I started writing a song for her," I said.

"For Dotty?"

"It's that one there," I pointed out, indicating the lines of tape above my bed. "I took some of the things she said to me, the little rhymes she uses, and I wrote a guitar picked melody to it. It's very beautiful. Well, I think it is, at least."

"What's it called?"

"It's titled 'Rhyme And Reason'."

"Well, I'll listen out for that on the wireless, son. Say, er, if you happened to play that song tomorrow evening after dark, Dot may well be listening from outside that window there."

"It'll be her last night here," I stated flatly.

"It will. You know, I'll leave this bottle and these glasses with you." We'd got through half of it. "And if you wanted to invite her in tomorrow evening for a little drink, well, I think she might like that."

I looked at him in the dim candlelight.

He nodded to indicate my understanding was on the mark.

"Tommy, she's going to be institutionalised, probably for the rest of her life. I've done all I'm capable of doing for her. I'm so utterly tired, son, and I have to think of my own wellbeing. My heart isn't so good, to tell you the truth. One more day is all I have to deal with.

"It would be nice, for her I mean, if that day was all it could be.

"To that end, I'll take her to church in the morning, and we'll get brunch at the diner, just like always. In the afternoon, she'll sit on the porch smiling at nothing as she always does.

"She'll go for her soak in the bath before dinner, and I'll cook her some beefsteak just the way she likes it, with gravy and biscuits and all of her favourite things.

"At eight, I'll tell her I need to do a little paperwork, and head off to my office. I'll suggest she get some air. The forecast is looking like a grand old day.

"You take as long as you need, son."

31.

I went to church with them on that Sunday morning. I sat alongside them on the cold, hard pew, with Dotty in the middle, and watched and listened as all of the hypocrisy played out.

Primly she sat, back straight, head high - a picture of innocence and respectability.

He matched her pose, that strong provider, his hand enfolding hers, tugging up when she should stand, and pulling down when she should kneel.

I sat throughout, an anger burning within me.

It was otherwise a joyous celebration; a perfect scene of good family within good community. I'm sure god must have seen how good it all was.

As we left, I was introduced to people. I smiled and shook hands. I ignored the looks I got from a couple of the ladies when their husbands were otherwise engaged talking business.

I thought of my sexual experience to date - from Janie with her snake collections, and Clarissa cheating on her husband-to-be, to Luca on his knees before me collecting a sample in the changing-room, to Lance's exploits, and the pimps protecting their asset.

My own mother taken advantage of - raped, I figured - by a man entrusted with the health and wellbeing of the community.

A handful of others so insignificant so as not to be worthy of mention.

It would be my lot. I was done with it.

The next sexual encounter I would have, I vowed, would be with someone who would be with me for the rest of my life.

It would be a happy thing. A real thing, with no pretence at play. That was what I wanted, I knew, outside the church that day. I wanted true happiness.

What was that? I didn't know. But I knew I was not going to settle for a half-measure of anything going forward.

But that would begin from the Monday morning. My next tryst, I knew, would come that night, with a woman who did nothing for me physically.

But it would make her happy, and I had a very strong sense that, come the Monday morning, she would never be happy again. She deserved that send off.

So I played the game for one more day, as I compromised myself one final time, and went to brunch at the diner, and sat and smiled and sipped my fruit juice and ate my fuckin' grits, and pretended to like it all.

In the afternoon, I finished painting the porch, and smelt beef roasting and biscuits baking in the oven. I heard the water run into the metal bathtub and absorbed all the sounds of a normal life.

A normal life that I would forever be on my guard against.

Because I sought happy, not fuckin' normal.

I played my guitar after dark, and sipped a little of the bourbon. And then a little more. I knew she was out there, watching me.

In the candlelight, I smiled at the window - at my own reflection.

Rolling my fingers over the strings, I sang the words I'd written with her in mind.

I saw no rhyme or reason in anything.

She entered, unable to resist temptation.

Her dress slid from her shoulders, fell at her feet, and she sashayed in front of me, nakedly dancing with her own shadow, because nobody else would dance with this plain woman who, on the outside, appeared to be devoid of passion.

And I gave her what she needed. All she desired.

I made her happy.

And, knowing what I now know, I'm fuckin' glad I did.

For, come the next morning, I watched him take her away, his for-better-for-worse.

By the time I imagine he returned, I was half way back to Delaware with more money in my pocket than I'd left with.

32.

Marcus Anderson letter published in 'Rooty-Tooty Magazine', July 1988.

May 14th, 1988.

Dear sir.

Along with Johnny Anderson, I co-founded Jury Duty Records in 1953. Tommy Histon was our first signing. In fact, the label came about because of Tommy Histon. He was the spark that ignited the idea.

Over the years, Johnny has been outspoken in his condemnation of Histon, and I wish to set the record straight, as he doesn't speak for both of us.

The truth is, I let Tommy down. If I could turn back the clock, I would handle things very differently. In short, I would back him to the hilt.

Histon was right. We were wrong. At the time, I knew that, but Johnny and I had an agreement that we would concur on business matters before proceeding. We didn't agree on Histon, and I had to side with Johnny for the sake of the venture.

I regret it.

Johnny was after the quick buck - the seizing of the moment. That led to him having a fairly short-sighted view of the music world. He was, in fact, the polar opposite of Histon.

For myself, I occupied a space somewhere between the two.

The night Tommy recorded 'Track Back...' I was in the studio with him, alongside our producer, Hank Silver. I contributed a couple of suggestions and some handclaps. That was it. Tommy ran the whole session, and Hank did what he was asked to do.

Never let anybody tell you that they offered anything more on that record. I was there, and recall it as though it were yesterday.

The truth is, I was awestruck. I'd never seen or heard anything like it.

Believe me, I don't say that for personal gain, as I sold any rights to those records a long time ago.

However, it is, I feel, important that the truth be known.

Now, sure, some of the things Johnny said were true. Tommy did defy us and use the remaining studio time, so we couldn't re-record that first album. Johnny wasn't likely to pay for more time, so the record remained as it was. It was pretty underhand of Histon.

Secretly, I was happy with that, and smiled at his cunning when unobserved.

And, yes, Tommy did threaten Johnny with a knife when he initially refused to honor the contract and allow him to record a second album. In point of fact, it was a letter opener, but it did have a sharp tip.

I managed to calm them both down, and Tommy asked us, "how much?"

"How much what?" Johnny snapped back.

"How much will you pay me not to make my record?"

Johnny offered him a hundred bucks.

It was agreed, so I went to the safe to retrieve the cash. We'd had some success in late-'53 through Marty Greengrass, and Johnny was adamant the smoother country-pop sound was the way to go. Looking at the revenue, it was hard for me to argue. Still, I found the balladry of Greengrass a little boring, if I'm being honest.

Besides, who has even heard of Marty Greengrass these days?

I handed Tommy the cash, and laid his cessation of contract paperwork out for signing.

I'm laughing now, but I wasn't at the time.

Histon set the money on fire and told us, "I have a f****** contract for two records. F*** you."

He dropped the burning notes on the floor and walked out.

We had no choice but to make 'Coda'. We released it, but gave it no support. As a result, it died.

The next morning, Johnny arrived at the office to find someone had taken a **** in his desk drawer.

That evening, a knock brought Johnny to his front door. A burning package lay on the step. Johnny stamped it out with his slippered foot. The paper carton contained dog ****.

I guess it was Tommy's way of letting Johnny know what he thought of him.

Still, he couldn't prove it was Histon, and had to make the record or risk legal action.

'Coda' was, and remains, a stunning record. Of course, at the time, we had no idea what it was about, but some of the lyrical content has been revealed over the interim. Musically, it puts me in mind of the baroque-folk of the late-sixties. The kind of thing Nick Drake would do, though that was much later.

Johnny cut and ran on me in '56, taking all the cash from the safe with him.

My only hope of Jury Duty surviving, I felt at the time, was through Tommy. 'Three Minute Hero' had been recorded in 1948-49, and was perfect for 56-57. I added eight years on to his recording 'Track Back...', and my heart sank when I calculated it would be 1961 before the world caught up!

As we now know, it was longer than that. It was probably 63-64 before folk-rock became a thing.

'Coda' took twelve to fifteen years.

In my opinion, none of that was luck. It wasn't merely fluke.

Tommy looked me up in 1957. He was in a bad way, with a horrific scar down his face. He looked like he'd been through hell. He kept asking me how many testicles Johnny had.

I asked him if he wanted to make another record. If he could have done something like 'Three Minute Hero', it may have saved me.

One look at him, though, told me that he wasn't capable of recording anything. I feel bad for asking, now I think back on it.

More so, when I consider what the next few years had in store for him.

Tommy Histon offered to give me two thousand dollars that day. Just like that. I didn't ask for it, and he asked for nothing in return. I didn't take it. It would have been throwing good money after bad, and barely scratched the surface of the level of debt.

Still, I've never forgotten his generosity.

As he walked out, he said, "make sure you hang on to those records of mine. Keep a few copies in a safe place. And don't forget that copy of 'Three Minute Hero' you picked up. One day, they'll see you right."

That was the last thing he ever said to me.

Sure enough, I turned sixty-five a couple of years back. I sold some copies of the Jury Duty pressings, and netted myself a nice retirement fund.

Still, I couldn't bring myself to get rid of one copy of each of his albums.

I'd let Tommy Histon slip through my fingers once before, and wasn't about to do it again.

Sincerely,

Marcus Anderson.

(Address withheld)

33.

I was offered a hundred dollars cash not to make another record for Jury Duty, but I had a fuckin' contract that stated two albums.

A hundred fuckin' dollars! That was my value to that shit-dripper Johnny Anderson.

They'd had some success in the year I'd been gone, through some crooning kid with lovey-dovey hair and face to go with his lovey-dovey shit-ass songs. He'd sold a few records and been played on the radio 'all over the country!'

I forget his name. Green Ass, or something.

It was liberating, to know I wasn't wanted, and that the record would receive no support.

I'd had half a mind to make the record a little more like what I knew they desired, and bring some of the 'Three Minute Hero' sound back.

When they tried to buy me out, I thought, 'fuck 'em, now I'll make the record I really want to.'

"Do you know your trouble?" Hank asked me when I swung by the studio.

"What's that?"

"The world is not ready," he said in his clipped and precise way.

"What should I do about that?"

"You do nothing," he replied, as he sucked on his cigar and puffed smoke out the corners of his mouth. "You do the record that will satisfy you. I see too many people selling their souls, making recordings they do not really want to do as they chase commercial success.

"That is all well and good short-term, Tommy. But, if they are lucky enough, they shall live to be my age. When they get to my stage of life, they shall reflect on their lives.

"Yes, they shall regret some of the things they did. But more, they shall regret the things they did not do.

"Take that from me. The old testament of old Hank."

If I required convincing, Hank's words would have done it.

With just the two of us in the studio, Hank and I worked on 'Coda' for longer than I'd worked on my other records combined. Hank only billed Jury Duty for the hours they allowed me. The truth is, we spent somewhere close to forty studio-hours on that record.

Hank did it, as he told me, "because it is different. And different interests me at my age. Everything else is copycat. So much so, that I barely hear it. There is only so much hearing a person can do in life, and I would rather not waste my allowance on hearing music I already heard a thousand times."

The whole album had been mapped out in the log cabin, but I would never have been able to pull it together without Hank's help and support.

There aren't many people in my life I owe a great debt to, but Hank Silver is most certainly one. He passed away in 1962, aged ninety-two.

Ten years on since I last set eyes on him, and every time I smell cigar smoke, I picture him in my head.

I don't know what 'Coda' is, or where it falls in musical terms.

The album has a theme, I guess, telling stories of all the characters I'd met in my life to that juncture, at the grand old age of twenty-two.

I titled it 'Coda' because it felt like the end of something. Coda is the name of a town, the last place on earth, where all these fucked up people live.

The notion came from watching Dotty in my cabin that Sunday night before she was driven away by Leonard. A final dance to a final movement.

'Rhyme And Reason' ended side two, as Dotty 'danced with her darkest true self, that candle tongues licked to life, until sickness came to be cast more bright, driven away by the shining light, rhyme and reason holding sway, as they drove the dancing girl away, rhyme and reason waltzing on, mercy me, for now she's gone.'

Yes, it was probably quite different to anything being recorded in 1954.

My drug exposure came into play on the opening track, 'Get A Shift On', as I reminisced about Lance, and his changing form. It was literal, becoming Rick, and so on, but also picked up on the transformation of his character on hallucinogens.

Clarissa was the inspiration behind 'Chianti', as I wrote about 'a bottle of wine, a stopper pulled free, and spilling red on the filthy street, a father's pride in a baby born, spilling red, pouring scorn.'

Janie was 'The Snake Catcher', though I rechristened her Jacqueline-Jayne, and wrote of the hypocrisy of her bad reputation, labelled by the very men who had established it and taken advantage of her. 'Laying the blame for Jacqueline-Jayne.'

The whole album was like that, and for the first time, I didn't knowingly borrow from anything. All songs, as far as I was aware, were original.

They were very unlike any song that had come before them.

Of course, Jury Duty hated the record. Well, Johnny did. But I knew that before I let them hear it. All they saw was money in flames. And, frankly, they may as well have burnt that money as release 'Coda', for all the sales it achieved.

Their game was short-term. Mine, I believed, was the long game.

Okay, so ten years on, I didn't think it would take this fuckin' long.

'Coda' received no reviews that I ever saw. Any airplay at the time went unheard by my ears.

That said, those alien fuckers must have got to hear it somehow. I figured they had someone vetting me down on the ground by that time.

Hank was right, though. Ten years later, and, of my three albums, that is the one of which I'm most proud. I don't regret making that record.

My face must have been a picture when Hank suggested putting violin on it. My experience of anything played with a bow was country style fiddle.

But Hank knew. He'd trained as a classical musician from the age of five, and took his seat in some of the best orchestras in Europe at the turn of the century.

Boy, could that man play violin. And viola.

His name was actually Hananiah, and he'd been born in Poland in 1870.

Come the war, and he was away touring with some-or-other philharmonic, when the Nazis came for his family.

Despite being over seventy, he re-entered Poland to search for them, posing as a Swiss national. He followed the trail to Germany, but to no avail.

In 1942, after many months of searching, he was identified as a Jew, but fled to Switzerland before making his way to Great Britain, where he remained until the end of the war.

At seventy-five, he went back to Poland one final time. He paid his respects to the wife, three children, seven grandchildren and a great-grandson. All were killed in the transportation and camps.

"They were not human, the people who did that to my family," he told me. "I do not know where they came from, but they were not of this earth."

I thought about Hitler only having one testicle.

His musicianship led to him being accepted into the United States, where he lived the remaining sixteen years of his life.

From first learning of his family's disappearance, he never once picked up the violin or viola again.

Until the night he played on my record.

"Why not, Hank?" I asked him.

He puffed on his cigar, shook his head, and said, "because when I play, I lose myself in the music. It is the only thing I think about. And I never want to forget my family for a second."

"But you played on my record," I pointed out.

"I did."

"Why?"

"My wife told me to," he said, and rolled the cigar from the middle to the corner of his lips.

I didn't say anything. There was no need.

He smiled. It was the only time I ever saw him smile properly. All other times, it was a tolerant smirk with a cigar in the centre of his mouth.

"She said she wanted to hear me play one final time," he added, raising a finger upwards.

He turned away sharply to the tape machine.

"Darned smoke got in my eye," he said, as he removed his spectacles, dabbed a handkerchief, and went about his business.

34.

Some fifteen-hundred dollars to my name was a chunk of change. At that time, I figured I was done with the recording industry, so began to think about an alternative future.

Twelve of the fifteen went into a bank account, where my royalties, such as they were, were also directed.

I opened myself a Post Office Box, just as Rick and I had once planned to do.

My half-formed idea was to see where the open road took me, and how long three-hundred bucks would last me.

Little did I know it at the time, but it would last me for eight years.

Walking, walking, riding trains, accepting the occasional ride in a car or truck when it suited, before walking some more. That was the pattern of my life for a year and a half.

By taking work where I found it, and living thriftily, I seemed to always scrape together just about enough to warrant carrying on.

I looked for a place to settle, but never found it. Similarly, I looked for a woman to settle with, but never found her either.

No real friends did I meet during that time, as I drifted from one town to the next.

To be honest, I didn't even know I was in Canada until someone told me I was in Canada. At some point, I must have wandered over the border unchallenged.

It was there, in the summer of 1956, that they first came for me. The fuckers.

I was in Nova Scotia, at a place called Shag Harbour. For some reason, I had it in my head that I was heading back to the USA that way, until I ran out of land.

After a night of rest, I planned on turning around and heading back north, then south before winter came on.

The lights were the first I knew of anything.

They came for me in the beams, at the speed light travels.

Time became an irrelevance.

In three seconds, I was half a million miles away.

Half a million miles in three seconds!

I'd wake up from time to time.

Light.

White light.

And music playing. My music.

I was there for years, being tested.

But when I was discovered, it had only been two days.

That's how it works. Here, we exist at the speed of sound. There, everything is light.

Sound takes nearly five seconds to travel a mile. Light moves nearly a million times faster.

Radio waves travel at the speed of light!

The fuckers could be anywhere. Everywhere.

They spoke to me, in their language, inside my head.

I knew their language. I always had. How?

The same way I knew anything. Through the books, and the teachings in the community.

Or instinctively. I knew a lot of things instinctively.

My father? Did I inherit the knowledge from him?

The fuckin' snake, I remembered. It was the reptile in me that made me different.

The snake and my father - they were the same entity as far as I was concerned. Each injected my mother unbidden around the time I was conceived.

Years on, but only two days later, they found me in a christmas tree plantation.

I'd lost a lot of blood, and was lucky to be alive, I heard them say.

One side of my face was opened up, from the corner of my right eye down to the point of my chin. In an arc.

That was how they got access to my brain.

I tried to explain, but nobody believed me.

Shit, I wouldn't have believed it, if someone had told me that.

For six days and nights I lay in a hospital bed. They were worried about releasing me, but I told them I was fuckin' going. I needed to get away from that place.

I went to my digs, paid for a room I'd never slept in, picked up my guitar case and bag from where they'd been stored, and walked out of there.

Because of my appearance, no offers of a ride came my way. I hopped a train for part of the journey, alighting near Toronto, and made my way on foot towards Niagara Falls.

It took me a long time to make that trip south.

Again, nobody checked me at the border, and I passed back through to the USA.

Note: In 1967, Shag Harbour was the setting of one of the most well known UFO sightings in North America. It's well documented, and worth reading about. Histon couldn't possibly have known about it in 1956, or in 1964 when he wrote his autobiography.

35.

Report, as published in the Nova Scotia Daily newspaper, August 28th, 1956.

Note: Prior to the discovery of Tommy's notebook, the details around his claimed abduction were unknown. Having the geographic location and approximate date, I was able to unearth the following report:

US Man Discovered In Plantation, Badly Hurt In Mystery Incident.

Tuesday, August 28: A US man, Theodore Histon, aged twenty-four, was discovered by loggers returning to work on Monday morning.

He'd suffered severe injuries to his face, and lost a significant amount of blood. He is reported as being in a stable condition in hospital.

A spokesperson confirmed: 'A man in his twenties was admitted to hospital on Monday morning. He is badly cut and somewhat undernourished. We believe he lay in the plantation for two days and nights, and is fortunate that the time of year is mild. He is receiving fluids intravenously, has been administered stitches to his injuries, and we expect him to make a full recovery.'

Asked what is believed to have caused the injuries, the spokesperson said: 'We have no idea. Mr Histon has no recollection of events, other than seeing bright lights. Beyond that, he seems confused as to what happened. We think that perhaps he was hit by a vehicle, possibly a motorcycle, though no tire tracks were found near the scene. We are hoping he will have better recall as he recuperates.'

Histon, of no known address, is believed to hail from Virginia, USA, and it is not known what brought him to the area.

At the plantation, this reporter spoke with a man who claims to have been one of a group who discovered Histon.

Not wishing to give his name, the man stated: 'The guy reckons he was taken by aliens! That's what he was saying when we found him. He was kind of talking crazy, but he was clear about that. He was in a pretty bad way, and his face was opened up all down one side. Craziest thing was, he reckoned they'd had him for twenty-something years, but he wasn't that old. I guess time don't matter up there!'

Asked what he thought might have occurred, he replied: 'There are some big machines operating up this way. And, yes, at night they're lit up pretty bright. By my thinking, the man was mistaken.'

Harbour police refused to comment, merely confirming that a 'man in some distress had been found' as otherwise described.

An inquiry is ongoing, and an open case exists at the station. Police have appealed for witnesses to contact them.

More as it becomes known.

A small follow-up item appeared in a later edition:

Monday, September 24: Following the discovery of US national, Theodore Histon, 24, on August 27 in a christmas tree plantation, police confirm that the case is now closed.

No charges were brought and no arrests made. The police report states: 'No evidence of wrongdoing. Investigation ceased.'

At the time of his discovery, he claimed to have been abducted by aliens from another planet.

His injuries, while severe, were not life-threatening.

Histon has since, it is believed, returned to the United States.

36.

It took all of my mental and physical strength to keep going, but I had to keep moving. I must have drunk fluids and eaten food, but I can't tell you what or where.

In New York state, I was accosted by a man as I rested in a doorway. It was dark and late at night, but time was an irrelevance to me. I'd lived for years in two days. I was twenty-four, but really I was twice that.

He was a large man who smelt of alcohol and the road. The truth is, had he tried to take my bag, I probably wouldn't have reacted. Indeed, had he been more concerned with taking my life, I would have been fairly nonplussed.

As it was, he wanted my guitar. That was never going to fuckin' happen.

I beat that man badly. I'm not proud of it. In fact, I wasn't even truly conscious of it.

One punch from him, and I dare say I'd have been spark out lying on the ground, such was his size and strength. From there, he could have snapped my neck.

But he never even got close to landing a blow on me. I saw every single movement in my mind half a second before he made his moves. By the time his fist came at me, my head was no longer there, and my own fist was connecting with him. Seven times I dodged and punched, and seven times he missed and I connected.

Through his eyes, I saw the will leave him. So I drove him back, until his form collided with a brick wall and he had nowhere to go.

Inside his range, I did my damage, driving my forehead into his face. I sank my teeth into his filthy skin, and came away with a chunk of his cheek that I spat back at him, before carrying on with my assault.

He fell to the ground like a dead elephant, and I kicked and kicked at his fat unprotected head.

I broke that man.

As he lay there whining, his breaths wheezy and his bones and teeth splintered, I saw the light shoot out of me and enter him. It left through the cut on my cheek, and entered him through the hole I'd made in his face.

I was free of the fuckers.

Somehow, I'd driven them out of me and into another.

Tiredness came on me, a relieved exhaustion after a great burden had been lifted.

My hands throbbed as I gripped my bag and the handle of my guitar case. My feet were seemingly too heavy for my legs to fully lift free of the ground, as I dragged myself away from the scene.

The police picked me up fifteen minutes later as I tried to get out of the town.

"Just fuckin' leave me alone!" I screamed as they wrestled me into the cop car, my guitar case shoved in alongside me.

37.

They had nothing on me, and I knew it.

A simple check with the hospital in Nova Scotia explained all of my injuries.

The man I'd beaten would live, but the cops were looking for a man with a guitar case. That was all they had.

If it hadn't been for the damned christmas tree, I would have been out of there in no time.

The smell of the thing, that sappy freshness, triggered something in me. I'd lived with that aroma for all the years they had me as their prisoner.

A smell is so redolent. I believe the sense of smell is the most accurate of all our senses when it comes to evoking memories. Or maybe that's just true of myself, and the snake in me.

So, that sap smell put flashbacks in my mind - images that were so real, I could feel them on my skin and see them right in front of me, even though I knew they weren't really present on the outside of my head.

The snake-like tentacle was back clamped to the side of my face, stretching from my eye to my chin, as tiny tongues pushed into my brain, looking for...

Looking for what?

Those tongues would coldly follow my blood vessels and nerves and go to all parts of my mind, constantly, for years.

They would show me things - things projected into my head telepathically, and I knew I was supposed to tell them what would happen next - to imagine what followed. But I never showed the fuckers!

I shut my mind down, so that they couldn't tap into my neurons and synapses and map the human brain. I hibernated for all of that time.

Because I understood. We had that ability, and they didn't.

And I knew with utmost clarity, that the man I beat was one of them. He was an alien.

He was my test, for the mapping was still active in me, right up to the point that the light left me and went back to the rightful owner.

Did they have what they wanted? As I foresaw every move he made, and dodged his blows whilst landing my own, did I allow them to see what they'd spent years trying and failing to see?

One lapse of concentration on my part, and all that I'd endured was for nothing.

"How many testicles did he have?" I asked as I was being led to my freedom through the police waiting room where the christmas tree stood.

"What?"

"How many testicles did the man have?"

"How should I know, buddy?"

"He only has one. That's why I did what I did to him."

"What did you do, son?"

Tapping my skull, I said, "I gave him back to himself, the asshole."

"So you did attack him?"

"I did what I had to do. It was self-defence. He attacked me, both last night, and up in Canada. But he now knows. He knows how to see the future. We have to finish the job, and kill the fucker!"

"Hold on there, boy!" the cop said, as he bent my arm behind my back, "are you saying you were trying to kill the man you attacked?"

I was face-down on the floor of the waiting room, the branches of the tree brushing my hair. "No. Yes! I mean, no, I wasn't. Not last night. He was trying to get information from me. But now I know that we have to kill him."

I was being dragged back into the holding area, my guitar case and bag left behind.

"You don't understand!" I remember wailing, as my hands scrabbled for anything on which I could gain purchase.

I was never charged with any crime. The slippery alien fucker didn't press any charges, and disappeared from the hospital one night. As far as I know, he was never seen again.

Things from my past came back to bite me. Why had I told the court that I'd killed Lance-Rick-Cecil? They didn't understand that he was the same person, those cops.

A psychiatrist sat with me in a room for a couple of hours over the following two days. All I did was tell the truth, as he jotted notes in his book.

Despite his recommendation to the contrary, they had to let me go. The 'victim' had absconded, and there was no tangible proof that I'd broken any law. In fact, given the state of my face, it was I who appeared to be a victim.

Pausing only to have my wound treated for infection, I walked away - still searching.

38.

Christmas came and went at some point, as did the new year. It was 1957. The weather got warmer, and life came back into the world.

I heard the music coming out of the radios in stores and cars. I heard the change that had taken place.

It made me laugh hysterically, as I knew the rest of the world had finally caught up to what I was doing eight years before on 'Three Minute Hero'.

The same people who had ignored my record were now clamoring for the 'new rock'n'roll sound that was sweeping the world.'

I'd play my old songs on the streets of towns and cities, and listen to the people tell me that I was just another Elvis wannabe.

One guy shouted about how I was ripping off Bo Diddley.

"Bo diddly-squat," I raged back, "I was doing this when Bo Diddley was still shitting yellow!" The police came and moved me on.

To anybody who'd listen, and plenty who didn't wish to hear, I'd shout, "I was the first! Tommy fuckin' Histon! I invented this rock'n'roll, but you weren't ready, 'cause you can't see as far as Tommy can! That's why they came for me, and not you! Consider yourselves fortunate that you're so backward at looking forward, else it could have been you!"

People thought I was pretty demented, I guess.

In Vermont, a man sat staring at me as I played for change in some piddly little town I was passing through.

Drink and tobacco had become my drugs of choice. No more amphetamines or hallucinogens for me. Bourbon was my nip, and I was at the stage where I'd sooner have a flask of that for supper than any food.

My work ethic was still healthy, though. I'd busk for as long as it took every day to afford a third-bottle and twenty smokes.

The staring man came over and told me I played well, to which I nodded my gratitude.

How much I'd changed! When Roberto and Clarissa Vertoni had done similarly, I'd seen only opportunity. In Vermont, I saw only a threat and the danger of being exploited.

He wanted to manage me, he said, and suggested we go someplace and talk about a deal. He was paying.

"I hear something in your music that sounds like the future to me," he informed me. That was a red flag, right there.

"Sure," I shrugged, "I'll see what you have to say."

He chatted away all the while as we walked to a bar, telling me about his big plans. I'd heard it all before, and knew it was horse shit.

"I'll make you a star! You'll be on the television shaking your hips like that Pelvis guy before you know it, all them gals screaming at you, and pissing themselves with excitement!

"We just gotta clean you up, and get you in a nice suit! Ballads, that's what gets them gals screaming the most! I seen it on the television, I tell you. I'll call myself The Captain, 'cause that other fellow got The Colonel sorted, and I'll take my twenty percent!

"Moody ballads is the long game. This rock'n'roll, as they call it - yeah, that'll get you through the door, but it's short-term. You trust me on that, you hear?"

At that point, I gave him an inspection to ascertain how many testicles he had.

I figured he'd got information on me, and was talking like Rick Doyle. He must have got that from inside my head, by accessing my memories.

He had two, but I swear one of them felt different.

He also had a knife, which flashed up into my face, and darn well cut me in the exact same fuckin' place as the aliens had opened me up.

Oh, yeah, he knew what he was doing. He knew where to strike. He was one of them fuckers!

I dread to think what would have happened to me if the people hadn't come to my rescue.

He hot-heeled it out of there when he heard them shout, and their footsteps slapped the sidewalk as they ran towards me.

The result? More fuckin' stitches, and another police investigation, during which they looked at me as though I were some kind of lunatic.

At the end of that, I was invited to leave the state of Vermont.

But I was happy departing there. The fact he'd come after me, told me that the fuckers didn't have what they wanted.

39.

I guess when we run out of places to go, we head back to where we began. Thus, I entered my native state of Virginia just as the blossoms appeared on the trees.

A failure was what I considered myself to be.

However, a check in at my bank branch cheered me a little. My twelve-hundred bucks had become two and a half grand in the three years I'd been gone.

Some of it was interest, but most of it was royalty payments. People had, to some degree, cottoned on to my back catalogue.

It wasn't enough to save Jury Duty. I called at the office and spoke with Marcus Anderson, after picking up my mail from the PO Box and discovering a letter from him.

Johnny had ratted away home to his mommy in California, and Marcus was desperate for a break, as the debts mounted.

He could see that 'Three Minute Hero' had been ahead of the curve, and was clutching at a straw in thinking 'Track Back And Trail On' or 'Coda' might do something similar in time to save his business.

Marcus asked if I'd consider making an album like 'Three Minute Hero', to cash in on the current state of music, but I hadn't forgotten the past. They tried to pay me off rather than make 'Coda'. Besides which, I could see Jury Duty was all washed up. I felt for Marcus, though. He wasn't a bad man.

I desired a label that would allow me to develop, not one that would force me to regress.

A library book I found contained a list of record labels in the Virginia and Washington DC area. I called in on a couple, but my physical appearance kind of scared people off.

After the final one I tried, somewhere up near Arlington, I decided to get myself a drink in a bar. Several large whiskeys later, I paid up and left, my guitar case in my hand.

Now, whether it was due to the drink I'm unsure, but I began walking in the wrong direction. It was only when crossing the Potomac river that it dawned on me I was heading north.

Turning, I trudged back towards Arlington Cemetery, looking up at Arlington House as I went. It was mid-afternoon, and I decided to pay the cemetery a visit, as it was a place I'd never been to.

Cecil, back when he was Lance, would talk about it, and his desire to be buried there, "with full military honors. Never fuckin' happen, though, boy."

"Why not?" I'd asked him.

"They can't admit to the things I done, see. A lot of it was what they call covert operations, and there ain't no record of my role in the official log. It don't bother me none. I knew the rules of engagement when I took them on.

"It was enough for me to be told by two presidents, boy. Fuckin' two! Roosevelt and Truman both shook my hand in the White House, and thanked me for my service. That was enough for me, I tell you."

It was a beautiful afternoon that June day, and after walking around for a long while looking at the white headstones, I climbed the hill and settled with my back against a broad tree.

Soon enough, I was dozing happily.

It was a dream. The noise was in my head. The wind that had whipped up was simply present, and not due to my propulsion through the sky.

A song played - one of my own from a few years before. It was on an album called 'Coda', and was about a friend of mine. His name was Lance and Rick and Cecil. Oh, and Kenneth! That was the name on the other identification card he had.

Kenneth John Eddy! The name was in my song, 'Get A Shift On'. I set a part of it there, at the cemetery near DC, as they 'laid the body of Kenneth John Eddy, who became whatever he decided to be, ending up president of the entire country, an ordinary man who altered shape, before meeting his fate in the Lone Star State, where a gunshot saw him lay alone in state.'

The noise! Above me.

The wind! Above me.

The fuckers were coming again!

My eyes snapped open, but the images remained. It was real. It was no dream.

A gun had been easy to obtain in Virginia. Given the trouble I'd encountered, I figured it would be useful to have.

As they swept over, their lights searching for me, their engines throbbing in my ears, I opened fire.

I didn't cease shooting until the chamber was spent.

It was sufficient. They veered away, banking out over the treetops.

There was my chance! I picked up my guitar case, held it over my head for protection, and ran in the opposite direction.

A bang and impact from a body launched me into the air; half a turn as I rode the breeze; clutching my guitar case to me in a bear hug as we flew together - me and my music!

My head smacked on a white grave marker as I came down on my back. Bouncing. Impacting again.

And then nothing.

40.

Primarily, they locked me up for my own protection. That's what they said in the court.

I was considered a danger to myself and others. Because of mental instability. Probably brought on by great trauma in my life.

Momma dying of a broken neck and burning right in front of me, they said.

The abduction and assault in Canada.

A grotesque alien baby I fathered, born dead in a trailer as I looked on.

Cecil dying the way he did.

Other shit.

Paranoia. Schizophrenia. Delusions. Drug abuse. Ungodly ways.

I tried to explain it all, but they had their minds made up long before I entered the courtroom.

"It all began with the snake!" I implored. "The fuckin' snake bit my Momma, and that gave me special abilities. That's all it is. I'm no danger to any person or thing belonging to this earth. Aside from snakes, of course.

"It ain't the things of this earth that need fear me! Oh, no siree! It's the fuckers not of this planet that I will always strive to defeat in any way I can. I do it for you! All of you! For, one day, they'll come and destroy you all!

"But I'll never show them! Trust me. You can do what you want to me; believe me or don't. It makes no difference. They will never get the information they seek. Never!"

That was the gist of what I said, when invited to make a statement prior to a judgement being delivered.

I don't know if it did any good or not.

Firing a pistol at a government helicopter is likely to land one in trouble.

Particularly when that helicopter is used to transport the president and high-ranking dignitaries to local air-force bases.

Even though the president wasn't on the helicopter, and neither were dignitaries of any rank, and I didn't actually manage to hit it, it was, I was informed, a worrying act. And, set amidst a catalog of similarly alarming events, not to mention a bizarre explanation in my testimony, I was to be transported to a mental health facility in Virginia for evaluation.

A report on my wellbeing would determine the next step, and how long I should be detained.

It ended up being four and a half years of my life.

Cecil told lies all the time, and everyone believed him. I told the truth, and nobody believed me.

I'd never made an attempt on my own life. Even so, I was considered a suicide risk. That meant no sharp objects, nothing I could string myself up with, and, because I was a danger to others, nothing I could use as a weapon.

As a result, they took my guitar away.

And I was fed a cocktail of drugs that took everything else away.

Thankfully, taking drugs had never been a problem for me.

Initially, I enjoyed the numbed state. Nothing mattered. Time oozed by, heavy and thick, and so did any thoughts I might have. Before any notion could form, it was lost in the process of revealing itself.

My molasses-mind seemed to slow everything. Even blinking was a drawn-out, deliberate act. Words were too dense for my mouth to handle, as I developed a gentle rocking motion in time with my pulse that came six times to every breath cycle.

Weeks or months passed that way. I don't know how long.

Questions were asked, but I didn't have an inclination to answer them. In my mind, I was forming answers, but they were sluggish, and never seemed to make it to my mouth. It was easier to simply nod and shake my head.

I smiled a lot, because that was how my lips shaped themselves when at rest.

In time, my medication was adjusted, and I could function a little better.

Eating became more enjoyable, as I had energy and desire to chew and swallow. Still, any creative thought was stymied. No music did I hear in my head during those initial few months.

A report was filed to the court, and told of my progress. I was 'responding well to treatment,' and should 'remain in the facility until a balance of medication could be found to enable me to function normally in society.'

I didn't want to be normal.

"Do you think aliens are coming to get you, Tommy?" they'd ask me in the white room I was taken to once a week.

"Sometimes," I'd snigger, and shake my head.

Shaking my head would make the dribble run from the corner of my mouth, so I'd wipe it away with the back of my hand.

"Tell us about the snakes, Tommy?"

"Sssss!" I'd hiss, and poke my tongue out before grinning.

I knew what I was doing, and was aware it was ludicrous, but couldn't seem to stop myself. Everything seemed so ridiculous.

"Is there a snake inside you, Tommy?"

"Snakes in all of us, by my reckoning, trying to get out."

"Is the snake in you a demon, Tommy?"

"Guess-sss so. Just have to keep it in. Not let it esssscape!"

"Are you happy, Tommy?"

I'd grin and nod that I was. My needs were so simple, and my brain so subdued, how could I not be? I was incapable of thinking of any need that wasn't being met.

In time, I was allowed out of my room to mingle with the other patients. Whatever they'd done with my meds enabled me a little more communicative ability, whilst still keeping me... I don't know the word. Flat, I suppose.

Imagination and invention remained locked out. Myopia ruled, as I could sit contentedly staring at a wall or door for hours on end. No more mental stimulation than that was required.

The television in the communal hall held little allure, beyond being a screen on which light danced around and sound came forth.

So, I'd sit and stare at that for hours on end, and think about absolutely nothing at all.

41.

Letter from Clarissa Vertoni. John Greene (THAS Chairman) contacted her in 2002, and received the following response.

September 22nd, 2002.

Dear Mr. Greene.

Thank you for your letter dated May 1st of this year.

Tommy Histon is a name I have not heard in a very long time. However, it is a name I shall never forget, and often think of.

I am delighted to learn that he is so fondly remembered in Britain and elsewhere, and appreciate you are attempting to piece together his short life.

It took me a long time to pluck up the courage to respond, as my life is much altered, and I am a vastly different person to the one I was back when I knew Tommy.

I am seventy-six this year, as you may be aware. The truth is, it is entirely thanks to Tommy Histon that I am able to see this age. It is no exaggeration to state that he saved my life on more than one occasion. For the fifty-plus years I have lived since, I owe him a great debt.

To answer your questions in order:

- yes, the record from the court regarding the events in New York and subsequent trial are accurate, if a little cold and sparse. There is nothing I wish to add to that.

- yes, I am aware of my father's opinions of Tommy, and, no, I most certainly do not concur with them. To add to that, I had no relationship with my father during or after his time in prison. I saw him once, in 1979, just before he passed away. I would prefer to keep the details of that private.

- no, I would not like to contribute to the Society other than through this letter. I thank you for the offer, but it is difficult for me to relive what I went through, and ask that you respect my desire for privacy.

- yes, I did see Tommy Histon once more after that day in court in January of 1953. The details of that meeting follow.

Before I get to my final encounter with Tommy, I should like you to know that I loved him. I only loved two men in my life; Tommy and my second husband, who I lost last year.

Ah, but Tommy!

I can close my eyes and see him sat on the sidewalk playing guitar that first day I encountered him. It would have been the summer of 1948. I was with my father, enjoying a meal, and I was distracted by the young guy singing.

My father wished to talk about my planned marriage, but I was far more interested in the music. Besides, it wasn't as though the marriage was my choice.

Indulging me, my father invited Tommy to join us. By the end of the night, a business venture was dreamt up, and Tommy would live in a trailer parked on the grounds of our family home.

That suited me just fine.

There was a magic between us, and one thing led to another. We became very close.

The stress of my 'forced' marriage was telling on me.

Anyway, as a means of coping, I began taking pills and other potions.

To be very clear - despite my father's claims to the contrary, Tommy did not introduce me to any drugs. In fact, I fear the reverse is true. It has eaten me up that I may have worsened his problems through that.

Tommy took to amphetamines in a big way, and became somewhat reliant on them for the year he resided in Richmond.

Yes, we became lovers, and I have no regrets concerning that. As I have stipulated, I was in love with him.

It is also true that I fell pregnant with his child. My dearest wish is that I could have given birth to his son. Sadly, it wasn't to be, as I miscarried in 1949.

That was the first time he saved my life. Had it not been for Tommy, I would have died that day.

As you correctly state, my father's business activities were investigated that same year, and he was arrested for tax evasion and money laundering. As a family, we lost everything, and my short marriage disintegrated as a result. It was a very low time for me personally.

It resulted in me slipping from grace, and falling in with some bad people in New York. As you know, it was there in 1952 that I next encountered Tommy, and he once again saved my life.

I spent six months in a rehabilitation home cleaning myself up and sorting myself out. Reconnecting with my mother made that possible. I wish for you to know that I have never touched anything stronger than mild pain medication since that time, and have expended much effort helping addicts in the years since. I see it as both my penance and my calling in life.

Tommy and I lost touch after the court case, and for a few years I was reluctant to revisit my past, lest it should lead me into old ways.

But I couldn't forget him, and had never had the opportunity to properly thank him for all he did for me.

So, in the fall of 1957, word reached me that he was spending time in a mental health facility in Virginia named Progressive Pines. Thinking, perhaps, it may be an opportunity for me to repay him, and to show there were people who cared, I visited him there.

The truth is, I wish I hadn't. I am haunted by what I saw. It breaks my heart that my last sighting of him was in that place in that condition.

Tommy had always possessed such energy and dynamism! That was what drew me to him in the first place. There was a cockiness that spoke of confidence, but it also smacked of compensating for vulnerability.

I also remember a maturity, when I think back on him. He was so young when we first met, but held a certain depth belying his years. Oh, he was naive, for sure, and given his upbringing, that was understandable. But that naivety gave him such optimism. There was no cynicism in Tommy Histon. He looked at the world with wide-eyed wonder!

Yet, there was also something quite feral in him. Yes, that's the perfect word. He was, to some degree, wild and undomesticated. I couldn't imagine Tommy ever being tamed.

He was also incredibly kind and thoughtful. I believe that was always Tommy's undoing - that willingness to put others' happiness before his own. He would have done well to be a little more selfish.

None of those traits were present in the man I encountered in the institution. He was an empty shell of a young man - a shadow was all that was left of him.

He had most definitely been tamed. But at what cost?

I was permitted to see him for a short time in his room. Prior to that, I had to remove my belt, shoes, hair fixings and brooch. My bag was confiscated, and I was searched for sharp objects or anything else that might be used as a weapon.

Finally, I was allowed in. He wasn't restrained. He didn't need to be. He could barely raise his head. Even so, an orderly stood watch by the door.

Tommy was seated on the floor in the corner of the room. For a fleeting moment I imagined him holding a guitar on a street in Richmond. But, no. This was a very different Tommy to the one of a few years before.

He raised his eyes when I said his name, his head bowed and bent over to one side slightly.

A vicious scar scored his face, and dark rings saddened his eyes. His hair was shorn to the scalp, and he was just skin and bone.

He didn't have any idea who I was.

"Tommy, it's me. Clarissa," I told him.

An oblivious smile was all I received in reply.

"What have they done to you?" I asked nobody in particular.

"Clarissssss-a!" he managed, and poked his tongue out like a snake.

"That's right! Do you remember me?"

He shook his head and dribbled from the corner of his mouth.

"This is wrong," I turned and said to the orderly. He ignored me and stood with his arms folded across his chest.

I'd imagined the encounter as I'd made my way there with my mother. I'd even dared to dream that we might pick up some kind of relationship.

"Pissssss!" Tommy said, and I turned back. He'd urinated all over himself and the tiled floor. Dark yellow flooded along the grout channels.

I had to go. I simply couldn't bear to witness him like that. It was so heartbreaking.

"Take care of yourself, Tommy Histon. And thank you - thank you for all you did for me," I said, as brightly as I could.

"Tommy 'The Pissed On' Histon," he stated inanely.

I turned to leave, and in a voice that hinted at old times, he said, "Made a messsss! Went all over the floor. Luca take care of it."

"You remember!" I enthused, spinning back to him, tears welling up in my eyes. Luca was an old acquaintance of ours.

No response came, as he stared down at the puddle formed between his knees.

With great effort and concentration, he moved a finger, dabbed at it, and raised it to his mouth.

"I'll leave you to clean him up," I said to the orderly as I departed.

"Looks like he's doing a fine job of that himself," the orderly smirked.

That's my final snapshot of Tommy. I never went back. I couldn't. I had to be a little selfish. My own health and state of mind remained far from ideal.

But, I confess, I thought of and prayed for Tommy every day.

It was early in 1965 when I heard of his death. It was in a list of deceased Virginians of note in a magazine I subscribed to.

'Tommy Histon - musician - aged thirty-two - in England by misadventure.'

That was it. No details. No mention of what he contributed. I'd discover more over the years as his popularity grew.

It numbed me when I saw his name.

And it hurt and infuriated me to read all of the nonsense people have said about him since.

It was that, ultimately, that led to me responding to your letter.

If I can leave you with some final thoughts, they are these: Tommy Histon was a fine man with an immense amount of talent, and he was as good a friend as I ever had. His kindness is my overriding thought when I think back on him.

To this day, I love him, and I wish to goodness I could have done more for him.

As I reached the door that day in the institution, through a strangled throat I said, "got to go, Tommy, Momma's waiting."

"You see Momma, Janie?" he asked.

"Yes," I told him, not daring to correct him, or turn and look at him.

"Ask her if she's proud of me?"

"I will, Tommy. I'll do that."

Sincerely.

Clarissa (nee Vertoni)

Enc. - a copy of a photo of Tommy, taken in Richmond in 1949.

Note: Despite John Greene making further efforts to contact Clarissa Vertoni in the years since, no response was forthcoming.

42.

In February of 2003, the following email was sent to the THAS following publication of Clarissa's letter on the website.

Dear Sir.

I write in regard to the letter published on your site concerning Progressive Pines Psychiatric Care Home.

I was a nurse at the facility from 1956 to it closing its doors in 1974. As such, I wish to take issue with the depiction portrayed in the letter.

Whilst I readily concede many institutions specialising in mental health left a great deal to be desired at the time Thomas Histon was a resident, The Pines was no such place!

The aim was to rehabilitate, and to use technology of a non-intrusive kind to allow sufferers to return to society.

Funding came from donations, in the main, and in all my time there, I witnessed nothing but kindness being administered.

The clue is in the name - it was a very progressive approach to mental health care, and many of the techniques have been globally adopted in the years since.

I think, perhaps, Ms Vertoni has guilt stemming from her inability to cope with her 'very good friend' and 'lover' experiencing problems. Sadly, it was something I witnessed often, that stigma attached to our patients.

Thomas was with us for quite some time, and I got to know him. I witnessed first-hand the great improvements he made during his stay.

I will concede that Ms Vertoni may have visited him during his early days at The Pines, and heavy sedation was used whilst a level could be found to suit. It was only done to protect the patient, staff and other residents. Every patient was different and unique, and working from the bottom up, rather than the top down, was deemed the more accurate way of finding the correct balance.

Under the care of the staff at The Pines, I watched Thomas thrive. Until, when the time was right, he was introduced back into society.

I am aware of his untimely death in 1964, and believe me when I tell you, it hit all of us who knew him extremely hard. However, Thomas had not picked up his latest prescription, and it is important to register that the facility had no control over that once patients had asked for release from our care.

Further, I can assure you without doubt, that Thomas was only as heavily sedated as Ms Vertoni describes for the minimum amount of time, if at all.

My recollections are of a happy, well adjusted young man, who integrated well with others during the vast majority of his stay.

He was only supposed to be with us for a short spell, but voluntarily remained for some four years and more. On release, he donated a generous sum to the facility.

Does that sound like a man who was kept in the manner Ms Vertoni describes?

Yes, I write to defend my former place of work. But, rather, I wish for you to know that Thomas was a pleasure to care for. Always polite and helpful, I still hear him playing his guitar, and it echoing along the hallways.

Best wishes.

E O'Donnell

Former Psychiatric Nurse

43.

"Psst!" came to my ears one afternoon, "psst!"

A single-frame image shot to my eyes - a copperhead lying on a mound of earth...

But it was gone before it could become anything animated.

"Psst!"

I raised my eyes but not my head.

"Mercy me, well look and see, if it isn't dear Tommy come to sing to me!"

A tune whispered to me, but died on the scant breeze it arrived on.

I knew her. I'd met her. But I couldn't think where or how.

Was she Momma?

No. Momma was beautiful. The woman in front of me could not be described as such.

"Dotty!" she said, and took a seat facing me.

"It's why we're here, I guess," I replied, but not to be funny. I was incapable of humour.

"That's my name! You lived with us in Williamsburg a few summers ago. Lordy, lordy, well I'll be! Dress me up in lace and tie me to a tree!"

I looked at her blankly. Her squidgy voice was familiar.

"Guess it's a southern thing! They must have you on the hard candy, Sweetie."

I nodded.

"Yes, well, we all begin on that, but it does get better. And when Honey gets better, her pussy gets wetter," she whispered, and wriggled a little on the chair.

Dotty smiled happily, and gazed out the window.

"Beautiful, isn't it? I do so love this time of year, when the doe comes skipping with her tail in the air!"

A memory stirred in me, a smell of paint in my nostrils, a taste of bourbon on my tongue.

"Spring brings the doe, followed by the buck, and once that happens..." she cooed as she hugged herself gently.

"There's gonna be a fuck!" I finished the rhyme.

"Oh, Tommy! You haven't forgotten!"

I grinned inanely. She was so unattractive, but she'd opened a door in my mind through... What? Sound and rhyme. And sex. All things that were instinctive within me.

"Are you allowed outside in the garden?" she asked me.

I didn't know. It hadn't occurred to me to try and go there.

"What colour is your wristband?" she further wanted to know.

I showed her because I couldn't think of the name of the colour.

"Yellow, like a daffodil or a buttercup, let's go outside where the flowers open up!"

I let her take my hand, and followed her on my shuffling soft-slippered feet to the great outdoors. The sun on my face and a breeze in my mouth and nose were glorious things.

It felt like years since I'd tasted them, but had only been eight months or so.

I was powerless to resist, as she knelt in front of me in a dense ring of evergreen bushes, and tugged my pajamas down to my ankles.

The warmth of her mouth was pleasant, but I felt nothing more than a comfort. It was the human contact I ached for. It had been so long.

My muddy mind stumbled back over time, trying to establish a line. It had been four years since I'd been with a woman. It was with this woman kneeling before me; this contradiction. On the surface, so sweet and innocent; so manly and plain; ugly, many would say. Certainly shapeless and undesirable.

Yet, inside, such a warm and caring nature. Such delicacy and character. And an appreciation for all natural beauty - a love of love, I might term it.

The medication prevented me from responding. I wanted to. For her, I wanted to show her that I saw through the outer shell of crustiness and lack of femininity, and that I saw the living, pulsing, throbbing, loving entity beneath.

She pulled and squeezed, tugged and sucked, tickled and teased, but no reaction came from me.

I was a void. I had been turned into something incapable of feeling. And there was no more base a feeling for any reproductive entity than sex.

Had that always been my problem - was I too sensitive?

Wasn't that also true of Dotty? In a different way, was she, too, over-sensitive to sexual desire?

Was Cecil-Lance-Rick overly concerned with how others perceived him, and so compensated by making up new identities and lives for himself?

To society, we are all freaks as a consequence, purely because we happen to feel and see things in a different way to the norm.

"As Tommy's cock begins to stir, so Honey's pussy starts to purr!" she sang in her jejune voice, a voice that belonged to a pre-adolescent girl, but came from a chemically overcharged woman in her early-fifties.

It scared me to feel anything. Yet, it terrified me more to feel nothing.

So I went with the overriding side of me, for it was as though my heart and gut were pulling in a different direction to my head. Chemicals could affect my brain, but they could not stem my spirit.

Dotty gently tugged me down to earth and straddled me, as I lay on my back gazing up at a pristine blue sky with one white cloud fluffily looking down on us with utmost approval. I knew the names of the colours all of a sudden.

She sang a song as she danced on me, "rhyme and reason holding sway, as they drove the dancing girl away, rhyme and reason waltzing on, mercy me, for now she's gone, rhyme and reason comes the season, rhyme and reason holding sway, crime and treason needs no reason, rhyme and reason come and play."

Music holds memories that cannot be extinguished, and through that tune things came flooding back. I saw lines of tape on a wall depicting the very song she sang. My fingers made chord shapes on the dry dirt by my side.

When the moment came, it was physically painful, and I roared with the effort, as Dotty clamped her hand over my mouth.

Everything poured out of me. It was incredibly liberating.

I lay there breathing hard and sweating, despite my lack of physical involvement. Dotty had done all the work.

Smiling up at that sky, with Dotty more comely thanks to her being silhouetted, I was, it shocked me to learn, happy.

For the first time in my life, in that place of all places, I was fuckin' happy!

44.

The facility wasn't for the criminally insane. Most patients had either admitted themselves, or been sent by family. A few, such as I, had been referred by the legal system.

Much of the funding came from pharmaceutical companies, delighted to have willing subjects on which to test their products.

Overall, it was a pretty laid back place, where drugs kept the majority in check. Occasionally, there would be a scene, but that person would quickly be back on the hard candy.

The staff seemed not to care what Dotty and I got up to on an almost daily basis. Perhaps they thought we were good for one another. I ticked a need in her, and she gave me the companionship I realised I'd always craved.

If I'd been asked, I would have said that I was a loner. My music and penchant for the open road were solitary activities. Even as a child in the hills, I was most content when alone on the rocky outcrop, gathering wood, or sat fishing down by the streams and rivers.

Momma had been the only company I'd required.

Dotty was twenty-five years my senior, just as Momma had been. Still, I asked her to marry me.

It wasn't a real wedding, and wasn't legally binding, on account of us both being certified crazy and living in a mental health facility.

Still, it was a day I cherish, mostly because of how happy it made Dotty.

She looked good, primarily because she wore a veil, and she swung her arms blissfully by her sides as her body turned in time all through the mock vows.

The ceremony was performed by the lead psychiatrist I'd been seeing since I'd arrived. He gave a long speech about the sanctity of marriage, and fidelity being an integral part of such an undertaking. He saw it all as part of Dotty's rehabilitation.

In the end, Dotty cut him short with, "mercy me, will you get us wed, so Honey can have Tommy's cock in bed!"

I was allowed my guitar and personal effects, and began thinking seriously about music for the first time in half a dozen years. I guess that was around late-1960 or early-'61.

Through the radio and television, I heard the music that was current. It didn't sound current to me, as the ballads were being crooned, and rock'n'roll was politely nudged aside.

My medication had been gradually reduced, an adjustment made every six months, as a level was sought at which I could, 'more ably function without episodes of delusion and paranoia.'

"How are you this week, Tommy? Are you happy?"

"Yes, I'm happy. Life is good."

"What do you think of when you see this?" A card depicting a cat was shown to me.

"A cat," I answered, and thought of Dotty saying pussy.

"And this?"

"A snake."

"And this?"

"An airplane."

"And this?"

"A space ship."

"And this?"

"My Momma."

"Why?"

"Trees always remind me of her. I was born in the hills, you see, and trees are to me what buildings are to you."

He smiled at that, the psychiatrist.

That was when they let me have my guitar. The strings were stretched out and flat, but I could rekindle my muscle memory all the same.

I asked for a roll of low-tack tape, and was allowed it. Someone brought it to me from the supply store. I began decorating my walls with ideas. They were no more than fragments at that stage.

One morning in late-'61, I went to find Dotty to ask her opinion on a little tune I'd come up with in the night. She wasn't in her room. Nor was she in the communal area.

I searched the gardens, sticking my head into all of the places we'd had sex over the years. I half expected to find her with another man.

She was nowhere to be found.

I asked the staff if they'd seen her, but they shook their heads and looked away from my eyes.

Something was fuckin' wrong.

That afternoon was my weekly assessment, so I bided my time till then.

"Where's Dotty?"

"She's gone, Tommy."

"Gone where?"

"Home. She's gone from here to pick up her life."

"This is her life."

"Well, not any longer. Her husband..."

"I'm her husband!"

"Now, Tommy, you know that isn't true. Her real husband came for her."

"Why?"

"Because she's improved, and he's better equipped to deal with her."

"Bullshit!"

"A lot of the improvement, I believe, is down to you, and you should feel very proud."

"This is bullshit. You have to get her back..."

"He's her husband, Tommy. He signed the papers to have her committed, and he's at liberty to reverse that decision."

"There's something wrong," I instinctively knew. Thoughts were rushing at me once more, my mind awash with flashes of any number of explanations.

"Money!" I said, bringing a fist down on the table, "it's always about money."

"Yes, there was mention of an inheritance," he informed me honestly.

"That fuckin' asshole."

"Tommy, it enabled him to give up work and care for her. That's all I was going to say. This is a good test for you. This is the first stress you've had in a long time, and now is the real deal. How you handle this will go a long way to determining your future," he warned.

I missed her. I missed that woman as much as I'd ever missed anything in my life except Momma.

Plain old Dotty, with her strange rhyming phrases and nymphomania, was as close as I'd ever been to being in love.

As a young man, I'd sometimes depict what any future love might look like. It never looked like Dotty.

I pined for her, and worried about her. But I kept a lid on things, as I worked all the hours available to me on my new record idea. Even when the light was extinguished, I'd lie in my bed and continue to build the picture in my mind.

That was home. It was the longest I'd lived anywhere in my life. Momma and I never stayed in the same cabin for four and a half years that I could remember. Perhaps the first place we had, after I was born.

It was also the cleanest place I'd ever resided in, and the food was better than any I'd lived on when I was on my own.

My health was good, both mentally and physically. The only drugs I imbibed were prescribed specifically, and I hadn't touched a drop of whiskey in all those years.

The music began to take shape in my room, but the lyrics wouldn't come.

How could I write words cocooned in that place all the time? Words came from experience and exposure. Lyrics and characters came from relationships and a broadness of view.

In addition, of course, it all came because of my talent for looking into and seeing the future.

45.

A letter arrived for me in May of 1962. It was from a legal office in Delaware.

It named me as the sole beneficiary of one Hananiah Silver.

A sealed letter was also enclosed with my name in blue ink on the envelope.

'Dear Tommy,

Well, if you are reading this, I am finally dead and gone.

In truth, I have been dead for a couple of decades now, along with my family.

All I have ever felt since is anger, along with a guilt - a guilt for not being with them, a guilt for not finding them, and a guilt for living in a world without them.

I have no living family.

I am leaving you all of my savings and my possessions, such as they are.

Use it, Tommy. Use it to find for yourself all of the things in life that I lost.

I have no sentiment left in me, so there is no more to say, beyond this - I enjoyed working with you very much, and you see the world differently to everybody else.

DO NOT let them take that out of you! This is very important. They will want you to be just like them, and never challenge anything - to never look at anything in a different way!

Ignore them, Tommy! You fight for what you love.

If I could live all over again, I would change only that - I would fight harder for the things I have loved! I would fight until I died!

Because losing them was death anyway.

Take care of yourself, Tommy Histon.

Hank

Hananiah Silver'

He left me over ten-thousand dollars and his violin.

"Are you happy, Tommy?" came the question at my next session of psychotherapy.

"Yes," I answered flatly.

"It's been a few months now since Dotty went. How do you feel about that?"

"People come and people go," I shrugged, "it's the way of life."

He nodded and wrote a note.

"Can I go?" I found myself asking.

"We have another five minutes."

"No. I mean, can I leave here? This place, I mean."

"Do you feel you're ready to leave?"

"Yes. How long have I been here?"

"Four and a half years."

Fuck me. It was a seventh of my life. I was thirty, I grasped in that moment.

"It's a long time," was all I said.

"Long enough, do you think?"

"I do. So, can I leave?"

He said, "yes. You're free to go. You could have left at any time in the last two and a half years."

"What? Why didn't you tell me?"

"Why didn't you ask?"

It threw me, that question. Why hadn't I asked?

"Because I couldn't think of anywhere I'd rather be."

"And now?"

"And now I can. Now I see a life ahead of me."

"What does it look like, Tommy, this life you see?"

I thought about the correct words. Not the words I believed he wished to hear, but the words that described what I aspired to.

"Settled. Content. Happy."

He smiled, stood, and shook my hand.

I'd need to continue taking the medication for the rest of my life. It could either be collected from the facility, or, in exceptional circumstances, prescribed via referral through a pharmacist.

"Every six months, Tommy. That's the deal. You come back and see me. Okay?"

"You must really fuckin' like me!" I jested.

A silence prevailed. I ended it with, "who paid for all this, doc?"

"For the first two years, the state. The government, more aptly."

"And for the last two and a half?"

"We receive donations that help support the facility."

"Charity?"

"I suppose."

And just like that, I was walking away with my head held high, my guitar case in my hand, and a bag slung over my shoulder.

Where to now, I asked myself?

46.

My first port of call was Delaware, where I took lodging and took stock.

At the first opportunity, I sent the mental health facility a check for a few grand.

My royalties had grown substantially during my time away. Radio play, and a major label artist covering one of my songs, had added a few thousand dollars. I was in good shape, both financially and generally.

As soon as I found my feet, I headed down to Williamsburg, and the house I'd stayed at with Leonard and Dotty.

I drove there, having purchased my first car. It was a '58 Buick Roadmaster Riviera in a green colour. It suited me well enough. I went for the hardtop because it was the only one they had on the lot. A fleeting thought came to me about keeping the fuckers out of my head, but I didn't dwell on it too much.

I didn't bother with getting a driver's licence. I figured I'd tell anyone who asked that I was from South Dakota. I assumed the law hadn't changed there.

Leonard and Dotty didn't live where they once had, but I was given a forwarding address in Staunton, Virginia, by a neighbour who recalled me.

So, I drove north up I-81, a road that didn't exist the last time I was there.

At Staunton, I asked directions, and found the property a mile or so out of town. It was a new build, on a couple of acres, and was a pretty impressive residence on approach.

Once up close, I saw that it was large but characterless; a box of a building, inside which I imagined each room to be devoid of angles and crevices and places to explore.

"Well, well, I know you!" Leonard greeted me as I emerged from the vehicle.

"Hi," I replied, and begrudgingly took the hand he offered.

"I want to thank you," he said, as he ushered me inside, "for what you did for Dotty in the facility. I don't know the details, and I'm not sure I wish to, but I know you looked out for her, and helped with her rehabilitation. So, thank you, son."

"Is she here?"

"Sure, sure! Come on in. Bourbon?"

I nodded. "I thought you were starting a new life, with another woman?" I asked, once I had a tumbler in my hand.

"And so I did. But the guilt, you know? It ate me up over the years, and I had to go get my Honey out of that place. Simply could not live with myself. How'd you end up in such a facility, Tommy?"

"I'm not sure," I lied. It wasn't a lie, in truth, because it was all a little vague to me. "Being stupid and getting into trouble, I guess."

"Well, you're here now, and it's darned fine to see you. Cheers!"

We touched glasses.

"Nasty scar on your face," he observed.

"Yep, part of the being stupid and getting into trouble I mentioned."

"Well, we all got things from the past we ain't right proud of, I figure."

"Where is she?" I asked again after a few minutes of awkward chatter, as he explained his early retirement.

"Oh, she likes to sit in the conservatory on the back and watch nature. You know Dotty!"

"I'd like to see her."

"Sure, sure, come on through. She's not been well lately, but she's up and about today."

Her appearance horrified me.

My appearance had no effect on her.

The skin on her face was a mass of acne-like eruptions, and she looked as though she'd aged a decade or more in the few months since I'd last seen her.

She was gnarled and twisted, with barely enough strength to hold herself upright, as her head rolled back to find support on the chair-back.

Black eyes stared at me, but I saw no spark of recognition. Crusty vomit had streaked down her knitted cardigan, and a pool of it sat seeping through her skirt to her lap.

She was rake thin, with hollow cheeks. Her inherent unattractiveness was accentuated to a ghastly level.

I recoiled and immediately felt bad. This was still Dotty, I reminded myself.

No sound came from her, beyond a gurgle in her throat with every laboured breath.

"What the fuck have you done?" I snarled at Leonard.

"She's not been well, as I said."

"Bullshit! What are you giving her?"

"Just a little bromide. Hell, it ain't that. You can get it in the pharmacy! She likes taking it. Loves it with a little honey when I add too much and it gets somewhat salty."

I stood shaking with rage, but the psychiatrist's words and the lessons I'd learned contained it.

Also, I knew I could not get into trouble. Not for myself, but for Dotty. I knew that if I acted rashly in that moment, she might die.

"She's had none of her old problems, I tell you. The bromide works just fine! Yes, there's a little sickness with it, but there is with most medicines. At least we can go to church without me worrying about what she might say or do!"

"Why didn't you leave her where she was?" I bellowed.

"It was costing me every day she was there, Tommy! And a preacher friend of mine from Georgia told me about the bromide as a cure. It was probably all they were giving her in the place, anyways, and charging an arm and a leg for it, an' all!"

"Enjoy your inheritance," I growled.

"Now, Tommy, don't be like that. It ain't the money per se. I needed that money to take early retirement and look after her. Now, how could I do that if I was working all the time, eh, answer me that?"

"Fuckin' asshole."

I scooped her up in my arms. She reeked of urine and acrid vomit. Her belly pressed hard and inflated against my hand, and she recoiled with pain and discomfort at the contact.

"Where are you taking her?"

"Away from you."

"Now, Tommy, son..."

"Get the fuck out of my way."

"It's on you!" he said, "I can't pay for her caring, not after buying this place! And I have another woman depending on me for financial support. Mind, I told you about her - a widow lady over in Charlottesville?"

She weighed next to nothing.

I wasn't hearing him. I brushed past, harder than I'd intended, as he bounced off me and impacted on the doorframe.

With her head pressed securely against my chest, I strode out the door, laid her in the rear seat of my car, and drove away.

47.

I messed up. I should have taken her to the closest hospital, rather than drive to the facility.

My plan had been to use my money to keep her there while they sorted her out, and then buy a little place and have her come live with me.

She'd been happy just a few months before.

We'd been happy.

Hell, I'd have checked myself back in, if I'd needed to, just so I could keep an eye on her.

Hank's words played on me:

'If I could live all over again, I would change only that - I would fight harder for the things I have loved! I would fight until I died!

Because losing them was death anyway.'

For three days I sat by her bed in the hospital they sent her to. The nurses brought me food and drink after they gave up asking me to leave.

I told them I was her husband, because I sort of was, I figured. They looked at me kind of funny when I told them that, but nobody questioned it.

I'm not sure I slept a wink during that whole time.

I was present as they flushed her system, and gave her an enema to clear the constipation that crippled her guts.

The bleeps of machines gave me solace. It was their silence that I dreaded.

Her hand was limply, lifelessly in mine when the time came.

She didn't open her eyes or say anything at the end. There was no little squeeze or faint smile.

It isn't like it is in the movies or on the television.

It was so much more soul-destroying than anything I'd experienced in my life, to lose someone you've only just realised you love. After it's too late.

If I could have turned it all back - time, I mean - I would not have gone to the night of the storm when I might have stopped Momma going to the cabin. And nor would I have saved Lance, or changed anything that had happened to me personally.

I would have gone to the day of our faux wedding. More importantly, to the evening when we lay in her bed in her room in a post-coital clinch.

"I love you, Tommy, with all my heart and all my body," she'd whispered.

And I'd pretended to be asleep.

In a barely audible hush of breath, she'd added, "no one ever once said that they love Dotty."

48.

I was searching again.

In addition, I was experimenting with my medication to see the effects. I began reducing the dose, and missing occasional slots entirely. I was always sure to keep a tally, though, so the numbers were right for the appointments every six months.

My problem, I deduced, was that the medication left me, to some degree, creatively stifled. Off them, I was creative in my music, but also creative in my thoughts. And not in a good way.

On a whim, I took a trip up to New York, and showed up at the record label I'd visited a decade before with Rick Doyle.

"Good morning, I'm here to see James Ardanian."

It was a different receptionist.

"And you are?"

"Tommy Histon."

"Do you have an appointment?"

"Yes, I do."

"I'm not seeing your name on the list, sir."

"Oh, I'm a little late."

She glanced through the sheet beneath.

"Still not seeing you on the list. What time were you due here?"

"I think it was at eleven."

"Today?"

"Ah, no. It was 1952, I believe."

"Very precise. Mr Ardanian usually leaves between five and six."

"Oh, well, can I see him anyway?"

"Was it for an audition?"

"Yes! Yes it was."

"Okay, I understand. You aren't supposed to be here at the office. I'm betting you're on at around ten to eight, down at The Chapter Club. You know where it is?"

"No," I confessed.

She handed me a piece of paper with an address on.

Now, to be honest, I hadn't had my full dose of medication that day, thinking I needed to be at a certain creative level for any audition, should I happen to get one.

So, feeling pretty pleased with myself for my blag, and imagining Rick Doyle would approve, I also skipped my evening pills, and went along to the Chapter Club for seven thirty, guitar in hand.

Nobody questioned me, or asked for anything at the door, and I was shown to a room with a basic stage, and approximately twenty men in suits sitting at tables drinking.

By nine, I was still sat waiting, having endured a succession of singers, both male and female, who had performed an audition that went largely unnoticed by the audience.

Simply because there was nobody else left, I was asked my name.

"Tommy Histon."

A couple of heads snapped up and stared at me through the smoke-haze and murky light.

"You ain't on the list," I was told by a man who had to turn sideways to fit his shoulders through the door.

"I have an audition," I informed him softly.

"Who asked you to come?"

"James Ardanian."

The large guy looked over at a wiry dark-haired man who stood no more than five-two in height. He looked like a child at the bar, though his face was craggy and careworn.

A nod from him allowed me passage.

An amp was present, but I had no cable, so sat on the edge of the stage and played acoustically.

As to what I played and sang, I don't recall, but it would have been a couple of tracks from 'Coda', or perhaps one each from that and 'Track Back And Trail On'. I played them pretty straight, I know that much. With it being just me and my archtop, I didn't have a lot of choice.

One thing I am certain of is, as I played, the hitherto disinterested men in the room paid attention.

A few leant to one another and passed comments, but never once turned their eyes or ears away from me as they did.

I had them. And I fuckin' knew it.

At the end of my two song stint, for the first time that evening, I heard applause.

"I've heard of you," one gentleman called out, "you had a couple of records out, as I recall."

"That's right," I replied.

"How'd they do?"

"Okay, I guess."

"Weren't they on that Jury Duty label, down in Delaware?"

"Yes, sir, that's correct."

"Well, seeing how that label went ass up a few years back, I'm guessing they didn't do that well."

"No, I guess not."

"You have something, Mr Histon, I'll tell you that. Here's my problem, though," chimed in Ardanian, "you aren't right for this time.

"Right now is all about youth - fresh-faced, pretty-boys, who appeal to the teenage girls for looks and sound, and appeal to the boys because, if they model themselves on them, they'll get the girls.

"Fact is, talent counts for nothing, Mr Histon. You're all wrong - you look wrong, and your words are wrong. You sing about things men like me want to listen to, and that isn't the audience you're going after.

"You sing about serious things with real poetry, and that isn't where it's at right now. Hell, we're almost back to post-war moon-June-fucking-croon as things stand."

A ripple of laughter trickled through the room.

"You're too quirky, Tommy. And too old. You are, speaking plainly, too different. And different is a hard sell."

"I can do many styles," I suggested, and hated myself for selling out. Hank would not approve. But I sensed it was my last opportunity.

"But you still wouldn't look right, Tommy. You aren't clean enough or innocent enough. I'm sorry, buddy, but that's how it is."

Sympathetic heads nodded in accord.

As I packed my guitar away, James Ardanian approached me.

He was chatting to a colleague in a strange language.

I recognised some of the words.

That was why I gave him an inspection.

He was horrified. As were the other men in the company, most of who represented major record labels in New York.

I tried to explain, that it was the language, and that I may have made a mistake - that I believed him to be an alien, and that I was protecting the rest of the assembled.

Someone said it was Armenian he was speaking. Whatever it was, there were familiar sounds.

The large man I'd encountered earlier advanced on me. He was maybe half a foot taller than I, so I had to reduce him a little by kicking him in his privates. After that, his face was on a convenient level to impact with my forehead, and my knee did the rest.

I hadn't even bothered to lay down my guitar case during the whole thing. It had been so easy, as I'd foreseen every move he was about to make before he could even think of it.

So, I walked away on my own terms, having, literally, alienated myself from every major player in the music business.

Those that weren't present would hear about it.

I'd finally done it. I'd finally fucked myself.

I recalled an image I'd seen in a book a few years before, where a snake is swallowing itself, its tail disappearing into its own gaping mouth.

Well, that was me, I figured.

49.

Excerpt from James Ardanian's autobiography, 'A&R-danian: My Life At A Major Record Label', first published in 1990.

The one that still gets to me is Tommy Histon.

He showed up at an open audition in New York one evening in 1962. I'd heard of him, most certainly. Indeed, I was a fan.

Thanks to my position, just about every distributed record in the USA was sent to the office. As a team, we'd divide them up and give them a listen. I'd picked out 'Track Back And Trail On' because it looked interesting. And so it proved to be.

A year or so later, and I spotted 'Coda' in the pile, and took that one as well. Again, I was pretty impressed by this kid from Virginia.

I went as far as checking him out, to see what else he might have to offer. Somehow, someone got me a copy of 'Three Minute Hero'. I was intrigued.

Calling the Jury Duty office number, I spoke with one of the two guys running the label. This would have been in late-'54, maybe early-'55.

I had a real feeling that rock'n'roll was about to break out in a big way, and I intended for Histon to come on board and be a part of that.

Unfortunately, I was curtly informed, "Histon is no longer making music, and we have no idea where he is or how to get in touch with him."

They tried to push a singer on me that they had on their books, some crooning kid, as I recall. I received a tape from the label, and a follow-up call, but I wasn't interested. We had a plethora of such artists on the books, and I didn't hear enough in the songwriting to warrant any deal on that score. We'd often take a good song from a demo, and pay to have one of our big-hitters re-record it.

In the early-sixties, that was precisely what I did with one of Histon's tracks.

So, having not heard anything of Histon in six or seven years since that call, he suddenly showed up at this audition.

Well, I was pretty blown away when I heard his name announced.

He played wonderfully, and sang two songs I was familiar with from his earlier records. It was one of the most impressive auditions I'd ever heard. The man could truly compose, and his delivery was sublime.

Sadly, he was a mess physically. He made Johnny Cash and Jerry Lee Lewis look like angels. There was an horrific scar down one side of his face, and his eyes were kind of crazy looking. He was also very jittery, and clearly not stable.

Music at that time was very clean-cut, and Tommy was the opposite of what we were looking for.

Still, I heard and saw something that made me excited.

Standing at the bar that evening watching him perform, I tried to project music over the next few years, and to imagine what direction it was likely to take.

There was an emerging singer-songwriter scene on the underground in the States, and I knew it was no different in Britain.

Every indication pointed at albums being set to become more affordable and popular, and that would change music, and allow more scope.

The recorded music industry, I had a strong feeling, was going to grow up in the sixties.

On a whim, I decided to sign Tommy Histon. I'd stick him on the pay-roll, and keep him close until his time came once more. I'd justify it by having him write songs in the meantime, as the guy had an ear for a melody.

Furthermore, I was considering launching a more experimental side-label under the umbrella of the major, and wondered if that might not be a better outlet for him.

I was outlining my plan to my cousin, who worked for me, as we walked over to him. We were chatting in Armenian, as I didn't wish to show my hand to the other label people in attendance.

Suddenly, and without warning, Histon had a hold of my genitals.

Well, all hell broke loose. A fight started, which Tommy won without breaking sweat, and he was walking out the door.

There was no way I could work with him after that; not without looking very foolish.

But the truth of it - I had to act more appalled and shocked than I actually was.

In those days, I was hiding my true sexuality.

So, I responded in a way I believed would best protect my secret.

Over the years, I learned more about Tommy Histon, and the mental health problems he suffered with. I discovered he spent several years in an institution just before I met him. In addition, I heard how he wasn't treated well by the music industry.

A shame and a guilt has dogged me ever since when I think of Histon. I wish I could have done more.

Word reached me that he was flying to England to make an album in 1964, and I was genuinely delighted for him.

I hoped he'd sort himself out, and find some success and happiness. Again, I imagined we might perhaps hook up one day, and work together.

The news of his death reached my ears, and I recall a heavy depression sitting over me when I was told.

Oh, I've missed many a top-selling talent over the years. But Tommy Histon is the first to spring to mind when I'm asked about 'the one that got away,' or 'the one you wish you'd signed.'

He was within my grasp, and my own self-protection stopped me following my better judgement.

And because of my reaction, I effectively finished him in America. He became a joke figure; a pariah; persona non grata.

He became all of the things I was terrified my sexuality might make me.

Yet, sitting here in my comfortable retirement, he remains one of the greatest talents I've ever encountered. I still listen to his records, and they sound as fresh today as they did back then.

If his missing album ever came up for sale, I would be prepared to offer a lot of money in order to own it.

Not to release it. Simply to own a copy.

I doubt there's anyone else in the history of recorded music I would do that for.

At the very least, I can say that I got to see him perform live on stage. That's something I shall never forget.

50.

Nature is to the mind what soap is to the hands.

Shenandoah in September of '62 was where I washed up. I rented a log cabin that reminded me of my time with Momma, with its wood-burning stove and lack of other amenities.

Water came from a stream and tasted of earth; light from a candle too dim to read by.

I'd sit in the near dark drinking whiskey every night and play on my guitar. I didn't need to see to do that. In addition, I taught myself to play the violin. Well, of a fashion. I liked the melancholiness of it, and it reminded me of old Hank.

For right around a year I remained there, connecting with nature, and venturing out in my Buick only when absolutely necessary. I'd have to leave to collect my medication from the facility, and to pick up supplies from a general store in a nearby town.

Dotty's death hit me harder than I knew, and more than I ever thought it would. My own sense of guilt was what ate me up, as I played things over and over in my mind, thinking of all I might have done differently.

As a musician, passing thirty felt important. It was a young person's game, and I was considered too out of step.

The feedback from the audition plagued me. The fact that I knew everyone in that room had enjoyed my set beyond all the others, yet wouldn't touch me, felt terminal. And that was before I screwed myself.

Between my earnings and the money from Hank, I could live for years in the way I was. I considered buying a house, primarily as an investment, and to save wasting money on rent. I'd never had a home to call my own. Still, something repelled me from being tied to one place.

Or, perhaps, I simply didn't know where I wanted to settle and establish a base.

I'd never managed to find anywhere I felt I belonged, despite searching for over half my life.

A tortoise became my companion. He showed up one late-September day, and we kind of bonded. Come the cold weather, he crawled into a box I fashioned for him, and spent the winter cocooned therein.

I checked on him regularly, and in the spring of '63, when the weather improved, I gave him a warm bath and offered him some tomato I chopped up. He was right as rain after that, and showed no inclination to move on.

My only problem that winter came not long before spring arrived. I was low on supplies, and didn't see the snow coming. My car got stuck in a drift as I tried to get to the store, and it was a-ways-away to go on foot.

For a week, I subsisted on hot water and pine needles for a little vitamin injection. A rabbit I snared probably saved me. It also reminded me of Dotty.

My medication ran out a day after the thaw came, so I had to run out of there and go get my supply from the facility.

Shelly, my tortoise, slept on while I was away.

I'd chat to him in his sleep, about this and that. Nothing important. Just things I thought about as they occurred to me.

At night, I'd make up stories for him as he munched methodically and meditatively on a bit of leafy green stuff, and I'd draw the bow over the strings of my violin and make soothing sounds.

A song idea came to me, which I called 'Hypernation Hibernation'. I played it for Shelly, and he seemed to like it. I reckon he nodded his head in time, at least.

I wasn't unhappy, but neither was I happy. Somewhere between the two, in a kind of limbo, was where I found myself.

The way I figured things, nobody I'd known was happy.

Momma certainly wasn't. Perhaps Janie was, but she was too simple to have aspirations. Her mind was too narrow to be capable of broad vision and wide open dreams.

Clarissa was desperately unhappy, I think, despite having wealth and all one could ever dream of in material terms.

Lance became Rick, and hid from Cecil, because he was unhappy with his true self. He made things up in an attempt to find a version of himself that he was happy with.

Poor Dotty was unhappy most of the time because she couldn't be the person she truly was at heart. That was unacceptable to society.

Leonard was unhappy with the reality of his wife.

Hank was unhappy because he lost his entire family, and blamed himself for being absent. And on it goes.

Juice! Juice Cartwright was a happy man. And he was alone in life, travelling to fruit farm and back again, always moving on. Until he died on the move.

Shelly seemed happy, hiding away in a shell and sleeping for months on end. He was in no hurry to get anywhere.

What would make me happy?

I had no idea. Playing music and making records was as contented a feeling as I'd ever known. I could always play music, if only for myself. But it had been almost a decade since I'd last set foot in a studio.

And I didn't see anything coming along to change that any time soon.

51.

Shelly had upped and walked out prior to hibernation in that year of '63. There was no ceremony. He wandered off like he usually did, and failed to return. I looked for him, but not too hard. He was a free spirit, and entitled to do as he chose.

The idea of him taking his abode with him everywhere he went appealed to me. It crossed my mind to buy a mobile home and keep on the move as he did.

I took his departure as a sign, and decided to do the same. I foresaw a bitter winter looming, and sought an easier ride through it.

The warmer the better, thought I, so I drove down to Florida's gulf coast before the first frost bit further north.

My only stop came in North Carolina, as I finally made it back to the fruit farm I'd worked at all those years before. I'd always planned on returning, but had never quite made it.

The owner and his wife were the only people I knew. At first, they didn't recognise me, and I had to explain who I was. They recalled me eventually, but I'm unsure whether they were just pretending to do so.

Still, I got to chat with them about Juice Cartwright, and they recalled him fondly. They were kind enough to offer me a coffee and some cake as we did. It was good to talk about Juice. It lifted a weight from me, paying homage to the first friend I ever had.

"Never be afraid of your own talent," I chanted in my head over and over as I drove south. The words came to me in Juice's voice.

"They shall regret some of the things they did. But more, they shall regret the things they did not do," came to me in Hank's accented tones.

Music. That was always the thing for me. Even as a child, it was the one pursuit that freed my mind and settled me down.

In the studio with Hank, and, even before that, down in Richmond, I'd been myself in those moments.

Music had brought all of the players in my life to me. Well, maybe not Lance. But it did bring Rick and Cecil.

Music was the first thing Dotty remembered about me. "Mercy me, well look and see, if it isn't dear Tommy come to sing to me!"

Music. Clarissa heard me busking on the street, and encouraged her father to sign me up.

Even Janie got off on my singing and playing guitar.

Men, too, though. Juice and I bonded because of it.

Hank, of course, and Marcus Anderson. Vertoni and Luca, and all of the people I met on the road. Countless others, too, whose names escape me, but faces do not.

Music gave me an income. Either directly through earnings, or indirectly through the inheritance I received from Hank. I'd survived for seventeen years because of it. And I had a fair old pile of cash in my bank account. I saw no reason why I couldn't carry on for another seventeen at least.

I'd need to subsidise it, to stretch it out. But that was fine, just so long as I was playing music and writing songs.

It was less important whether anyone ever cared to hear them or not. It was worth doing for myself, because that is the real me. My self-worth was sufficient to fuel my motivation.

That's what I'd do. That was the plan. I'd get to Florida, and play on the streets for change. Perhaps I could get myself a residency someplace, and play in an outdoor bar down by the beach on the Gulf of Mexico.

Hell, I'd rent a small beach house or trailer, perhaps a mobile home a la Shelly, and watch the sun set every night as I strummed and picked away. Beyond that, nothing much mattered.

Any high notion is always, in my experience, off-set by a low. It keeps us balanced, I reason.

Those names came to me again - Hank, Cecil, Dotty, Juice, Momma.

They were all dead.

The voices I heard in my head never came from the still-living. They always came from the deceased.

"Never go back in life, Tommy. Keep going forward. Keep heading to your future," Momma said to me.

"No one ever once said that they love Dotty," Dotty whispered simultaneously.

"Who do you want to be?" Lance shouted over both of them.

"Fight for what you love!" Hank added to the wall of noise in my ears.

Only the departed did I hear.

And I knew in that moment that it was because I would be joining them soon.

52.

Reputations can be good or bad. And sometimes both at once.

Ever since Bobby or Johnny Somebody had covered one of my songs, that was how I'd get introduced at the gigs; as the guy who wrote such-and-such that Johnny or Bobby had covered. That name would get the biggest cheer of the evening.

Of course, I'd leave that song out of my set, which pissed off every fucker except me.

Still, the reference was enough to draw a few people through the door. And once they were through the door, they'd drink and smoke and barely pay me any heed. I was background noise.

I heard of the changes that were coming - The Beatles over in England, Bob Dylan in the USA. All I thought was, 'shit, I was doing that ten years ago.' Still, I liked the new direction. I certainly preferred it to the Bobbys and the Johnnys and the watered-down Elvis I saw in a movie once.

Then, on November 22nd, 1963, Lee Harvey Oswald shot and killed John F Kennedy.

Someone connected that to a lyric I wrote on 'Get A Shift On', from my album 'Coda', on which I borrowed a name from Cecil's identity cards.

Kenneth John Eddy. Shot dead in the Lone Star State.

A DJ over in Texas picked up on it, and began playing the song.

One night, just after Thanksgiving, they tracked me down to the bar I played in. A phone call came in, and I was called over after I'd finished my set.

I had no idea who I was talking to, or that I was live on the air.

"Is that Tommy Histon?"

"Yes, sir. Who's this?"

"This is Davie D Davidson on the Big D over in the Big T. How are you this evening?"

"I'm fine, thanks."

"Just to be clear - you are the same Tommy Histon who released an album called 'Coda' back in '54, correct?"

"That's me."

"Well, let me start by saying that I've been a fan of that record for a while now."

"Well, thank you very much."

"Tell us about the song 'Get A Shift On'?"

"Oh, well that was about a guy I knew. A friend, I guess you might say. And he was always reinventing himself, you know? So, get a shift on referred to him shifting identity, as well as the jobs we worked and the shifts we took on. It had two meanings, if you follow."

"Okay. But he was president of the United States, correct?"

"Well, if he decided to be. That was the point - that a person can be whatever they decide to be."

"A president who was shot and killed right here in Texas?"

"Well, yes, that was part of the song. Be careful what you wish for, I guess was the message."

"Kenneth John Eddy. Sounds a lot like John F Kennedy, wouldn't you say?"

"A little, I suppose."

"And the song is ten years old?"

"Yes, it's getting to that age," I confirmed.

"You don't find that a little strange, Tommy?"

"I haven't thought about it too much. Sometimes things are known, you know?"

"Known, you say? What do you mean?"

"Well, I've always had a certain knack for seeing events that have not yet come to pass."

"You can see the future?" he exclaimed.

"Well, yes sir, I believe that we all can, if we use our minds in the right way."

"We?"

"Humans."

"You believe that all humans can see the future?"

"I do. My Momma could, and I've met others who know how to tap that stream."

"So, I need to be clear, Tommy - you foresaw JFK's assassination ten years before it took place?"

"Well, not exactly. I must have seen a president getting shot in Texas, and had a friend who sometimes used the name Kenneth John Eddy. Those two things were merged. That was all it was."

"Erm, okay. Do you know why Kennedy was shot dead, Tommy?"

"I've thought about that, as it happens."

"And what did you think?"

"Well, it seemed to me, and I ain't saying I'm right about this: But Kennedy said 'we choose to go to the moon in this decade,' right?"

"I believe he did, Tommy."

"Well, I don't reckon them fuckers up there wanted us going into space, or anywhere near the moon. That's what I believe."

Silence.

"Apologies to anyone offended by the language Tommy Histon used there. You say, erm, them up there. Who are you referring to, Tommy?"

"The aliens. Those fuckers are listening to everything broadcast over the airwaves. They can't see the future like we can. So they monitor everything to see who can predict events. They took me for that purpose."

"Aliens took you?"

"Yes sir."

They'd stopped broadcasting by that point, but continued to record the conversation. It would be bleeped out and broadcast many times afterwards.

"Okay. Erm, they took you to do what - what did they do to you up there?"

"They opened up my head. I have a scar to prove it. They probed my brain so they could discover how I do it."

"See the future?"

"Yes sir. But I didn't show the fuckers. I kept it hidden from them."

"Well, erm, ah, that must have been tough."

"It was. They held me for a long time, many years, even though it was only a couple of days in earth time."

"Ah, why is that?"

"We operate at the speed of sound. They at the speed of light. But radio waves, they carry sound, but travel at the speed of light, so that's how they get to us. That's how they keep track of us and know what we're up to."

"Okay."

"And they have bodies on earth that live amongst us."

"Really? Aliens are living here on earth? Are they, erm, little green men?"

"No. They look just like us. Except for one thing."

"What's that? How can we spot them, Tommy?"

"They're always male, and they only have one testicle."
"One testicle?"
"Yes sir. That's how you tell them fuckers from us."
"Well, that's, erm, fascinating."
"See that guy who shot Kennedy?"
"Oswald?"
"Yeah, that fucker."
"What about him?"
"I'll bet a million bucks he only has one testicle."
"Okay, thanks for your time, Tommy."
"My pleasure."
There was a bit of a furore over all of that.

Note: I've heard this interview in full, and Histon's account of it is almost exactly what was said in the exchange. Any small differences were too negligible to be worthy of correction.

53.

My residency was cancelled. Nobody would touch me.

From what I could understand, people were more upset about me cussing on the radio than anything else I might have said.

At Tampa Bay, a man approached me whilst I was busking. He looked smart in his suit and tie, and carried himself with an air of authority. A crop of bright and unruly red hair was swept back in a Jerry Lee Lewis style, but the breeze off the ocean kept messing it up. He had hair that would go only where it wanted to go.

In his Irish accent, he introduced himself as William Delaney, "but call me Liam." So I did.

He offered to buy me a drink, so we could talk business, and revealed that he knew who I was, and that he saw my tarnished name as being something to capitalise on.

"Folk know who you are," he told me in his jaunty manner, "and that's more than can be said about most people. That's a foot in the door, right there!"

I informed him that I had an album ready to go. "It just needs lyrics and something to hang it all off."

"Well, best thing we can do is ride the wave of your current notoriety. Strike while the iron's hot! That's what I say," he gabbled. I had a little trouble understanding him, as he spoke so rapidly.

Liam knew where and how we could get everything done. His problem was cash-flow. Only so much money could be transferred from Ireland every year, but he'd just bought a home near Tampa, and was due his citizenship any day.

"Ah, I don't suppose it'll hurt any to wait a wee while," he said as he ordered us both another bourbon. "Shame, though, because now is prime time, by my reckoning. What, with all the talk about you and whatnot."

I could see that what he said made a certain sense. It was true, after all, that I'd never been so well known.

"We'll be partners, Tommy, you and me, and we'll start our own record label. We'll build an empire, to be sure, and it'll be fifty-fifty down the line!" he said, chopping his hand down on the bar.

It was naive of me, but I was so eager to make another record, I gave him three thousand in cash.

And I never saw Liam Delaney again.

Showing up at the address he gave me, I was told it was a rental property. The previous tenant had paid only a week's deposit, and flitted without paying the outstanding balance. He was described as a "red-headed guy from across the pond."

I went to the studio in Tampa he'd mentioned, but nobody there had a clue who he was.

There was most definitely no session time booked for me.

Another year arrived, and I entered it with a defeated outlook to go with the usual uncertainty. I wondered if I was destined to spend what time I had left living in a nomadic fashion.

I didn't fit anything or anywhere.

Whilst it crushed any creativity in me, I went back to my medical regime so that my mind might settle. It made no difference to me, as nobody wished to hear Tommy Histon play music.

Driving aimlessly, I found myself heading north into the storm of winter. Virginia and her homely familiarity once again coaxed me, and I was seemingly powerless to resist.

Motels became my residence for a few nights at a time, before I drove on to the next town that got in my way. I was in no rush to reach my home state. Moreover, I stalled all the way. It took me a week to cross the border and leave North Carolina, and I was in sight of the 'Welcome' sign.

Inching along through snow and ice, sleet and wind, I slept in the car when I had to, swaddled in a blanket.

I had no idea where to go; so very alone was I on this earth filled with people.

In late-January, I washed up in Delaware. Checking in at my bank, I picked up my royalty statement. My reputation had had a detrimental effect on my income.

My time had arrived. The world was ready for my back catalogue. It would fit perfectly with all that was going on musically in 1964.

But my time was all behind me.

I nearly missed it. Amidst the mail sent to me from outraged people who heard, or heard about, my radio interview, sat an envelope all the way from England.

A new label, Chemisette Records, was being formed in a place called Brakeshire. Would I be interested in recording an album for them?

It went on to explain that they would pay for me to fly over, house me, give me full use of their own studio at Norton Basset, pay me a small advance on arrival, and a percentage of all record sales after costs had been recovered.

The letter was a month old. There was a number to call. So I called it, and spoke with a man named Baz Baxter.

I was polite. I didn't cuss. But I was sceptical. My medication was doing its job. My thought was that word about me hadn't reached the United Kingdom.

But Baz Baxter and Ally McIntyre knew exactly who I was and what I'd done.

The difference was, just as with Liam Delaney, where others saw damaged goods, they saw opportunity.

Reputations, as I said, can be good or bad. And sometimes both at once.

I'd require a passport. How the fuck did one go about getting one of those?

54.

I paid a legal man a great deal of money to get me the necessary paperwork, including a passport. For a birthdate, I made up February 29th.

A couple of weeks later, when that date arrived, I celebrated my birthday for the very first time. I was thirty-two.

Approximately.

By way of celebration, I got myself a bottle of bourbon and some cigarettes, and spent the time alone in a motel room unrolling lines of tape. I stuck them to the walls and over anything mounted on them.

All that was missing from the album were lyrics and a concept. Melodies and harmonies, timings, rhythms and instrumentation, were all in place. It simply required a theme to bring it all together.

My tickets arrived by courier.

Was it real? Was it happening?

I'd been asked for nothing, so began to believe. I was flying to England on March 19th. My first time on a plane, but not my first trip up there.

The days crept by. I drank whiskey, smoked, and stared at the tape, but nothing would come. I ate food when I remembered to.

I'd get ideas over there in England. I could start afresh, in a place unknown to me, and in which, more importantly, I was relatively unknown.

I watched The Beatles on The Ed Sullivan Show. It appeared as though there was something going on across the Atlantic.

I began to dream. Perhaps there lay the place I'd always been searching for.

The lines of tape intrigued me. I'd stare at them for hours, but was incapable of adding or subtracting.

My medication was set to run out a couple of days before I was due to fly. My intention had been to drive over to fill my prescription, and to advise them that I was going away. The trip was only scheduled for seven weeks, but one never knew. What would happen if I ended up staying for longer than six months? How would I get my refill?

And I knew - I knew that I could not finish the album if I was on the meds.

My mind had to be free, because freedom of thought was everything. Without that, we may as well be dead.

I said it out-loud in that motel room. "My music is more important to me than my sanity. My well-being is secondary to my creativity."

Freedom of expression was more vital to me than my actual freedom.

So, with a clear mind, and fully medicated, I withdrew the contents of my bank account in a mix of USA and British currencies. It was just under eight-thousand dollars in cash.

On the morning of March eighteenth, I took my last pill, loaded my meagre possessions into my Buick, and drove to New York to catch my flight the next day.

I said goodbye to nobody. And I doubted that anybody would even notice that I was gone.

Parking the Buick on a side street some distance from the airport, I left the key in it, and walked the rest of the way. Someone could have it if they chose to.

If not, it would be there for whenever, if ever, I returned.

Tommy in Florida, Oct-Nov 1963.

PART FOUR: Kimono For Kip

55.

Sleeping pills got me through the majority of the flight. I have little recollection of it, other than being woken with a tray of food and a smile. My joints ached from being cramped in one position for so long.

For the first couple of hours, though, I spent my time writing about my early life in this very journal. I had a compulsion to document all I have experienced.

On disembarking, I stepped out into moist drizzly air. It was a cold damp that pierced me and numbed my very bones.

I was just thinking how I should have packed a coat, when I looked at the passengers ahead of me in the terminal.

The shock of red hair sticking up in all directions was unmistakable.

Much to the annoyance of people 'queuing', I went charging through the line, and grabbed a hold of him.

Same hair, same build. Different guy.

Despite my apologies, I was taken away to a room by two men in uniform. They asked me plenty of questions, and I tried to explain about the radio interview, Kennedy, the moon, aliens and testicles, but I'm not sure I made much sense. I was still groggy after the flight.

They understood that a man very similar in appearance had stolen money from me.

Still, they searched my bag and my person. Thankfully, I'd hidden my cash inside the lining of my guitar case, otherwise that may have been a problem. The whiskey, cigarettes and change of clothes I had in my bag were, apparently, fine.

"What's inside your case, Mr Histon?" one of them inquired.

"My guitar in that one. And my violin in that one," I pointed out.

"No, your suitcase, sir. We can't find it."

I looked blankly at them.

"Do you have any other luggage?"

"No."

"According to your papers, you're here for seven weeks. Correct?"

"That's the plan."

They let me go then.

A man said, "welcome to London, sir," and I was through, my bag on my shoulder, guitar in one hand, and the violin tucked under my arm.

The instructions told me to wait in the hall, and look for a sign. I guessed they were a faithful nation, the English.

After a while, a man approached me and asked if I was Tommy Histon.

"That's right. I'm waiting for a sign."

He showed me a piece of card with my name on.

"The car's not far. I'll take that," he stated, and went to take my guitar.

I decided to let him have it, but I kept pretty close to him. My cash was in there. I'm not sure he was comfortable with me being that close.

England was like some parallel universe. The cars were back to front. The roads were back to front. The sun didn't exist during the daytime.

"Where's the sun?" I asked the man.

"Shan't be seeing it today," he muttered, "probably not for the weekend, neither."

"What's your name?" I asked next, wondering if he was Ally or Baz.

"Trevor."

"You're supposed to be Ally or Baz."

"Definitely Trevor, mate. I'm just paid to pick you up, and take you to this address." He showed me a piece of paper.

I kept a very close eye on him for the duration of that drive.

England was very busy, I noticed. The sidewalks were as busy as the roads. People dashed through drizzle from one doorway to another. They liked to cover their heads with black umbrellas.

"Hey, buddy?" I said.

"Yes, sir?"

"Do people cover their heads with black umbrellas so they can't be observed from above?"

"Nah. None of that bollocks here. It's just to keep the rain off."

I liked that answer. I began to relax.

England, it seemed, was my kind of place.

If only I knew what bollocks meant.

56.

Interview with Miles Lovatt-Crane, who Tommy stayed with on his arrival in England. First published in 'Legends & Cult Figures', 1998.

Histon was dropped at a house I shared with three friends in March of 1964. He'd landed in England that day. We housed a few musicians over the years, as we were part of the scene. Sometimes they would be overseas arrivals, and other times touring parties.

Tommy Histon most definitely sticks in my memory!

He seemed jittery on arrival, and looked at us strangely as we asked him questions about America and his music, and generally tried to make him feel welcome.

We smoked some weed, as we did with most guests back in the day. Tommy was happy to partake, but I began to notice it made him more edgy.

Our use of the word 'bollocks' was of some concern to him. As were our questions about Kennedy.

After disappearing into the kitchen, he returned to the sitting room, and calmly asked us what bollocks meant?

Well, we found that hilarious.

"You don't have that word where you come from?" I recall asking him.

"Never heard it before on this earth," he said in his soft, breathy voice.

"It means testicles," I informed him, and we laughed heartily at that.

Histon merely stared at us with his head cocked over inquisitively.

Without warning, he whipped a knife free from the waistband of his trousers, and held it at the throat of Imogen, a girl who was living with us.

"Now, I need you three to line up against that wall there," he instructed, "or I'll make damned sure none of you will reproduce with this female human here."

We did as he ordered. Imogen was terrified, trembling and crying.

"Now, drop your pants," he added.

We didn't move.

"Drop your fuckin' pants - trousers, or whatever your fuckin' word is for the things covering your legs," he growled.

We complied.

Pushing Imogen away, he approached us as we stood in line with our trousers round our ankles. As you'll gather, we had no idea what was going on. I remember thinking that he was going to castrate us.

Imogen was struggling with her asthma, and we were all confused and fearful.

With the knife point pressing into my ear, he felt my testicles.

"Two. And they feel attached. Over there with her!" he instructed me.

He then subjected the other two men to the same inspection.

Seemingly happy with what he discovered, he relaxed a little and lit a smoke.

Nobody spoke to him for the next hour until a car showed up to collect him.

On leaving our home, he turned back and tried to explain, "I'm sorry about the trouble, but I had to be sure..."

We shoved him out and slammed the door on him.

It was one of the most bizarre and alarming experiences of my life.

I must say, it was a relief when he didn't turn up two months later for his return flight.

All of that said, I'd discover his music later in the sixties, and have been a fan ever since.

And at least I have a Tommy Histon story to tell.

57.

An excerpt from Bill Goods' letter to his son, Danny, describing his time spent with Histon in 1964. It was first published in the book 'Worldly Goods' in 2019.

On a Friday in the spring of that year, I left work early, and drove down to a house in Middlesex where I picked him up.

Hopping in the driver's side, I noticed that he was standing motionless by the passenger door.

Ah, I thought to myself, I'm supposed to open the door for him.

Leaping back out, I scooted round to his side.

"Why is this car back to front?" he asked me.

"Oh, all cars in England have the steering wheel on the other side."

He nodded. "This is earth, correct?"

"What?"

"Planet earth. This is the planet earth?"

"Erm, yes. This is definitely earth."

At that, his hand shot out and grabbed my genitals.

He began to rummage, his eyes averted, and the lids almost closed.

I tried to pull away, but he held me firm, and examined me.

"Two," he announced, releasing me.

"Two what?" I asked, in a state of shock.

"Testicles. You have two."

"Erm, yes. Why? Is that important?"

"Very," he informed me, and let himself into the car.

We set off towards Brakeshire. I was to deliver him to a hotel in Tredmouth, before picking him up the following morning at eight-thirty, and taking him to Ally Mac's place.

How hard could that be?

"The testicle thing..." I ventured, as I drove north.

"Had to check. My apologies for that."

"Why?"

"To make sure you ain't one of them," he said, and pointed upwards.

"Them?"

"Aliens. They only have one. It's how you tell 'em from us."

"Right."

"It's on account of their momma's only having one ovary."

"Okay."

"Shrind el pas ng-ng-ng tormu belzee," he said, as though it were a continuation of the conversation.

I must have looked at him like he was completely bonkers.

"You don't understand that?" he enquired.

"Erm, no." I chuckled.

"If you did, I'd slay you here and now."

"Right."

"If you had one testicle, and understood that, you'd be dead in a fuckin' heartbeat."

"Then I'm glad I don't."

"What's your name?"

"Bill."

"I'm Tommy."

"I know."

"How do you know?" he snapped, scowling at me.

"Because I'm employed to drive you to your hotel. And it helps if I know who I'm picking up."

"Okay," he accepted, and somewhat relaxed. "You know how you can spot them aliens?"

"Through the testicles?"

"They study us, and they know all that has gone before. But they have no clue what will happen even a second from now."

"Right."

"See, now, I know that you will have to hit them brakes hard, and slow this car in twenty-four seconds from now."

"Right."

We waited, the pair of us, the wiper blade whipping water from the screen. I couldn't help but count those seconds in my head. I was determined not to brake, no matter what.

As I approached my count, a car slid on the wet surface ahead, veering into our side of the road.

I hit the brakes.

And Tommy Histon laughed for two minutes solid.

We finally arrived back in Brakeshire. It was late, and he refused to stay at the hotel that had been booked for him. Apparently, it was the wrong colour and shape.

He suggested I drop him at an all-night bar, and he'd sort himself out.

This was 1964, and there were no all-night bars in Tredmouth. It was close to eleven, and the rain was still lashing down.

All I wanted was to sit down and have a beer before hitting the hay.

"Look, you can kip at mine," I offered, mainly as a way of achieving that end.

He could have my bed, and I'd take the sofa.

No answer came. His eyes stared at me unblinkingly, his head slightly over to one side as we drove through the city centre.

"Say that again," he growled.

"You can kip at mine," I repeated.

In the blink of an eye, a knife point was pressing into my ear. Apparently, that was the only way to kill an alien.

"How do you know that word?" he asked, his voice slow and low.

"What word?"

"Kip."

"It's... It's a word. An English word."

"No it fuckin' ain't."

"It is!" I insisted. I was starting to get a bit worried.

"Only one way you could know that word. You fooled me with the testicle."

"No! Look, I'll stop and ask someone. It's an English word that you might not know in America."

I went to pull over alongside a man walking home.

"Not him," Tommy hissed, "he could be one of yours. Him over there. We'll ask him," he said, pointing at a man striding towards us.

The hand holding the knife dropped down out of sight, and he wound down the window on his side.

"Hey buddy," he called out, "who's going to win the Grand National tomorrow?"

"Team Spirit, if I'm lucky," the man smiled back.

"Ah, you can see that. That's good. Real good. Now, you know the word kip?"

"Kip?"

"Yeah, kip. You know that word, buddy?"

"Yes, it means sleep. And that's what I'm going to do right now."

As the man walked on, Tommy called after him, "you going to the Grand National?"

"Not me, no."

"Good," said Tommy, "I'm glad about that. They'll be watching from the sky. Wouldn't want you getting hurt by any fire falling from above."

We drove away, Tommy Histon happy that I was human, and delighted to be able to kip over at my place.

En route, I asked him, "so, what does kip mean in alien language?"

"Potassium permanganate," he answered without pause, and lit a cigarette.

"Right," seemed like the only suitable reply.

PS - I put half a quid on that horse at eighteen to one, and it came in!

58.

A few hours were spent at the house Trevor dropped me at.

Again, the word 'bollocks' was bandied around. I had to ask what it meant, and was informed it was slang for testicles.

Well, that, along with their questions about Kennedy, had me a little concerned for a while.

Once we'd worked things out, time passed uneventfully prior to me being collected by a car in the evening. I spent much of it reading the sport in the newspaper.

The driver's name was Bill, and we hit it off pretty much right away. Well, we did once we'd cleared up a couple of minor misunderstandings.

He was a young man in his early twenties, and I recognised something of myself in him. My former self, at least. And the man did love his music. I'd say that he had a passion for it, and I always respond well to anybody with zeal in their make-up.

We were driving along a straight stretch of road, and I had a little flash of something with regard to him. I saw his hands grip the steering wheel, and the car lock up for a brief period of time.

Now, I've analysed this over the weeks since it happened, and wondered if I didn't simply piece it all together because of what I might term unperceived-perception.

Either way, I told Bill that he'd have to hit his brakes in so many seconds.

And he did.

I guess that must have shocked him a little, the fact I knew he would.

The truth is, though, I reckon I saw only what was going on in reality. It was raining hard, and there was sitting water on our side of the road. I watched a truck plough through it, sending a wave to the other side.

Now, the vehicle in front of us was a truck, and I knew a similar thing would happen when we reached that point. As a result, I also reasoned that any oncoming vehicle would hit that displaced water and either attempt to avoid it by veering over, or be pushed over by the impact.

Either way, young Bill would have to hit his brakes.

The number of seconds was what my brain calculated it would take all of that to happen. My ability to do that came from the lines of tape and planning of musical composition. I'm not sure which came first, but I, as a result, saw things in a very strung out way.

So, right on the count, Bill hit the brakes, and his knuckles went white in the headlights of the encroaching car as they gripped the wheel.

Bill's face was such a picture, I laughed hard for a minute or so.

Anyway, we arrived safely in Brakeshire without further incident.

The hotel that had been booked for me reminded me of the hospital Dotty had been sent to. I wasn't too keen to revisit all of that.

I saw my time overseas as a chance to reset; to begin again, I suppose I might term it.

Bill understood, and kindly allowed me to sleep over at his place. It was a strange thing, but he used the word 'kip', meaning sleep here in England.

Well, that word sparked something in me. I recalled it as being alien-speak for potassium permanganate. It all helped reignite me.

The pills were flushed from my system, and I could feel the electrical charge and buzz of creative energy zipping around my brain.

Thanks to the newspaper I'd read, I was aware the Grand National horse race was due to take place the following day. That, too, had ignited an idea in my mind.

Words - whether they be horse names, kip and its interpretations, aliens, or the ocean I'd flown over the previous night - they all merged into sentences and phrases, that naturally found rhyming bedfellows with one another.

Flashes from my past coupled up with the present, and I began to fill in all of the missing pieces for the album I had on rolls of tape in my bag.

Spending two nights with Bill allowed me to play around with those phrasings, as I sat and picked on my Gretsch to an audience of one.

When I first sang 'Take The Sea Air' and 'Which Way?', and Bill commented on the beauty of them, I knew I was on to something.

I asked him, "does it sound like anything you ever heard before?"

"No," he replied, and he had a fair few records in that apartment of his.

I calculated that it was only Friday night, and I'd left the nation of my birth on the Thursday.

It felt like so much longer, and I began to wonder if something didn't happen up there in the sky after all, even though I remembered only sleeping.

Momma sprang to mind, too, probably because I was so far away from where she spent her whole life.

Yet, here, in this country foreign to me, was where our ancestors hailed from.

Strangely, for the first time in my life, it felt like I'd arrived home.

59.

They're a peculiar species, the British, with their strange words and liking for warm beer, amongst other quirks.

On the Saturday morning, Bill took me over to meet one of the partners in Chemisette Records. His name was Ally Mac, and I'd never met anyone like him before in my life.

He opened the door to us wearing a purple silk ladies garment.

'Purple silk' danced around my mind as I looked at him. I'd read those words in the Grand National runners.

Bill seemed a little nervous of Ally, I noticed, and kept pretty quiet.

"What's that you're wearing?" I asked as I shook his hand.

He locked his eyes on me, as though he were looking into the most shadowy part of my soul.

"Why," he replied quietly, "don't you like it?"

"I like it a lot," I told him, "just wondered what it was called."

"A kimono. It's Japanese."

And the title and missing parts of my album swamped me in a moment, the chemical formula for potassium permanganate being $KMnO_4$.

The whole story lined up in my head, and I felt a surge of euphoria.

And all thanks to a man dressed as a woman who scared me more than any human I'd ever met in my life.

An intensity bubbled within him, like a pressure cooker. I certainly wouldn't wish to be in the vicinity if it ever blew up.

"Would it be possible to have a couple of minutes alone?" I asked him.

"Of course," he said, and I followed him through to his office. To my surprise, he knew what I wanted.

Allowing the kimono to fall open, I gave him an inspection in the flesh.

He was all good.

"I wish I didn't have any," he said calmly as I went about my work, "not even one."

Nodding my understanding, I smiled at him.

He smiled back, but there was no warmth in it. Cold steel formed him, and mercury ran through his veins.

Yet, if I could pick any human to be by my side in a crisis, I would choose Ally Mac. It was strange, that instant sense I had of the man.

"A thought came to you when you saw my kimono," he said.

"It did."

"Anything to do with the record you're going to make for me?"

"It was."

And I knew that he was just like me. He could see the path ahead, and tell what the future held.

"Do you trust me, Tommy?" he asked.

"Yes," I replied, because I absolutely did, despite having only just met him.

"Thank you. Then trust me on this. All of my staff have been vetted by me personally. You can trust each of them, too. Understood?"

"Yes."

"If you have any problems, you come to me. Clear?"

"Yes."

"When you meet Baz Baxter, same thing. We spent some time in prison together. I've seen him stripped naked many times. He's one of us. Okay?"

"Yes."

"You control only the music. I control everything else. Crystal?"

"What?"

"Crystal clear?"

"Yes."

"Make me the best record you can, and we'll be fine, you and me."

"I will."

"Do you know the trait of personality I value above any other in people, Tommy?"

I took a second, and answered, "loyalty."

"Incorrect. Do you know why I spent seven years in prison?"

"No."

"Because a man stole from my father. He was a newsagent in Tredmouth, and the man worked there. He took money from the till. He denied it. He denied it to my father. And he denied it to the police.

"He then denied it to me.

"Now, the truth is, I didn't care so much about the theft. That could have been sorted out, the money paid back, and all would have been well with the world.

"But he fucking lied to me.

"As a result, once he'd confessed, I broke both his legs, both his arms, several ribs, his jaw, and a vertebrae in his spine.

"So, what's the trait of personality that I value above all others, Tommy?"

"Honesty."

"Correct. I think you're the same as me. Am I right?"

"Yes."

"How was your flight?"

"Fine."
"Tea or coffee?"
"Coffee."
"Hungry?"
"No."
"Tired?"
"No."
"Good. Because you begin work on Monday. The hotel?"

"Didn't suit me," I answered, as I followed him back to where Bill stood waiting.

"We'll get you another for tonight. I'm told the accommodation at the studio will be ready by tomorrow."

"He can stay with me," Bill offered, "and I'll drop him at Norton Basset tomorrow as planned. It'll be simpler that way."

Ally expressed his appreciation to Bill.

"Okay with that?" he said to me.

"Yes."

"Good. So, drink your drinks. I'll go and get changed now we've completed our introductions."

On the way back to Bill's, he and I got chatting about Ally and his time in prison.

Bill asked me, "do you know how much the man stole?"

I shrugged.

"Seven shillings."

"What's that in American money?"

"About a dollar."

60.

Bill and I had a blast that Saturday evening at his place. We ate fish'n'chips out of newspaper, which was very fuckin' strange.

Mine was wrapped in the sports page, and those Grand National runners caught my eye once more.

He drank warm beer, and I my whiskey, as we talked and played records Bill liked. I liked them, too. He had good taste in music, at least.

We were celebrating, as Bill had won a few bucks, or quids, on the Grand National, thanks to my help.

Later, I got my guitar out and worked up the title track of the album, 'Kimono For Kip'.

It was based on my time on the railroad, and the mechanical repetitiveness of a colossal engine containing many smaller parts moving far more rapidly. It was fast paced, and I imagined those trains being similar to Crobegs (another National runner), built by aliens and sent from the skies to destroy humankind.

As far as the album went, I was ninety-five percent of the way there. The rest would have to be worked out in the studio.

Bill offered me his bed for the two nights I was with him, but I refused. As I told him, "hell, I slept in worse places than this sofa half the nights of my life."

Laying my guitar down, we chatted.

I told Bill Goods as much about my life as I believe I'd ever told anybody. Only the psychiatrists knew more, I reckon.

Looking back over these few weeks I've been in England, I'm unsure whether that was because I trusted him, or because I knew it was temporary; that I'd not be here for too much longer.

He told me his life to date, as well, and the plans he had for his future. He wanted to own his own business, as a mechanic, and desired a wife and children.

The happy existence he sought was how I saw him. But then I saw the sadness that would inevitably come to pass, if you allowed yourself to get too attached to any person or any thing.

I didn't tell him that part, though.

"What about you, Tommy? How do you see your future going?" he asked me.

"Oh, I don't really think of any future beyond the next few weeks and the album."

I again stopped short of telling him that, thereafter, all I saw was a cold, dark corridor of nothingness.

Sunday morning arrived, and Bill and I drank tea and coffee respectively. It was instant coffee granules, as that's all they have in England.

He didn't mention going to church, which was fine by me. I hadn't set foot in a church since that Sunday morning with Dotty and Leonard some ten years before.

Why was I thinking so much of the past?

Throughout that Sunday morning, I kept recalling the words from the fortune-teller Lance had visited.

Was it possible to change one's destiny? If I made an album Ally Mac and Baz Baxter adored, why wouldn't they offer to put out more albums? I could either stay here, or come back once a year for a few weeks just as now.

Wouldn't that, though, be dependent on it being financially successful? After all, they're in this as a business.

Ah, but I shook all the thoughts away. Come the following day, I'd be back in the studio for the first time in ten years.

That was enough.

So, I enjoyed the remainder of my time with Bill, and come late-morning, we loaded my gear in the car and chatted happily all the way over to Norton Basset.

Bill helped carry my bag and instruments in, and I was taken to comfortable living quarters that smelt of fresh paint. They sat above the most state of the art studio I'd ever seen.

Hank would have loved it.

Rather than Hank, I was shown in and around by a middle-aged guy named Oggy. He was overweight with a beard capable of doubling as a habitat for many a woodland creature. His teeth were brown and rotten, and despite the abundance of hair on his face, he possessed not a follicle on the top of his head.

He was also heavily tattooed, and had spent a chunk of his adult life in the navy, I would come to learn, specialising in sonar and anything to do with sound.

Oggy was the sound engineer and co-producer, along with myself.

"Are you one of Ally's people?" I asked him.

"That's right."

"Then you're all good, Oggy!" I beamed, and winked my understanding.

61.

Studio Engineer and co-Producer, Patrick 'Oggy' Ogden, 1993 CD sleeve notes.

Anybody who cares to ask receives the same answer: The most talented artist I ever worked with was Tommy Histon.

That was true the first day I spent in the studio with him, and it's true now, nearly thirty years on.

It was his vision that set him apart. He walked in on a Monday morning, and knew precisely what he wanted in terms of sound. All parts were mapped out, either in his head, or on rolls of tape that he stuck all over the walls of a room.

All that said, I didn't quite understand that in the beginning. We had a few problems initially.

I was nervous as a kitten, because it was set to be the first release on Chemisette, the new imprint set up by Baz Baxter and Alistair McIntyre.

They'd spent a small fortune on the facility out at Norton Basset. It was rigged up in a large old house, with a studio and control room on the main level, and living quarters on the upper floor.

I rarely stayed there, as I'd bought a house not far away in Oakburn. It was a bit of a change from London, where I relocated from in '63.

I built the four-track studio for them, though I thought it two tracks too many. As it turned out, it would set them up nicely for the next few years. And it was simple enough to make it eight and sixteen track later on in the sixties.

In a converted outbuilding, they had me install a record manufacturing plant. It was a slick operation, and didn't come cheap.

I was employed because I had all the skills, both studio recording, and vinyl pressing. I could cut lacquers and create stampers and all the rest of it. A one-stop-shop, as it might be termed nowadays.

Even the centre labels were printed in-house, and a small room out the back was where they were left to dry before being applied to the records. Only the sleeves were outsourced.

The construction work had been completed the day before Tommy arrived. I was tired and stressed, if I'm honest, and probably not at my most welcoming!

Ally in particular, 'got' Histon. He knew that to get the best out of him, you had to give him free rein.

Still, I didn't want to fuck up. Baxter was a big pussy cat, really. Don't get me wrong, he knew his business, and could get things done. I liked Baz. He always had a smile on his large, jowly face, and a joke to hand for any and every occasion.

McIntyre was the energy. Ally was like a coiled spring next to Baxter's languid easygoingness. Personally, I never had any problems with Ally, but I know plenty who did.

It always amazed me that the two men could get on so well, as they were so different. But they were both smart enough to know that they needed each other to succeed. One compensated for the other's shortcomings.

Ally Mac could not have conducted business transactions, as his manner was too brittle and abrasive. Frankly, he was bloody terrifying, and nobody would have dealt with him for fear of any repercussions should they displease him.

Underneath, though, Ally was a very fair and decent man. He was simply pathologically honest, and expected everyone else to be the same.

Baxter employed me, and most of my dealings were with him.

However, Histon was Ally's project. Baz wouldn't have touched him, given his reputation and lack of commercial success, but McIntyre heard something that he thought was genius.

He was correct, in my opinion.

Histon always operated within good songs. That was his great strength. It wasn't different for the sake of shock or to be contrary - it was beautiful melodies presented in a way never done before.

He saw the world differently to anyone else, and he refused to be told no. Everything was possible for Tommy Histon. It just needed a means of achieving.

But - and I have to reiterate this - the songs in simple form, are stunningly pretty. The lyrics, once you interpret them, are heartbreaking and challenging.

We look back on the album now, albeit only in demo form, and have more of an understanding. It was his swan song. And I think he knew that, deep down.

It's autobiographical, but woven around this end of the world alien thing. Well, that would have alienated him, I think, had the record seen the light of day at the time.

I didn't know what half of it was about. I didn't need to know. For me, it was all about the sound. Lyrics were never my thing. That said, I knew there were hidden references in that album that nobody has fathomed to this day.

What should he have done in the spring of 1964? As I said to Ally and Baz at the time, they'd have been better off spending their money on securing the rights to his two fifties albums. That was the sound of the next couple of years, before all the psychedelic stuff came along.

At first, I didn't like Tommy Histon. He was strange. He had a very odd view of the world. I respected him, though. No question there.

He was like that saying. What is it? Reasonable people conform to the world. Unreasonable people expect the world to cater to them. Unreasonable people are the only ones who will change the world, as a result. Something like that, anyway.

Very quickly, though, he won me over. After a week or two, I can honestly say that he became a friend of mine. He was a very generous man, once you tapped into him. Generous of spirit, I mean.

I'll go further than that. By the time we were done, I can honestly say that I loved the bloke.

He was so controlling, though. For the first few days, we were going at each other all the time, butting heads. We were like a married couple. I'd been in studios for years, and knew only one way of doing things. That way worked.

That knowledge was why Baxter had sought me out and employed me. I'd moved up from London, and staked a lot on the label being a success. As a result, I was keen to press home my beliefs and practices. They'd worked for all of recorded music history, after all.

I wanted to play it safe, and take no chances.

I didn't take too well to some cocky, brash, weirdo telling me how to do my job, frankly. I was used to being my own boss in the studio.

But I'll tell you this now. I learnt more from those few weeks with Histon than at any other time in my life.

And those lessons would set me up nicely for what was to come. I made a good living, with Chemisette and others, once the world caught up to what we did on 'Kimono For Kip'. I owe Tommy a great deal for that. He showed me the way. He showed me the future!

When I heard what happened to him, I was terribly sad. I always had a sense that he'd be fine, if he could just get his head straight. He needed help. A psychiatrist, I mean. We know now that he stopped taking his medication. That was the real tragedy. It was all so unnecessary.

Oh, but the record itself! It was criminal what Histon did, destroying it like that. I'd spent so much energy on it. And for him to do that...

It was a fucking good job he offed himself, because I dread to think what Ally Mac would have done to him if he hadn't!

Ally never let on, but I sensed he was raging inside, in that contained way he had. It was hard to tell with Ally, as he always seemed like he could go ballistic at the slightest provocation. But I imagine he was absolutely fucking livid.

They must have lost a fortune on that record. Okay, they clawed some of it back by selling the demos I'd backed up to tape, but it wouldn't have made much of a dent.

What was the finished record like? It was acid-folk and space-rock long before such things had been invented. Krautrock wasn't first conceived in Germany in the late-sixties. It was done by Tommy Histon in Brakeshire in 1964. They should have called it Brakerock.

He'd improvise all the while, getting sounds out of objects he'd find lying around.

Joe Meek was doing a bit of that down in London at the time, and that's as close a comparison as I have to what Tommy did. But it was more psychedelic than anything Meek ever did.

Look, I'm probably remembering it better than it was. The passing of time, and hindsight, have a tendency to do that. Besides, given all the changes in music over the intervening years, particularly with regard to technology, it'll probably sound dated and tame. Even a bit clumsy.

Remember, too, that it suited me to big that album up over the years, as it kept me in employment.

But I still have a sense that it was something special when put in the context of 1964.

His process was bonkers in itself. Tape, tape and more tape. There was the tape all over the bloody walls. Then there was the tape we recorded to. How he kept it all straight in his head, I have no idea.

Mark it! Cut it! Splice it! That was virtually all I heard for a month. Countless bits of tape stuck together and lined up with similar worms of tape.

Tape worm, I used to call him!

But it worked. Somehow, it all came out alright. And then he destroyed it. All that work, gone in a moment of madness. Like I say, criminal, really.

If I could go back, I'd get Tommy some help. That's what I'd do. Fuck the record. In the great scheme of things, it isn't that important.

Look, I'm old now, and half deaf. I can't work in recording like I used to. I'm also half blind, which somewhat screws me when it comes to cutting vinyl. The shakiness of my hands doesn't help! Ah, it's no loss. It's all gone fucking digital now, anyway. People like me are dinosaurs.

But Tommy - he'd have moved with the times. No, fuck that. He'd have been setting the times.

You want to know what music will sound like five to ten years from now? Listen to Tommy Histon.

Except you can't. That's the tragedy.

That's the thing I'd have changed, if I could.

We spent sixteen hours a day together for a month and more. I never saw it coming. Any of it. I honestly never got wind of him being suicidal. If anything, he seemed happy.

It does make you wonder if someone did him in.

No way on this earth he would have destroyed that album, in my opinion.

But that was the point, wasn't it? It wasn't of this earth as far as Tommy was concerned. All his demons came from up there.

He was a basket-case, really.

And then I think - would he be as well thought of had he lived, and had that album been released? I honestly don't think he would. Nobody was ready for it, and the rejection would probably have killed him anyway.

People love the story around it. There's a kind of morbid fascination, along with a 'what if?'

It's the unknown that draws people in. The hope that 'Kimono For Kip', the finished album, will show up one day.

And, no, before you ask, I don't have a copy.

If I did, I'd have retired long before I was fucking forced out.

The business changed, and not for the better. I lost interest after punk, to be honest. Occasionally, over the years, I'd hear something, and think - yes, Tommy might have done something like that. But not often.

I suppose I only really appreciated what we achieved many years later. But I can't share it with anyone, as only he, Ally Mac and I ever heard the finished recording.

There are no personalities nowadays. Not really. There are no Tommy Histons. As infuriating as he was at times.

And every world needs a Tommy Histon in it.

62.

Oggy, I sensed right away, would require a little steering round to my way of thinking.

We had some stand-offs at first, but the fact I had Ally's backing negated any support he could get from Baz Baxter.

He stormed off a couple of times, and Baz had to coax him back.

He'd constructed the studio himself, and had done a grand job of it. There was no doubting his technical ability. It was his narrowness of mind that I struggled with.

Oggy had cut his teeth in a live-take environment, and had only welcomed two-track recording because, "it was usually the singer who fucked up, so at least I could save the important bit."

"Then why did you build a four-track studio?" I asked him.

His face went purple, his eyes blinking rapidly. "Because that's what Chemisette wanted. I told them it was a waste of money."

To my thinking, a four-track could be filled. That track could then be played back as one track, and three more tracks added to it. Thereafter, that could be played as a single track, or even as two, leaving two or three more to add to.

"Why can't you see its infinite potential, Oggy!" I shouted at him during one of our discussions.

"But... But... What about the sound quality?" he bellowed at me.

"Anyone who will listen will play it on a shitty record player with an inbuilt speaker and a worn-out needle. It doesn't fuckin' matter."

"I'm employed by Chemisette to get usable recordings! What you want doesn't really count!"

"But it's my record. Listen, I know I can be an asshole, but I need your support."

"It's arsehole. Arse! Not ass! That's a fucking donkey, you fucking donkey's arsehole!"

"You know your problem, Oggy?" I asked him in a conciliatory tone.

"And what's my problem, arsehole?" See, he didn't have to add arsehole.

"Fear of the unknown. Fear of pushing the boundaries!"

"Bollocks."

"Is it because you're overweight?"

"I'm big-boned."

"When did you last manage to lay eyes on your own penis?"

"You're full of shit!"

"Your arms can't even reach your own ass to wipe it! That's why you smell."

"Arse! It's arse, you..."

Oggy went to the pub.

The plan was to use session musicians to lay down all of the rhythm tracks. I would play guitar with them, and overdub a vocal. That was it. A guitar overdub then might be allowed, leaving one track for add-ons, as Oggy termed them.

My vision was to play everything myself in many overdubs.

I'd begin with a basic beat to set time, all of the beats per minute noted on my wall tape. Rhythm guitar would come next, along with vocal, then bass, percussion, organ, violin, and anything else I had noted down.

It required seven tracks as a minimum. More where I had layers of guitar. There was no way I could do it in only four.

I followed him to the pub that day, and joined him in drinking warm beer in heavy dimpled glasses. We sat in silence at a table for some time.

He went to the bar at one point, and came back with two more pints. One was shoved in front of me with a grunt.

I reciprocated fifteen minutes on.

Half way through my third beer, he started giggling. It was infectious, so I joined in.

"You're right about me," he said.

"I didn't mean it, Oggy. You don't smell of shit."

"Thank you for that."

"Well, if you do, I can't detect it over the stench from your underarms," I smiled at him over the round wooden table.

He chuckled, before composing himself. "Look, I was in the navy for years. It was all about following orders and sticking to a tried and tested practice."

"I understand."

"It was enough of a change for me moving up here from east London. I don't do change very well."

"Is that why you never change your clothes?"

"Fuck off."

"Look, as I said, I'm an arsehole. But this is my record. Help me make it the way I hear it, Oggy. I can't do this without you."

He nodded.

"Why did you move up here?" I asked him.

"My old lady died."

"Your wife?"

"Don't be fucking stupid. Who'd marry me? No, it was my old mum. She was big-boned like me, and her heart gave out on her."

"I'm sorry, Oggy."

"Thanks. Thing was, she looked after me. She did my washing, and cooked and cleaned. Between her and the navy, I never had to worry about anything like that. Truth is, I'm having a bit of trouble coping, I suppose."

I felt terrible, then, for the things I'd said.

He continued, "so, I thought to myself, when Baz got in touch, why not start afresh up here? Too many memories down there, Tommy. Too many ghosts."

"Momma died when I was fifteen."

"Did your father bring you up?"

"No. I never knew him. Well, I did, but that's a long story. Anyway, it's irrelevant, as he died at the same time as her."

"Christ in heaven. What of?"

"They burned in a cabin in the woods. I watched it happen."

"Is that how you got that scar on your face?"

"No, that was fuckin' aliens opening up my head to see if they could work out how I can see the future."

"Oh, right. Do you want another pint?"

"I knew you were going to ask that."

"Do you want one, or not?"

"Please."

Oggy and I never had a problem after that day in the pub.

In fact, one day when Baz Baxter queried the cost of the tape we were getting through, Oggy told him it was necessary.

When he cut the acetates, he even inscribed them with a little in-joke reference to it in the run-off area - 28, 40, PostP.

It referred to the twenty-eight different instruments and objects used in making the album, forty warm beers that he estimated accompanied each song on average, and a reference to me using the term 'post it Patrick!' whenever we had what I wanted.

Without Oggy, I must concede, the record would have been unachievable, or certainly unlistenable.

Somehow, he made it work.

63.

Bill Goods had mentioned a music store to me. It was in the city of Tredmouth, a few miles south of Norton Basset.

According to Bill, they had a relationship with Baz and Ally, and a selection of the latest musical equipment, including electronic keyboards. I was keen to pay the store a visit, as I had a mind to use them on my record instead of piano and organ.

A couple of days after my arrival at the studio, I took a bus there when Oggy had gone home following one of our discussions about working practices.

Whilst there, I figured I'd get myself some clothes from a new boutique in the city, 'It's Tred Dad!', owned by Baz Baxter.

I appreciate I wasn't at my smartest that day. The young man attending the music store followed me closely, and, I have to say, wasn't very helpful.

Feeling a little anxious, I left and made my way to the clothing boutique.

Ally Mac was there, picking up a pair of Yves Saint Laurent thigh-length alligator-skin boots.

"Hello, Tommy," he said in his intense way, his mouth moving to the absolute minimum.

"Hey, Ally."

"What are you doing here?"

"I need some clothes," I informed him.

"You don't look very happy about that."

I told him of my experience in the music store. He went perfectly still and silent for a count of ten. He didn't even blink. I began to worry that something had gone wrong with whatever mechanism drove him.

"Wait," was all he said when he regained power.

He disappeared into a room behind the serving counter. The man who was in there left and the door was closed.

Within two minutes, Ally was back.

"You were too early. That was the trouble. You should have gone an hour later. Buy some clothes. By the time you're done, you can go back. All will be well."

"Okay, Ally. Thanks," I replied, and picked out a long charcoal coat I liked the look of. It wasn't inexpensive, but it was soft and warm, with a silky lining, and mohair in the wool mix that made it real nice to the touch.

In addition, I got some new pants, boots, a couple of collarless shirts, and a cap to keep the infernal rain off my head. I figured I'd look more like an English gentleman with that gear on.

Even though I say so myself, I walked out of there looking just swell, as I caught sight of my own reflection in the storefront windows.

Back at the music establishment, a different man opened the door for me, and said, "Mr Histon, if I'm not mistaken, we've been expecting you."

I was invited to take a seat and enjoy a coffee, as I took my time, and to feel absolutely free to discuss any requirements I may have.

Any instrument I deemed useful would be mine for the borrowing, and delivered to the studio at Norton Basset within the hour.

"How much will it cost?" I asked.

I was informed, "Mr Baxter and Mr McIntyre are very good friends of the establishment, and seeing how you're working with them, it will be our pleasure to supply you with anything you require."

"Thank you!" I enthused.

As I played around, pressing keys and testing the sound ranges of those electronic keyboards, I was struck once again by the similarities between Ally and myself.

He knew I was just a little early. Looking an hour ahead of time, he saw all of what I was set to experience.

I switched from a Mellotron to a Gibson G-101, and wondered to myself if he'd ever encountered the fuckers.

64.

"You seem miserable today, Oggy," I observed, one afternoon in the pub. "More miserable than usual, I mean."

"It's my birthday tomorrow," he replied miserably.

"And this is a bad thing?"

"I always get down on my birthday."

"Why?" I asked him.

"Because it marks another fucking year having passed, in which I've done fuck all of what I thought I might do with my miserable fucking life."

"You cuss a lot."

"Fuck off. Another pint?"

"I'll get them. Think of it as your birthday gift."

On my return, I asked Oggy, "so, what is it you wanted to do in life, but haven't?"

"Oh, you know, fall in love, get married, have kids, be rich and successful, and other things."

I thought about how I might help him with his unfulfilled dreams. "Okay, so what are the other things?"

"Do you know what attracted me to recorded sound?"

I shook my head.

"Ah, it's fucking stupid, really. Don't listen to me. I'm in a maudlin mood, that's all it is."

"Go on, Oggy, I want to know, buddy."

"You'll laugh."

"I won't."

"Well, I always wanted to be on stage. That was the thing."

I laughed, but he was oblivious to it.

A light came on in the big tattooed man. His eyes shone as he stared off at the dartboard and imagined himself up on stage.

"Doing what?"

"Anything, really. Singing. Banging a fucking drum. I just wanted to be, for one day at least, up there in the bright lights. I was never even picked for the school nativity fucking play. My old girl never got to see me up on stage. Too late now, gawd rest her dear old soul."

Oggy made a silent toast to his mother.

"Can you sing?"

"Anyone can sing, Tommy."

"Sure, buddy. But, erm, some people sing better than others."

"Old mum used to say that I could hold a tune."

I'd heard him singing in the studio, and had found myself wishing he would hold the tune.

"How old are you?"

"Fifty."

"Fifty tomorrow?"

He nodded miserably.

So, for Oggy, I lined up a gig for the following evening at the Baker's Dozen in Norton Basset. I was breaking the law, as my entry permit only stipulated recording work in the studio, but I got around that by billing it as a live performance by 'Pat & Tom'.

We didn't rehearse, because he didn't know it was taking place until we arrived.

"Cor, look at that!" he chimed as we arrived at the pub, "live music! Well, fuck me!" he added, staring at the handwritten poster on the door.

"What?"

"Pat & Tom. Could be me and you, that! I bet they'll be shit."

We weren't shit. I'd dropped my guitar and a few percussion instruments over at the Baker's earlier in the day.

As soon as he discovered 'Pat & Tom' were he and I, he dashed back to the studio to get his portable reel-to-reel recorder.

Oggy mostly shook things and banged other things together, most of which were attached to his body. But he accompanied me well.

I let him take the front centre stage, and somewhat hid myself in the shadows as I sang and played guitar.

He danced around plenty, and the fifty or so people present had a good time.

On 'Which Way?' and 'Take The Sea Air', he belted out the second vocal line, and did a pretty good job of it.

I mainly stuck to songs from 'Kimono For Kip', because they were the ones he knew. But I did throw in a couple from 'Track Back...' and 'Coda', as well as the more bluesy 'Slitherin'', which Oggy particularly enjoyed dancing to as he made hissing sounds. At one point, he lay on the stage, writhed around, and flicked his tongue at the audience. Someone had to help him back up on his feet.

We walked happily back to the studio house after closing time.

Oggy said, "never thought I'd actually enjoy a fucking birthday again in my life."

"Why not?"

"My old mum died on this very day. Two years ago."

"I'm sorry, Oggy."

"Nah, don't be. Thank you, though, Tommy. Thanks for everything. Do you reckon she was looking down at me from heaven?"

"I'm sure she was, buddy."

65.

Oggy left at around five-thirty every evening for his dinner and a couple of hours break. He'd return before nine, so we could work through the night recording.

A couple of local girls began hanging around the grounds of the house after a week or so of my residence. I guess they wanted to catch sight of the American singer rumoured to be ensconced therein.

I'd head out, lean on a fence and chat to them. I must have been a bit of a disappointment. I am, after all, no Johnny, Bobby or Elvis.

Still, I signed their autograph books, and answered their questions about America as best I could. And I had to reiterate many times that I definitely did not know The Beatles.

At least, I did once they'd worked out Tommy Histon was the American singer, and that I was he. Initially, I believe they thought I was part of a backing band or management team.

They'd never heard of me, and had certainly never heard my music.

The night of the gig at The Baker's Dozen changed all of that.

I'd seen the girls dancing in the pub, trying to look cool and older than they were. I'd also seen them get an older guy to buy them drinks. The effect was a flush in their faces, and an increased level of confidence.

A third girl accompanied the two regular girls. I'd seen her before, but couldn't quite place where it was. I guess she looked different with make-up on, and dressed in her best clothes.

Now, I freely admit that she beguiled me. She was dark of skin, as though a light rub of coffee had been applied to her. Her hair shone brightly, like a polished chestnut, and was cut to a mid-length so that the natural waves kissed her neck and cheeks.

I found myself desirous of doing the same.

She smiled at me without disturbing her lips, her eyes alone conveying it.

For the first time in my life, I blushed with something more than mere embarrassment or shame when she did that.

As a result, I sank further into the shadows, and allowed Oggy to shine brighter.

I played with my head down for a little while, but couldn't help glancing up in the hope of seeing her once more. Each time I did, she seemed to be wherever my eyes rested.

At the end of the gig, I looked for her, but couldn't spot her.

Later, as I sat enjoying a bourbon at the studio house, I heard giggling from outside.

Figuring it was the regular two, I ignored it for a while. But I couldn't get their friend out of my head, so decided to take a look.

"You were great tonight, Tommy!" they screeched.

Well, two of them did. The third, the girl I'd hoped to see, simply nodded her approval.

I so wanted to hear her speak.

"What did you think?" I asked her.

"I thought you were very entertaining, Mr Histon," she replied, and I knew in that moment where I'd met her before.

She helped out in a general store down in the small town. On account of that, she always wore a head-covering, and was dressed in clothes befitting the job.

I'd noticed her figure and kindly way, but had missed quite how beautiful she was. Her shyness and age had always masked her from me to a certain extent.

"Please, call me Tommy," I insisted.

"Tommy," she repeated, and gave me a sense that she restated my name so she might never forget it.

I could have wept in that moment.

It shocked me, that rush of emotion.

Despite all I'd been through, I'd only cried once in my life.

66.

"You!" a man's voice cut through the dark. He advanced rapidly on, pointing a finger at me.

"Yes sir," I answered.

"Stay away from her!"

"Sir, I give you my word that nothing..."

"She's fourteen. Stay away from her," he interrupted me, snatching up the hand of the girl, and pulling her away from her friends and myself.

I knew him from the store, and began to understand he was her parent or guardian.

"Dad!" she said, resisting him. I felt her embarrassment and anger.

I also felt a compulsion to protect her.

Thoughts began flooding my brain. It was all I could do to resist the urge to act.

Two days later, when she showed up at the studio house, I should have sent her away.

I was powerless.

We chatted. That was all. Smalltalk.

I showed her around the facility. She seemed interested. It was educational. She was in her school uniform.

Nothing happened.

The next evening, she came again.

I let her sing into a microphone and recorded her. She had a very pleasant singing voice. Almost as attractive as her speaking voice. Almost as attractive as she was.

She tasted my whiskey. I had it sent up from Tredmouth through Baz Baxter. I couldn't get on with scotch.

I played her one of the songs from the new album, 'Never Come Down'. She listened through headphones, sitting on the control room floor.

She swayed her body in time, and smiled at me with her eyes.

Her legs were folded in front of her, side on, feet to her left, and her knees to her right.

Her short blue school skirt rode up, showing her thighs. A trough existed between them. Bare flesh.

I turned away. Averted my eyes.

Nothing happened.

The next evening, we danced, that was all. We danced once to my music.

At the end, she kissed me.

She kissed me. Not me her.

It caught me off guard. It was only a peck on the lips.

I should have said something to her - told her that it was wrong. Inappropriate.

I was over twice her age.

Nothing happened.

I should have sent her away after that.

But I so wanted to be around her.

I'd never known anything like it.

Her father came then.

He pointed a gun at my head.

It wasn't the first time. I thought of Lance-Rick-Cecil. He never got his settled life. A wife. Seven kids.

It was all over a woman, Clarissa, indirectly. It was all about sex. My protecting her led to it all. I couldn't let something like that happen again.

When I whipped the gun from him, I was sure to point it upwards, where it could do no real harm.

There was no bang. Nobody got hurt.

Nobody died. Not that day.

"Nothing happened," I assured him, once the gun was safely in my possession.

They went, then, father and daughter. Wordlessly.

And that was that.

67.

Today, I am writing this, my story, in real time.

I am no longer in the past or the future.

My album was completed yesterday. All we have left to do, is design the jackets.

I lie thinking on my bed in my room in Norton Basset.

At this stage in the past, on completion of a record, I felt a rush of achievement-fuelled adrenaline.

All I feel now is a terrible depression.

It's because, I know, I don't want it to be over. I don't want to leave. I don't wish to say goodbye to any of this - the process; the people; the place.

Her.

He went to Baz and Ally, her father. He told them things that weren't true. I understand that he was protecting his daughter. I told Ally as much.

I think he believed me. I sincerely hope he did.

Ally stopped him going to the police and the newspaper.

There are, I have come to realise, no aliens here.

I am safe in Britain.

Even without my medication, I am functioning normally.

I don't know why. Did something happen on that flight over? Was something about me determined finally, so that I am no longer of interest to them?

Has the snake in me finally worked its way out?

Ally Mac came to see me last night. We had a good chat after a play-through of the album. He was delighted with it.

We discussed the girl. I told him about my feelings. And my fear of them.

"We're alike, Ally, you and I," I told him. I was happy in that moment. Ally was talking about possibilities to come.

"You're booked to fly home in early-May," he reminded me. "But it's not the end."

We talked of the future. How music was changing.

Ally said, "people like the Beatles; they're writing their own songs. Technology is making things possible. People are pushing the boundaries. They're experimenting in the way you have. This album of yours? It's years ahead."

Laughing, I told him, "shit, Ally, this place! I can't see things here. How do you do it?"

"Do what?" he asked me in his hard manner.

"See the future."

"I don't."

"You don't?"

"No, Tommy. Nobody knows what the future holds. And why would anybody want to? That's a boring fucking life, if you ask me."

But I did.

And right there, for the first time, a light came on in my head.

I was the exception. I was the freak.

Am I the alien?

68.

Author's notes on a 1974 television interview with Baz Baxter and Alistair McIntyre.

Mick first told me of the interview. He recalled seeing it at the time of broadcast. It was believed lost, but in 2017, a copy was shared on the internet.

Picture and audio quality isn't great, as it was captured using a 16mm video camera pointed at the television screen.

The show was titled 'Give Us A Brake', and ran from 1972 to 1974. The episode in which Ally and Baz appeared would prove to be the final installment. Make of that what you will.

It was hosted by Tony D'Anthony, a slick-as-mud presenter, well known in the sixties and early-seventies as the self-proclaimed 'man with his finger on the pulse of Brakeshire.'

Mick's opinion of him was, "he was a twanker."

"A twanker?"

"It's a word I made up."

"Why?"

"Because you can't say twat or wanker these days."

"Why not?"

"Because some cunt will get offended."

Mick was right, Tony D'Anthony was a twanker.

He spoke with a slight American accent, even though he only spent six months there in the early sixties, and claimed to have met an uncountable number of 'stars' during that time.

In fact, pretty much any USA celebrity you cared to mention, old Tony had an anecdotal story about them that was never very amusing or even entertaining. Or particularly believable.

He'd cut his teeth on radio in Brakeshire, hosting the Breakfast Show on BrakeSound, before moving into television via the parent company, Brake Broadcasting Ltd.

'Give Us A Brake' was a ten minute interview segment, aired on a Monday at 10:50 as part of the local news. Its aim was to promote local events, whether that be via Brakeshire celebrities, or through touring musicians playing in the county.

Despite D'Anthony's best efforts to make it more 'Parkinson', it maintained the feel of a Public Information Broadcast.

It also went out live.

A last-minute cancellation led to Ally and Baz being invited on. It made sense, as they were local, available, and Tommy Histon's 'Kimono For Kip' demo tracks had just been released on Salvage Yard.

Salvage Yard was a London-based label with a knack for unearthing rare gems by cult artists. Oggy Ogden knew the owners, and facilitated the hook-up with Ally and Baz.

As a result of the demos being released, Histon's popularity had never been greater. Particularly in Brakeshire, where the songs were recorded.

This is what unfolds:

Colour television suits Ally Mac, who looks striking in a cerise trouser-suit, flared at both the cuff and hem. A few frills adorn the deep V-collar, and a silk scarf in vivid orange clashes perfectly. His wig and make-up are tastefully applied, and not over the top, and the white tasselled boots and dangly ruby earrings finish him off splendidly.

Looking at Baz Baxter, it may as well be in black and white. His suit is black and his open-neck shirt is white. His shoes match his suit which match his socks.

Still, his big open-mouthed grin is more approachable than Ally's utterly expressionless stare into the camera. The only time Ally ceases staring into the camera is when he glares contemptibly at D'Anthony.

As for the man himself, he wears his cowboy boots, lest we should forget he spent time in America, and a red jacket over a tight black polo-neck sweater. It makes his head look too far from his shoulders. White flares connect the pieces.

D'Anthony begins with a brief introduction that's scripted and accurate regarding his two guests.

It's when he gets to Tommy Histon that he begins to show his lack of preparation.

"So, Tommy Hilton," he kicks off, addressing Baz, "he, like I, arrived in these parts via the good old U S of A, is that right?"

"That's right," Baz confirms in a jovial 'delighted to be on the telly' voice.

"Histon," Ally corrects, his head snapping to D'Anthony and his eyes locked on like a heat-seeking missile.

"Yes, Tommy Histon. That's what I said, Mr McIntyre. Perhaps you should remove your hair, as it seems to be affecting your hearing - ha-ha-ha!" Just from the way he says 'Mister', you know he has a problem with Ally's transvestitism.

Ally doesn't rise to the bait.

"So, what brought His-ton to the area, Barry?" D'Anthony pushes on, "other than a transatlantic flight, I mean, ha-ha-ha!"

"Ha! Well, he came to make a record for us. We'd just launched a label at the time, Ally and myself..."

"Chemisette Records, isn't it?"

"That's right, Tony. And..."

"That's an article of women's underwear, is it not?"

"It is. So, we paid to fly Tommy over, having set up a studio..."

"Right here in Tredmouth, folks!" D'Anthony cuts in.

"Norton Basset," Ally counters.

"Do you wish to say something, Mr McIntyre?"

"The studio. It's at Norton Basset."

D'Anthony, you can clearly see, hates being picked up on his mistakes. Just as evident is the fact Ally has worked that out.

Referring to his notes, D'Anthony asks, "this record's titled 'Kimono For Kip', isn't that a fact?"

"It is," Baz confirms.

"Kimono - that's an article of ladies clothing, if I'm not mistaken." Despite him not asking a question, he directs his comment at Ally.

As a result, Ally simply stares at him and remains silent.

By this stage the tension is palpable. Baz continues grinning all the while. He's seen it all before.

"His-ton destroyed the recording," D'Anthony squirms on, "and if that's the case, how come the record is now being released ten years on?"

"Ah, well, he only destroyed the finished recording. We still had the demonstration versions on tape," Baz explains.

"You know, when I was in the States, I met the popular singer of the time, Jerry Hallam, after he invited me over to his beautiful home in Memphis. Now, there was a man's man, if ever I met one! His wife, Stephanie, was as beautiful as his home, I might add. She was all woman!

"He gave me some demonstration tapes he'd recorded, and I treasure them dearly. Indeed, I believe those rather basic versions are more precious to me than the finished songs."

"Well, it's unlikely, in Tommy's case, that the finished songs will ever be heard, so the demos are as good as it gets," Baz continues. He really is trying his best.

"What were the completed songs like, Barry?"

"I never heard them. Ally did. It was his project, to be honest."

D'Anthony looks appalled at the prospect of having to speak with Ally.

"What did you think of them, Mr McIntyre?"

"They were very impressive."

"Were you annoyed when His-ton destroyed the album?"

"Not really."

"Why not? I'm sure I would be, had I spent a great deal of money on flying him over and recording an album like that."

"Tommy wasn't well. He had some issues."

"Well, many of us have issues, it's clear to me, Mr McIntyre.

"Barry, he killed himself shortly after, isn't that correct?"

"That's right, Tony. It was very sad."

"You know, during my time Stateside, I met many stars who are no longer with us. It breaks my heart, it really does." He gazes sorrowfully into the camera.

"So, Barry," he continues, gathering himself, "you're married, correct, with children?"

"I am. I have a daughter aged eight, and a son aged six."

"Wonderful, and I can see what they mean to you by your face there! It really is a joy to witness! What about you, Mr McIntyre?"

"I can see what they mean to him, too."

"Ha! Yes, but are you, erm, married?"

"No."

"We chat about all manner of subjects on this show, Mr McIntyre, so there's no need to be afraid."

"I'm not afraid."

"Are you a homosexual?"

"Not yet."

"You either are or you aren't, Mr McIntyre, that's my understanding of 'it'. As I said, don't be afraid, we're all friends here, ha-ha-ha!"

"I like women. At the moment I'm a man. I hope to become a woman. When that happens, I shall still like women. At that point, I shall be homosexual. So, I repeat: Not yet."

"Well, best of luck with that! So, just out on record, is the Tommy Histon missing album, recorded right here in Tredmouth, and available from all the record emporiums in the area. Be sure to check it out!

"Thank you to my guests, Barry Baxter - it was a pleasure, Barry," D'Anthony says, leaning forward to shake Baz's hand. "I'd like to thank you, too, Mr McIntyre," he adds, and flutters a hand somewhat dismissively.

As is customary at the finale, the host and guests rise and assemble in the bar area of the studio, as a buxom barmaid pours them drinks. It's all done to show a certain bonhomie!

Behind the scrolling credits, Ally approaches D'Anthony. A conversation takes place, though you can only see the backs of their heads.

Baz looks on from his position along the bar as he tips a beer to his lips, still smiling, still seemingly delighted to be there.

The camera zooms in on D'Anthony and Ally Mac.

A very clear brown patch spreads at the rear of Tony D'Anthony's tight white trousers.

Within a week, D'Anthony was fired from the channel amidst a sex scandal that hinted at bondage and orgies.

He was never heard of again.

69.

Oggy suggested I join him for celebratory warm beers, but I declined his invitation. Rather, I told him I'd see him in the pub later.

Walking down to the studio, I sit in the chair I've sat in for hours alongside Oggy. Well, that was where we sat when we weren't on our hands and knees on the floor cutting and splicing audio tape.

My mind races. Why do I feel different here?

The future has caught up to me!

When I did 'Three Minute Hero' in 1949, it was what we now term a rock'n'roll album. Well, then Elvis came, along with others, and, come the late-fifties, rock'n'roll was old hat.

By then I'd recorded 'Track Back And Trail On', which was similar to what the likes of Dylan have been doing for a while. 'Coda', similarly, is perfect for right now.

Yes, the more I think about it, the world has finally caught up to Tommy Histon.

I am old hat; a music irrelevance, as things stand; a footnote nobody much cares about.

But what of 'Kimono For Kip'?

That's ahead of right now. Oggy said it - he talked about the record being like nothing else anybody was doing.

Ally Mac said a similar thing.

Am I the anomaly?

Am I the alien?

Of course, I can't win. If I am the alien, I have to do something about that. If I am human, the aliens will come again when they hear the record.

But it's more than that. The nothingness I keep seeing for myself is tied in to this album. It is only following the release that I see a darkness lying in store for me.

I've found the closest thing I've ever known to happiness. I am content right now.

Thus, I cannot take the risk.

I begin by picking up the spools of tape in my arms, and carry them out to the back yard.

It's a clear evening, but cold as a result; no blanket of cloud to insulate.

The tape spools rattle as they drop into a barrel.

Back and forth I go, loading a box with the acetates Oggy cut that very afternoon.

Stripping my lines of tape from the walls, I ball them up and add them to the box.

Oggy taught me well. I know my way around the studio and pressing plant. He showed me the whole operation, from start to finish.

Tomorrow is the day we were set to produce stampers and metal parts for the actual record pressing process.

Even the labels, depicting a snake consuming itself, are tossed into the barrel.

Finally, I mix in all of the paperwork pertaining to 'Kimono For Kip'.

A dousing of paraffin, the lighting of a cigarette, and a discarded match does the rest.

I stand and watch it burn for a while, warming myself in the heat it kicks out.

The smoke is dense and noxious as the tapes melt.

Upwards it drifts, on this still night, where any breeze will snatch it up and disperse it all over the planet.

But it shall never escape the atmosphere, and shall always be trapped here on earth.

It shall never travel at the speed of light, the sounds contained thereon, and shall not break through to unimpeded outer-space.

It shall never be heard by anything wishing to exploit it.

Stoking the pyre with a metal bar, I ensure everything is consumed by fire.

Fire has taken so much from me.

When satisfied all is ash, I pick up my belongings and walk away.

70.

Since I first saw and smelt it as a fifteen year-old, the sea has captivated me.

I sit and watch it come and go, the rhythmic back and forth of water on the shore. It feels like the end of a journey, at the point it meets the beginning of another.

And I write this, my final chapter.

This water - is it Irish Sea, North Sea or Atlantic Ocean? It's an irrelevance. It's all part of the same thing; an interlinked body that pulses and ebbs and flows in line with lunar and solar cycles, frothed and skewed by winds sourced from the same.

Momma was buried in the ground and devoured by parasitic creatures dependent on the process of decomposition.

She became soil that was taken up by plant life and transformed. Water washed her from earth and vegetation up on the slopes of the hills of my formative years, and, as gravity dictates, she flowed downstream and downriver, to this expanse of ocean dividing Virginia from Britain.

She is everywhere. She is present. She is with me.

I took a wrong turn. I exhausted the land once more. I ran out of places to move on to, and I'm so terribly reluctant to go back.

This place called Anglesey may as well be Nova Scotia. Both may as well be the end of the earth.

No music fills my ears. My thoughts are, for once, my own, constrained by a motorcycle helmet I covered in foil to contain my own self - to protect others from me.

My guitar was sold, finally, to a music store in Liverpool. I didn't get much for it, but I didn't do it for the money. Money's never much mattered to me.

I did it to sever myself from the last enduring relationship I have. For eleven years and more, that Gretsch was with me, and we experienced some things together. They are things I no longer care to think about or remember.

My words are almost written; my story almost told.

Any legacy I desire exists in four vinyl albums and this book. Three are dated and from the past. The fourth, as with this book, shall come to light when the world is ready, and only then.

Because things always do. Nothing is completely lost. Energy can neither be created nor destroyed, only transformed.

As I walked up the headland, a dozen snakes crossed my path. They regarded me, before slithering away in fear, seeking the safety of their lairs.

The water draws me in. It is the antidote to fire. Flames cannot harm me here.

"Momma," I call out, my voice weak and soon whisked away, as I project my words out to this mighty sea, "did I make you proud?"

Beyond the crash of water on stone, no answer reaches my ears.

And so I decide to go to her.

TTMH. May 2nd, 1964.

The last known photograph of Tommy Histon.
Baker's Dozen pub, Norton Basset.
April 1964.

Epilogue.

i.

More from Bill Goods' letter to his son, Danny, first published in 'Worldly Goods' in 2019.

A few weeks after I dropped him at the house over by Norton Basset, I was awoken one night by a rhythmic rapping on the door.

I got up, went down, and opened up to see Tommy Histon standing on the step. He had a crash helmet on his head, that appeared to be wrapped in tinfoil. I invited him in, but he declined.

In his hand was his guitar case. It, too, was wrapped in tinfoil.

"Can't stay. Got to run, Bill. They found me, the sons of bitches," he informed me, his index finger pointing upwards.

"Just come in, Tommy. We'll talk about it." I could see he was in a bad way mentally. His eyes were staringly mad and bloodshot, and there was sweat coating his face.

"No can do, Bill. They can't trace me with this on," he said, tapping his helmet, "but I need to draw them fuckers away from you, buddy. You still have things to do in this world."

"Do I?"

"Oh, yeah, boy. Me? I'm all used up. I have nothing more to offer. Well, let them fuckers come for me now. I'm ready," he said, and pulled up his shirt to show that he had a pistol tucked down his waistband.

"Shit, Tommy," I said. I'd never seen a real gun before. "We can sort it out, whatever it is," I urged him.

"I need a promise from you, Bill," he said, letting his shirt flop back down, and taking my hand in his.

His irises found my pupils, and I noticed the little tremor in them.

"What do you need, Tommy?"

"I need you to take this," he said, and squatted to open his guitar case.

He held out a twelve inch package that I knew was a record. I went to take it, but he held firm and didn't release his grip.

"That promise I mentioned," he said.

"What do you need me to do?"

"I require you to take these two copies of my record. One is for you to play, but only ever when you're alone. The other is the master - that should never be played by you. That is for someone else, who will collect it from you.

"When the time's right, this record will be taken by the right person, and you have to let them have it. Will you promise me, Bill?"

"I promise."

"You are the custodian, understand?"

"Yes."

"You're a good man, Bill Goods. Thank you for everything."

He walked off into the night.

For nearly fifty years I kept my promise, Danny. And now I'm dying, and this record will go to you. The second copy has never been played. The first has only ever been heard by me.

Two weeks later, I was called over to Ally Mac's. Baz Baxter was present. I remember being happy as I drove over towards Millby on that bright morning, and the prospect of spending more time with Tommy.

They told me that Tommy Histon's guitar case had been found on a beach in Anglesey. It was empty. The only other thing at the scene was a foil covered crash helmet.

His body washed up a day later.

It looked as though he'd walked out on the rocks that jutted out, and stabbed himself through his ear before slipping into the sea.

"Did you see him in the last two weeks, Bill?" Baz Baxter asked me.

"No," I replied, because I hadn't. It had been a little longer than that since he'd knocked my door.

"And he didn't give you anything?"

"Sure. He gave me an inspection," I said, and they chuckled.

Nobody ever came to collect the record.

Note: Bill's timings seem a little off here. We know Tommy entered the studio on Monday, March 23rd. At least a month was spent with Oggy in the studio, and his birthday was on April 18th, when the gig was recorded.

It's unlikely that the acetates were cut before that date, given Tommy's state of mind at the culmination of the recording process, and resulting conversation with Ally Mac.

Tommy, we now know from his own notes, died on Saturday, May 2nd.

The thinking is, Tommy visited Bill around April 24th, handed him the two acetates, and headed to Liverpool. Did he have his guitar at the time of the visit? Bill doesn't actually mention seeing it in the case. Why Tommy continued to carry the empty case is anybody's guess.

Word of his demise didn't reach Baxter and McIntyre until later that week, so perhaps around May 9th. It was probably after he missed his flight home, booked for May 8th, and outstayed his work permit.

Another anomaly in Bill's account, is Tommy telling him that aliens had tracked him to Brakeshire. Going on his own written testimony, by that stage Tommy believed he may well be the alien.

Bill could have misunderstood, but his description is pretty clear. Still, he wrote this account towards the end of his life, fifty years after it took place.

Tommy wrote his story at the time. Thus, I'm inclined to go with Tommy's version of events.

It is strange, though, that he makes no mention of the visit to Bill Goods. Was that to best protect the record, should the notebook come to light soon after May 2nd?

After all, he couldn't have known Ivan Roberts' dog would find it, and Ivan would take it home with him, where it would remain 'lost' for fifty-five years.

Anomalies remain that shall probably never be fully explained.

ii.

Tommy Histon's legacy, and regard for his music, has grown and grown over the ensuing decades. As recorded music caught up to what Tommy had done, so his contribution would be admired globally by those in the know.

Word spread, slowly but surely, on the underground music scene. It was aided by the emergence of the cassette tape during the seventies, as it made sharing easier.

Little by little, Tommy achieved the recognition he deserved, but never experienced, during his lifetime.

This was further enhanced by the release of the 'Kimono For Kip' acoustic demos in 1974. It comes as no surprise to discover they were released on the same day Progressive Pines Psychiatric Care Home closed its doors.

Histon's reputation and notoriety did his legacy no harm, either. There are countless tales on the internet of things Tommy did.

For this book, I've only included testimony from people who match Tommy's own timeline, and have a certain ring of truth about them.

What is inarguable, is that Tommy had mental health problems. He probably should never have flown to England.

Strangely, though, as I sit here typing this, I can't think of how to finish. There's a nagging loose thread in my mind. It hints at me having missed something.

There are elements of Tommy's story that don't quite add up.

Ah, but perhaps that's down to me not wanting it to end.

After all, what would I do if I didn't have the day's writing to read to Mick every evening?

iii.

Thanks to the local paper, I'm fully informed of the planned wind farms to be installed on Anglesey.

On the headland near Cemlyn Bay, I can appreciate why someone would wish to do that.

This was where Ivan Roberts walked on the morning of May 2nd, 1964.

The sea is grey and dull. White birds ride the wind, their feet dangling beneath them as they look for a glint of light to indicate the scales of a fish.

A lone man walks two dogs. They run off-lead and dive into the waves; they're braver than me.

He doesn't linger, arcing round the furthest point and heading back to the car park.

Good. I want to be alone.

A map available through the THAS shows the approximate spot where Tommy's personal effects were discovered.

I drop down from the grassy high ground. It's only a short way. Two strides cover it, and my feet scrunch on the pebbles. They're as grey as everything else on this day.

Somewhere here is where he set down his empty guitar case and crash helmet, and decided to end it all.

To best ensure I cover the spot, I begin walking side to side as I advance toward the sea. Rain, or darts of ocean, stab my cheeks anew on every turn. I'm glad I wear glasses for the protection they offer my eyeballs. I wish I didn't wear glasses because of the drops obscuring my vision.

Stopping where tide meets boots, I bend and touch the water with my fingertips. Shit, it's cold.

I take a picture on my phone to show to Mick. My hand won't stop shaking.

My scarf gets tugged higher up my face, but it only serves to deflect my warm breath on to the lenses of my spectacles, where it mists and further blinds me.

Turning my back to the wind, I begin trudging back.

"Why am I here?" I ask myself.

And then I see him!

"Tommy!" I call out.

The crash helmet spins and faces me.

I wave.

He raises his hand.

I jog as best I can on the scree under my feet, the wind propelling me along.

Christ above, it's actually fucking him!

No, no, no, no, no! He'd be nearly ninety, for fuck's sake. It can't be him.

My bloody glasses are all mist and droplets, adding a tinfoil sheen to everything.

"Sorry, I thought you were someone else," I pant once on the grassy headland once more.

"Are you here for Histon?" he asks me.

"Yes, yes, I am!" I shout back.

"Wrong place, my man. You need to be just over here a wee bit." I think he might be from Scotland.

I walk beside him for a minute or so.

"What made you come today?" I shout over the roaring elements.

"I come every week."

"Every week?"

He nods. Blimey, and I thought I was a fan.

"There," he says and points a gloved finger. Motorcycle gloves. To go with the silver helmet on his head.

"Where the birds are?"
"Aye. That's what you're here for, right?"
"What?" I call out as though he's quarter of a mile away.
"The terns!"
"The what?"
"The terns!"
"Oh, I thought you said Histon!"
"Who?"
"Tommy Histon!"
"Never heard of him, pal."

iv.

"Thanks for seeing me, Mr Roberts."

"Ivan, please," he says, as I shake his bony hand, feeling the swollen knuckle joints.

"I'm sure you get people bothering you all the time, since Tommy Histon's notebook was rediscovered."

"There were a handful at first, but not so many these last few weeks. Still, when you said you were writing a book, I thought, well now, I should let the man hear my story first-hand regarding all that!"

"Can I get you a drink, Ivan?"

"Thought you'd never ask! I'll have my usual. They know at the bar."

It's a nice place, I note, as I wait for Ivan's 'usual' and a pint for myself. We're in the club that's part of the complex, with a view of the sandy beach.

That sand makes it more inviting, as does the brightness of the day. As do the high glass windows that keep the bitterly cold wind out.

"How much?" I screech after receiving the drinks and being told how much.

"Thirteen-fifty. Three-fifty for the pint, and a tenner for the large single-malt."

I get another ten pound note out.

Ivan looks happy with his drink. As he bloody well should.

I decide to push on, in the hope we can be done before he's ready for another.

"So, I spent yesterday in Holyhead," I begin.

"Yes, I've been there once or twice," he says, and means it.

"I visited the local paper."

"Oh, right."

"I saw the report from the week after Histon."

"As you would. It was big news around here!"

I smile. "I also looked at the following week. And the next few months."

"Right. Thorough, then, eh? That's the way to be, if you're writing a book, like."

"There was no mention of a body actually being found. It was merely hearsay, according to the reports."

"Is that right? Well, the nuclear people kept it under wraps, I expect."

I nod my head and watch him over the top of my pint glass as I take a sip.

"Here, now, you're not a bloody journalist, are you?"

"No," I laugh, "just a guy trying to write a book about a man's life."

"And death, like," he adds.

"And that."

He's anxious, licking his lips, a finger tapping on his glass. A little tremor ripples the surface of his expensive beverage.

"The guitar case was reported as being found on the beach. As was the crash helmet," I inform him.

"Covered in tinfoil, they were!"

"Just like the book was."

"That's right. The dog came a-bounding over with it. You know, at first I thought it might be a fish. Or a snake!"

"Yes, so I read in an interview you did when the book came to light."

"And then I thought it might be treasure!"

"Yes, you said that as well."

"Well, I'm not sure there's much more I can add. Sounds like you know it all," he says, a tone of annoyance in his voice.

"Did he give you anything else?" I drop in.

"Just the book..."

"I thought the dog found that?"

"Yes, that's what I meant. Look, I should probably be getting on, like, if you have all you need from me."

"You met him, didn't you?" I ask, trying to sound confident; trying to sound as though I know more than I do.

I could never bluff. I always lose at cards. It takes a surprising amount of effort to maintain eye-contact and keep my face completely still.

He's weighing me up, matching my visage and meeting my eyes unblinkingly.

Ten times my pulse booms in my temples.

Did he count his?

He pushes his glass towards me. It's empty.

Taking it, I nod and stand.

Another tenner leaves my wallet.

All the while, I watch him from my half-turned position at the bar, lest he should do a runner.

His lips move, as if he's practicing what he's going to say to me. Will it be the truth, or is he rehearsing a lie? Surely the truth wouldn't require learning.

Unless he's been telling the other version of events for so long, he needs a little refresher.

"I'm in my seventies now, you know?" he informs me as I place his drink on the table.

"I know. You were born on February 4th, 1949," I think it a good idea to tell him. It all helps to make me look like I know more than I do.

Nervously, he says, "you aren't the law, are you?"

"No. Just a writer. Why?"

"Well, now, see, now... I haven't been totally honest with all that there Histon business, tell you the truth."

"You mind?" I ask, placing my phone on the table between us, my finger poised over the record button.

"I'd rather you didn't."

"Fair enough," I decide, putting it away. I don't want anything to stop him now.

"What happened, Ivan?"

He takes a deep breath. "I was fifteen, and I had a girlfriend, see. She'd finished with me the night before. Broke my bloody heart, she did. Left me for an older lad with a job and a car, and what have you."

I know all this, but I cradle my pint, and let him talk it out

"Funny thing, like, but I can't even remember her name now. Second name, I mean. June was her first name, because she was born in June.

"So, I was heartbroken that night and the next morning. I hadn't slept much. I lay there crying like a baby most of the night. Daft, really, looking back on it.

"I had an urge to get out and get some air. So, I took the dog. Smashing dog, she was. Trained for the gun by my father, like. Springer spaniel. A retriever. Could hold an egg in her mouth, and not break the shell. A raw egg, I mean! Lovely dog.

"Up on the headland, I didn't expect to see a soul. Suddenly, this bloke appears from down on the beach. To be honest, I didn't see him until I heard the dog growl a bit of a warning, like.

"I remember thinking to myself, he'll be up to no good, out and about that time of day with a bag in his hand. Smuggler, maybe? Something to do with the power station being built aways over? A bloody murderer, or similar, I thought! For a second, I was afeared for my life, I'll tell you that.

"Then he says to me, 'hey, buddy!' Well, I knew right off he was an American, like. Or Canadian, I suppose he might have been.

"'What do you want?' I says to him, thankful the dog was glued to my side protectively.

"He came closer, and I saw he was in a bad way. He was shaking with the cold. His eyes stared manically, the irises flicking constantly, like, from side to side. That said, he watched me all the while.

"There was a scar down his cheek. This side, I think," Ivan says, drawing a finger down the right side of his face, from the outer edge of his eye to the point of his chin.

"'You work for the nuclear people?' I asked, thinking they probably had Americans involved.

"'Not me, buddy,' he replied. 'You look upset. Everything okay?' "

"I told him that my girlfriend had broken off the relationship the night before. And laughed at myself, in that way you do, you know? I recall adding, 'I never saw it coming.' "

"He said a funny thing - he said, 'it's good you never saw it coming, buddy.' That perplexed me, that did, so I asked him 'why?' "

"Well, I can't recall precisely what he said then. But it was along the lines of him having things all upside down. And that he thought it was them assholes who couldn't see the future. He pointed at the sky when he said that. I looked up, but there was nothing there except a bird.

"He went on, a bit bonkers, like, saying how humans aren't supposed to see anything except the past and the here and now, kind of thing.

"I assumed he was an escaped lunatic, or similar. Especially when he started talking in a peculiar language. I looked at him funny, then, I'll tell you that. Strange thing was, the dog went right to him when he spoke it! I wondered if he was trying to speak Welsh. It wasn't like any of the Welsh I knew."

"Another?" I ask Ivan Roberts, as he drains his glass for the second time.

"Please," he replies, and I sense that this time he genuinely needs it.

On my return, he says, "you know, I'm glad I'm doing this."

"What's that?"

"Telling the truth, I suppose. A lie is a burden, I'll tell you that. It's a strange burden that gets heavier the longer you carry it. Well, either that, or we get weaker as we get older. I think carrying this fib all these years gave me this arthuritis, I do!"

"Please, carry on," I invite, his drink remaining untouched in front of him.

"So, when this man said to me, 'why did she ditch you, this chick of yours?' - I told him the reasons.

"It was surreal, talking to this crazy American stranger on the headland near Cemlyn Bay. In fact, if it hadn't been for the money and notebook, I probably would have ended up thinking I imagined it all."

"Money?" I slip in.

"Yes. When I told him about June, and why she'd dumped me, he told me he could help with that. 'Help with what?' I said to him.

"'Well, buddy, correct me if I'm wrong, but it seems to me that she might come back if you had money in your pocket.'

"I nodded at that. So he opened up a foil package he had in his shoulder bag. Inside was the notebook you know about, and more money than I'd ever seen in my life before!

"I know there was just under two thousand pounds there, because I counted it when I got home."

"What did he want in exchange?" I ask.

"He asked me if I knew what folklore was? I admitted that I wasn't really sure.

"He explained it like this, see. He said, 'folklore is stories, buddy; stories passed on by word of mouth. Tell 'em enough, and they become truth. Tell 'em in the right way, and people will attach themselves to them - fight for them; kill for them; die for them. Tell 'em long enough and hard enough, and they become a means of control. Like religion, and everything else with an agenda.'

"'Right,' I said, looking at the money. 'Wanna test the theory?' he said, looking at me looking at the money. 'It'll be June's birthday soon,' he added.

"I asked him how he knew that, and he smiled. I suppose it was obvious, in a way, that she'd be named after the month she was born in. It's like people called Holly being born near christmas.

"'So, wanna test the theory?' he asked again. 'Sure,' I replied.

"All I had to do to earn the money, was agree to keep the book safe until someone came for it, and to start a rumour that a body had been found in the sea off Cemlyn Bay. 'Tell 'em he stabbed himself in the ear, and slipped into the sea.'

"'Tell everyone who'll listen,' he told me, this Histon bloke, 'and tell 'em the fuckin' nuclear people are keeping it quiet, because they don't want anything to hold up the power plant. You understand?'

"I did. Easiest two grand I'd ever earn! People want to believe bad things, I'd come to realise. He knew that, this Tommy Histon.

"Funny, really. I've thought of him often during my life. Particularly lately, like, what with this fake news and social media, and what have you."

Finally, Ivan Roberts picks up his untouched large single-malt.

I sense he doesn't have more to say.

I have a million questions in my close-to-exploding brain.

"Where did he go?" is my first one.

"No idea. I took the package and went home. As far as I know, he remained on the headland. It was that, I think, that made me consider he perhaps did die that morning. It made the story easier to tell, I suppose, the fact that I half-believed it myself."

"You never heard from him again?"

"Never. I waited for someone to come for the book, but, in time, I forgot where I'd put it, to tell you the god's honest, like."

It's an irrelevant question, but I find myself asking, "what happened with you and June?"

"Nothing. I was so scared of having the money, that I kept it tucked away for a long time. Mind you, it did pay for my first car a couple of years later. And that did lead to me meeting my wife. She passed away, see, a few years back. Cancer. I blame the bloody power station. She did like a swim in the sea on a warm day. We do get warm days here occasionally, you know?"

"Did he give you anything else?"

"No. Nothing."

"What do you think of it all?" I ask.

"What?"

"Tommy Histon. The fact people believe he died here."

"It's sad, isn't it?"

"Why?"

"It's sad that all these people come to pay their respects, and, as far as I know, it's all for nought."

"But you never thought of coming clean before now?"

"Oh, I thought about it. I even suggested to a couple of locals - my daughter amongst them - that Histon may not have died up the road there. Well, they looked at me like I was stark raving, they did! And my daughter, Gwenda, said about economics, and how many of her guests at the B&B came because of it. She said, 'no sense in spreading a story like that!'

"So, I kept my trap shut. But I'm glad I finally told someone."

"Thanks," I tell him.

"What for?"

"For trusting me, I suppose."

"I don't. But it makes no difference, really. People will believe what they want to believe. He was right about that, was Tommy Histon."

I shake his gnarled hand again, and rise to leave.

"Thanks for the drinks," he toasts me.

"You're welcome." That's the best thirty quid I've ever spent.

"Hey!" he calls to my departing back.

"Yeah?"

"How do you know this isn't all a part of it, like?"

"A part of what?"

"The folklore. How do you know this isn't part of what he planned, for after the notebook came to light?"

v.

It's the FA Vase fixtures that give me the notion.
There it is in the listing: Histon Football Club.
It's a whim, embarked on because I have nothing better to do at this moment in time. My expectation is low.
I'd rather given up on it all. There was no trail to follow after Anglesey.
Can Ivan Roberts even be trusted?
Perhaps he resented the attention directed at others, particularly Tommy, while his involvement remained unheralded.
If he was willing to take the two grand that day, does he sniff an opportunity for more now? That said, he didn't ask me for a penny. Three large drinks was his price.
But there was no report of a body being found. Not in the local, or more national media. Only the music press reported it, and that came a little later.
There is no known grave to visit, either here or in America.
For years, I've been reading and hearing the 'conspiracy theories' surrounding Tommy. I dismissed them, as did most others I know in the circle. Theories were all they ever were. But they persisted.
The speculation covered Tommy not dying that day. But it centered more around a cover-up by the government and the nuclear plant.
More commonly heard, are the suggestions Tommy was murdered that day in 1964. Fingers have been pointed at Ally Mac, Vertoni, and even the pimps Tommy helped put in prison back in 1953. None of it rang true, though.

For my part, ever since Mick had told me Tommy died in '64, I'd never seriously questioned it.

Tommy's own story suggests the same outcome.

Or does it?

The THAS had dug into the matter. Like any detective worth his salt, John Greene followed the money. Tommy's royalties had been directed to a mental health charity since his departure to England. There was no next of kin.

Surely that implied he intended taking his own life, or foresaw his own demise?

In 2019, it became known that Bill Goods was the named beneficiary of the publishing income emanating from the 'Kimono For Kip' tracks. In light of his death, the backdated royalties went to his four surviving children. It was deemed a gesture of gratitude for Bill's kindness to Tommy.

In short, none of the income led back to Tommy. The trail ended there.

The on-line phone directory is my playground for a while. I punch in T Histon in Histon, Cambridgeshire to begin with. There's nothing. It's far too obvious.

I play around with his full name. There's a Marshall. Several, actually, within a couple of miles. It appears to be quite a common name in the area. But no Theodore or Thomas. Nothing looks or feels right.

Having exhausted all permutations, I scan my file lifted from Tommy's notes, and begin entering every name I see there. There are hits for McIntyre, Anderson and Baxter. The list of 'remote possibilities' grows longer.

Thinking about Tommy, it occurs to me that a phone wouldn't be high on his list of needs.

If Ivan Roberts was to be believed, Histon disappeared. He faked his own death, so that he might begin again.

To what end?

Not once, in all the intervening years, did he surface as the person he really was. Even as his star rose ever higher.

So - what? - he desired to be reborn. He wished to reinvent himself, and leave all that had gone before in the past.

It's in the lyrics of his final song - 'Never Come Down'.

I will be yours,
If you'll be mine for me,
Till the end of days and hours,
What little flowers remain untrodden unbowed.

The Beau of Normandy,
Offers his hand to thee,
All choice is thine, you see,
To choose which way to go and who to be.

Never come down,
Keep your feet off the ground,
Don't lay on her mound
Until she's born again amongst the trees.

Never come down,
Keep your feet off the ground,
Don't give up on your dreams
Until she flows once more amidst the streams.

Nancy took Laurie to Spain,
That they might begin again,
But cruelty will win her game
To crash and fall and hit the ground in flame.

FOLKLORIST: THE TOMMY HISTON STORY

Hello is goodbye for me,
Upward is downwardly,
The way she should go is clear
But lying in her way is all her fear.

Never come down,
Keep your feet off the ground,
Don't dare close your eyes
Before she rains on you from cloudy skies.

Never come down,
Keep your feet off the ground,
I'll keep standing by
Until she comes again once more to die.

What more can I do for you?
I shattered my head for you,
I followed my dreams
And schemes that always led me on and back to you.

I've had enough, I think,
Of all of the thoughts I think,
It's time to close my mind
And transport to a future I've defined.

Never come down,
Keep your feet off the ground,
Don't lie in my way
Until she's born again in nature's way.

Never come down,
Keep your feet off the ground,
Get out of my way

Until she's here again this time to stay.

Now we know his story, as detailed in his notes, the song changes meaning somewhat.

'Don't lay on her mound' is not the sexual reference it was always presumed to be. It must refer to the snake he encountered lying on top of the mound of earth his mother was buried beneath.

Tommy sees himself as part-snake. The fact he shattered the head of the reptile is literal. But the line is also figurative. His head was mentally shattered by her death, and the headstock of his guitar was shattered in the act.

'Hello is goodbye.' 'Choose which way to go and who to be.' 'Transport to a future I've defined.'

He wished to continue living on his own terms.

'Get out of my way, until she's here again this time to stay.' He wished to keep living for a woman. A woman who was coming back to him.

Plus, the final line of his own book reads, 'and so I decide to go to her.'

Her.

His mother, or someone else?

Ivan mentioned a shoulder bag. That was never reported as being found at the scene.

Altering tack, I shift my focus to spouses. Tommy wanted love. He did all he did for a woman, I am convinced. A female figure to settle him down to normalcy.

No. Not normal.

Happy - he always wanted happy.

'Settled. Content. Happy.'

Whoever that woman might be, she'd set up the phone. She'd look after him.

I tap in Sarah Marshall. Janie Marshall. Clarissa Marshall. The search asks me if I mean Clara? For some reason, I click yes.

And I discover that Ted Marshall, husband to Clara Marshall (nee Waters), resident of Histon, Cambs, died in 2019 at the age of 87. It's the right age, but a hell of a longshot.

Even so, I print off directions, and set off to Histon, Cambridgeshire. Specifically, to the address I have listed for Clara Marshall - and the house she's lived in for over fifty years with her loving, and loved, husband, Theodore.

Known to his nearest and dearest as Ted.

vi.

Histon is a village I've never visited prior to today, but it has a familiarity. It could easily sit in the flat terrain of west Brakeshire, rather than south Cambridgeshire.

"Can I help you, mate?"

He's wearing shorts in winter. Always a dangerous sign. They best show off his tattoos. He's a big guy, I'll give him that.

"Sorry," I say, because it's what we're conditioned to say.

"You from the agent?"

"Agent?"

"Estate agent," he elucidates.

"No, sorry."

"You were staring at the house."

"Yes! Sorry about that. I was looking for the people who live here. The Marshalls."

"Long gone, mate. We're fixing this up. Modernising, and all that. To be rented out. Or sold."

"Oh, right. Do you know anything about the previous owners?" I fish.

"Nothing. I'm from Cambridge. Just a contractor. I fix up properties for the new owner."

"Understood."

"I thought you said you knew them - the previous lot?"

"No, no, just that I was looking for them."

"Well, the husband died, I heard. So the lady cleared off to somewhere more manageable."

"Clara?"

"Yeah, that's her name. She moved back to Brakeshire, I heard."

"Brakeshire? That's where I'm from."

"Good for you."

"Moved back, you said?"

"Look, mate, I met her once, very briefly. And I'm fairly sure she said she was from there. That's all I know."

"Why did you meet her," I ask, "if she'd sold the house, I mean?"

"She showed up. Said she wanted to see if she'd forgotten anything. Like I said to her, we'd gutted the place by then. There was nothing of any value, I can tell you that. I told her that, an' all."

I don't know what else to ask.

He fills the pause with, "tell you what, even at her age, I would! If you know what I mean. Very tasty! Hey, are you planning on seeing her?"

"I might. Yes. Why?"

"Well, there was one thing. I hadn't really gone through the attic when she came. Hang on," he says, and jogs back into the house.

It's a nice looking property, probably enhanced lately by the fresh paint and external work.

Detached and private, with a half acre of land distributed evenly around it, it feels remoter than it is. Even this time of year the high hedges remain green and full, screening it on all sides. The driveway I stand on is angled, so that you have to enter in before anything is revealed.

Did Tommy Histon cut the grass here?

I count the rooms via the windows. It must be three-bedroomed, with an upstairs bathroom betrayed by frosted glass. Downstairs, I imagine a dining-room, living-room, kitchen, toilet, and perhaps a spacious hallway on entry.

Wooden fences stop me seeing in the back.

"Never even saw it at first," the big guy says as he re-emerges, "it blended in with the lagging, being dark up there, and with it being wrapped in foil."

My heart skips a beat.

"I opened it," he says, "just to see what it was. Anyway, she may want it. Clara, I mean. It's just photos and stuff, by the looks. Nothing I could make head nor tail of. But it might be... What do you call it? Sentimental value."

"I'll make sure she gets it. Don't suppose you know where in Brakeshire she is?"

"Oh, Christ, now you're asking. Say some places, and I'll know it when I hear it."

"Tredmouth?"

"Nah. I've heard of that. I hadn't heard of this place."

"Millby? Oakburn?"

"Two words, it was."

"Jemford Bridge? Palmerton Chase?"

He shakes his head.

"Norton Basset?"

A click of his fingers accompanies, "that's it!"

So, the woman I believe to be Tommy Histon's widow, went back to the place where he recorded his final album, and left behind a foil-wrapped package.

It can't simply be coincidence.

Then again, this does relate to Tommy Histon, so who knows?

vii.

It's a modest bungalow in a cul-de-sac ringed by modest bungalows, an easy stroll away from the small town centre at Norton Basset.

She is not Clarissa Vertoni. I know that instantly. She has olive in her colouring, unlike Clarissa's whiteness. Besides, Clarissa would be in her nineties.

Her hair is lightened by grey, but dark where pigment remains, and her eyes remind me of drops of warm toffee.

"Do I know you?" she asks me.

"No. No you don't. I was down in Cambridgeshire yesterday, and the builder on your old house asked me to drop this in to you. He found it in the attic."

"Oh, and you drove all this way?"

"Ah, I live in Tredmouth, so it wasn't far out of my way."

"Even so, it's very kind of you. What is it?"

Rather than answer, I hand her the bundle, now safely stored in a padded envelope.

She turns it over in her hands, and peers inside. There's no sign of recognition on her face; no jolt of excitement or cloud of concern. She looks perplexed, if anything.

"It was already wrapped in the tinfoil. I put it in the envelope."

"Tinfoil. How strange?"

Was that a little twitch of worry at the corner of her mouth? She resets her face before glancing up at me.

"Is this a joke?" she asks tentatively. I get a sense that she's hoping it is.

"No," is my simple reply.

"I'll have a proper look later," she decides.

"I did take a little peek at the contents," I inform her. "Sorry about that."

"Oh, I'm sure it won't be anything you shouldn't see!"

"And I'm sorry for your loss, Clara."

That comment brings him back.

I imagine she tries to block him out when in company. But my expression of condolence forces her to depict him in her mind. She blinks away the moisture that springs into her eyes.

"Thank you," she whispers.

She could pass for mid-fifties, comfortably, but must be quite a bit older than that.

And she's incredibly beautiful. Everything about her oozes gentleness and dignity. She appears taller then she is, and has perfectly sculpted features. Nothing about her is too large or too small.

Her eyes are clear and bright, and form little smiles that preempt her lips taking on that shape.

I'm utterly captivated by her voice.

I can't do this. I can't do what I came here to do.

"I should go. I just wanted you to have that," I say, and nod my appreciation for her time. "Sorry to disturb you."

"I was fourteen when I met him," she says to my back as I walk away.

The hairs on my neck stand up.

I stop dead in my tracks, but don't turn round.

She continues. "He was thirty-two. Nothing happened. Not like that. I wanted it to. But he insisted we wait until I was of age. He was such a good, good man. I've never met another man who would have done what he did.

"He waited for me for over three years. He found a way to change his identity. Someone from his past gave him the notion to do that."

"Lance," I say.

"That's right. He simply didn't want to be Tommy Histon any more. I think he was sick and tired of being that person."

Finally, I turn to face her.

And I can't help but rush to her and allow her to lean against me, her body convulsing, as, silently, tears stream from her toffee eyes.

"I shouldn't have come," I say into the top of her hair.

"Well, you did," she manages, her voice surprisingly calm despite the emotion. "I had a thought someone would piece it together. As soon as I read about the record being discovered, and the notebook being found."

She needed to talk about him. She needed to tell someone.

"What do you want, Clara? What do you want to happen, I mean?"

"I want him back."

I can't do that for her.

"I need a cup of tea!" she says brightly, clasping the package between her hands. "Would you like one?"

"I'd love one. Thanks."

viii.

Did Tommy Histon sit on this chair? Did he drink from this cup?

"How was Tommy? Cognitively, I mean," I ask, as delicately as I can.

"Oh, generally fine. He had little episodes, but he found a peace in life. He had to take medication right till the end, but, over time, they got that sorted out, and he lived a comfortable life."

"As Ted Marshall?"

"That's right. But there was always a cloud sitting a little way off, and threatening to blow over us any minute. All it would take was for someone to connect the scar on his face with the one on Tommy's. Or for someone from the past to bump into him in the street.

"He grew a beard to disguise it, but the hair wouldn't grow where the scar was. So, I made him shave, and covered it with make-up!

"You know, for years he didn't have a clue how well regarded he was. It was only when I got a computer, and looked him up, that we had any idea."

"How did that make him feel?"

"Chuffed, I know. Quietly chuffed, I suppose, that he finally got the recognition he deserved. Or, rather, his music did. But worried, too, that the interest in him might lead to him being discovered."

"How did he explain his American accent?"

"He didn't. He was always such a good mimic, and his accent was half-English anyway, living in the hills as a child in the way he did. Part of his cover-story was spending a few years in Canada before moving here during the war, so any strange phrasing was attributed to that. Nobody ever twigged."

"Why live in Histon? Just because of the name?"

"I suppose. And because that was where his family were from. Originally, I mean, before they moved to America a couple of hundred years before he was born. His name, after all, came from the place.

"But it was far enough from Brakeshire for both of us to feel safe. Well, as safe as we could ever feel. And the more time that passed, so the more we relaxed."

"Both of you?"

"Yes. I left home to be with him. My parents believed I'd emigrated to New Zealand just before christmas of 1966. I went there, but, unknown to them, returned in July of '67 to be with Tommy.

"My father was glad to see the back of me. The police had questioned him after Tommy disappeared, because he'd made threats and so on.

"He threatened Tommy with a gun. It was fake, but Tommy couldn't have known that. Tommy disarmed him in a heartbeat! I was so impressed by that, as a fourteen year-old girl. Whoosh! And it was safely in Tommy's hand!"

She smiles wistfully at the memory. I notice how often she says his real name. She's not been able to say it to anybody in fifty-five years.

"How did you get away with them thinking you were on the other side of the world?"

"I had a friend there. I'd send her letters and birthday cards, and so on. And she'd post them on, as if they came from me. I was adopted, and in '69, my step-parents moved to Canada. I visited a couple of times."

"You must have missed them, though?"

"I did at first. My mum more than my dad, I suppose. But I chose Tommy. I couldn't have both. They didn't approve. And they wouldn't have kept our secret."

"Did you have children?" I ask, and feel clumsy for the question.

She shakes her head. "It never happened. Not through a want of trying or wishing."

"Clara, what do you want me to do?" I ask again.

She takes her time as she takes stock. "For so long, I've kept it a secret."

Recalling what Ivan Roberts, said, I add, "and it weighs heavy, I bet?"

"Yes. It does. When I first saw you and the foil-wrapped package, I was filled with dread. But now it's dawned on me - the secret was kept for Tommy's sake, because I feared for what exposure might do to him. Well, he's dead. I suppose he died that day on Anglesey, and that allowed Ted Marshall to be.

"And now Ted Marshall is no more. Perhaps it's time people knew Tommy's story. Does that make sense?"

"Perfectly. You know I'm writing a book on Tommy? That's what led me to you."

"Really? From his notes?"

"Yes."

"The truth, then, finally? Rather than all the nonsense on the internet," she proposes.

"Exactly."

"Then you should make it the complete truth."

"And what about what's inside the envelope?" I ask.

"Those too. It's time people knew it all."

"Okay," I agree.

"He always said someone would come when the time was right."

She slides the contents out onto the table between us, and we set about laying them in the sequence denoted in Tommy's hand on the reverse.

Cropped polaroid photographs begin to fall into place as a picture forms like a jigsaw puzzle.

It's a depiction of an album titled 'Hereafter'.

Lines and lines of sticky tape are revealed, on the walls of a house in Histon. They denote every drum beat, plucked guitar string and lyric; every cymbal, key depression, bass and other sound. Hyphenated numbers spell out the melodies.

As composed by Tommy Histon.

So that "the fuckers might not hear it and come looking for me."

ix.

We chat as we build the puzzle.
"What else did Tommy do with his time? With his life, I suppose I mean?"
"Oh, he was a quiet man. He kept himself mostly to himself. Don't get me wrong, we'd talk, the two of us, all the time. And he said that was enough for him.
"I needed more, so pursued my career. I had my own interior design company."
"Did Tommy work?"
"Yes. He would repair old furniture for me. He could usually be found in the garage working on some project or other. He loved working with wood, and he had a talent for it. He learnt to cut dovetail joints and so on. There wasn't much Tommy couldn't restore to its former glory."
"And did he always retain an interest in music?"
"Mmm, no, not at first. I got him a guitar as a fortieth birthday present. So, 1972. That rekindled his interest, I think. He made his own guitar one winter, a few years after.
"He'd never perform, though, for obvious reasons, and would only play for me, or when he was alone."
"Did he keep track of music trends?"
"No, not really. Actually, I suppose he did. He always had the radio on in his workshop or room. But he bought very few records over the years. I probably had more than him. He'd always let me choose the music we listened to."
Clara drifts away. I imagine she's recalling an evening they spent together, and the music playing. I leave her to go there on her own, and finish my tea.

After a silence, I ask, "how did he do it? How did he fake his own death?"

"Alisha made it all possible."

"Alisha?" I know that name.

"Ally Mac, as she was known for years. But Alisha for the later part of her life."

"I don't understand."

"Of course you don't. That was the only way it would ever work, if nobody knew."

"Ally Mac knew?"

"Tommy went to Ally, and talked things through. He was too smart to cross Ally Mac. You probably wouldn't know, but Ally was someone you didn't betray."

"I've heard and read the stories."

"He told Ally about me, and that we wished to be together, but only when I was old enough to know my own mind.

"It was a violin that clinched it. Tommy had inherited it a few years before. He knew it was worth a lot of money. And so did Ally.

"That violin enabled our love."

"Ally Mac knew?" I repeat, trying to work it all through in my head, and relating it to all I know about the characters involved.

"Yes! Tommy said, 'I don't want to be this person any more.'

"To which Ally replied, 'nor do I,' and they set about their plan.

"The violin was sold, and they shared the money. It facilitated both of them achieving their dreams."

"How do you mean?"

"Well, it allowed Tommy to become Ted Marshall, and be with me. And, years later, it enabled Ally to become Alisha, and all that involved."

"Ally let Tommy destroy the album?" it suddenly occurs to me.

"Yes. As I said, he knew the value of the violin. There was no guaranteed return on the record. Ally made a smart business decision, and took the safest option."

"So, who knew about all of this?"

"Ally, Tommy and myself. Other people added to the myth, and Tommy made sure that he rewarded them. The young man he encountered in Wales was paid handsomely. There was a man in Brakeshire, Bill someone..."

"Bill Goods?"

"That's right. Tommy felt bad for visiting him and using him in his scheme, so he registered the royalties to his album in his name, and left him the two surviving copies. Tommy couldn't quite destroy it completely."

"Bill didn't know the truth?"

"No, but he was part of the folklore, as Tommy termed it. His biggest surprise, I think, was that neither of the two cashed in. The book and records remained a secret until just after he passed away."

I want to ask how Tommy died, but can't bring myself to. Instead, I opt for, "how did he disappear?"

"Ally got him a new identity, but I don't know the ins and outs."

"And Baz Baxter - he wasn't aware?"

"No. Ally settled that financially, so the company didn't suffer. Baz hadn't wanted Tommy in the first place, so never asked too many questions."

"Ally Mac made it all happen," I state again, for no other reason than I'm still processing it all.

"She'd look in on Tommy every so often. Ally was often down in London, and always made a point of calling in on us."

"Nobody ever twigged? Even though there was no actual body?"

"No. Tommy knew the power of folk stories. Through Ally, and the lad he met in Anglesey, it was enough to sow the seed. The risk was, that somebody would blab. But they never did. Or, if they did, nobody believed them."

I'm speechless.

All the pieces of the puzzle are in place, and laid out before me.

I sense that it's time for me to depart. I have the full story now. Well, perhaps not full, but as much as I need.

As I rise, I turn to Clara, still sitting at the table.

"Was he happy?"

She touches the photos with her fingertips, and a playful little smile accentuates her charm, as she straightens a couple ever so slightly.

"Tommy used to say, 'happiness is when you have no need to look up or down. No need to look backward or forward. No need to look to the side, or even too deeply inside yourself. Happiness is when everything in the world you care about is right in front of you, and you can stop searching.'"

"Yes," she adds, "I think he was happy."

I'm glad he found a place to settle in the end.

"I'll make sure you see the book before it goes to print. If there's anything you aren't comfortable with, I'll remove it. It's been a pleasure meeting you, Clara."

"Likewise. If you don't mind me saying, you don't look too happy yourself," she points out.

"Ah, is it that obvious?"

She shrugs.

"A friend of mine. He had a stroke a couple of months ago."

"I'm sorry. How is he?"

"Recovering. Slowly. But I fear he'll never be the same as he was."

She regards me for a few seconds. "He's still the same person. Ted was always still Tommy on the inside. It made no difference that he was no longer a musician. If you love someone, you don't care what they do."

"Thanks," I say, "for your time and candidness."

She walks to the door with me. "He'd tell me every day that he loved me. Every single day for over fifty years.

"If I was away, he'd write the three words on a piece of paper, date it, and seal it in an envelope, so I could read it on my return. On my trips to Canada, I'd return to a whole stack of them.

"He told me there was someone he knew - a friend. A woman, I mean, from his past.

"Well, his biggest regret was not telling her that he loved her when he had the chance.

"He vowed he would never get caught in that way again."

"Thank you. See you soon," I say.

"I hope your friend's okay."

x.

A vivid red drape jacket hangs in the room where Mick can see it. It enfolds a black shirt trimmed with red stitched detailing. On the floor sit his black leather brothel creepers.
They are his carrot; his incentive. His dearest wish is to don them and take Trudy jiving once again.
I tell Mick about the last two days. He listens. He likes to hear what I get up to. It isn't as though he can get out and about at the moment.
As a result, I come round most days and tell him my tales.
Speech is difficult for him, but his right arm is much improved. He can make signs with it - a thumb up for yes, a swipe of his hand for no, and a wanker sign for anything else.
I tell him about Tommy and Clara until, eventually, I run out of words.
"I'd better get going, Mick. I've not eaten since this morning."
He gives me a thumb up.
I stand at the door looking at his twisted mouth, and his slim form, his muscles wasting away through inactivity.
I can't show him my pity. It would destroy him.
Before I can stop myself, I find I've uttered the words, "I love you."
Vulnerability causes me to blush furiously, my throat painfully tight.
With a huge effort on his part, I witness his mouth stretch, and his neck go taut as he forces himself to speak.
"Fuck you," he slowly says, and I hang my head and laugh through my nose.
He's always had the ability to annihilate me.

He's still Mick.

Along with Tommy Histon, he's still my hero.

"See you tomorrow, mate."

He swipes his hand in the 'no' gesture.

"You don't want me to come?"

He swipes his hand again.

"Okay, Mick. If that's what you want."

Shit, the bloke must be so ashamed for me to see him like this. I shouldn't keep coming.

I turn to leave, and jump as I nearly bump into Trudy standing by the door.

"Say it again, Mick," she orders him. "Remember what the speech therapist said. Push your tongue against the back of your teeth."

Another monumental effort buckles his face.

"Thank you," he forces from his mouth, and Trudy insists I stay for my tea.

The end.

For more information on Tommy Histon and his music, please visit-

https://chemisetterecords.wixsite.com/mysite

or search 'Chemisette Records'.

Facebook - come join us at 'Tommy Histon Appreciation Society'.

Thank you for taking the time to read this book. It is very much appreciated, and we sincerely hope you enjoyed it.

A **Morning Brake** Publication.
Contact chemisetterecords@gmail.com

Other works by Andy Bracken:

Novels set in Brakeshire and elsewhere:

- Folklorist: The Tommy Histon Story
- Worldly Goods
- Across The Humpty Dumpty Field
- Reflections Of Quercus Treen and Meek
- The Book Burner
- Clearing
- The Decline Of Emory Hill
- What Ven Knew
- Gaps Between The Tracks (deleted)
- Beneath The Covers (deleted)

Non-Fiction:
- Nervous Breakdown (The Recorded Legacy Of Eddie Cochran)

Printed in Poland
by Amazon Fulfillment
Poland Sp. z o.o., Wrocław

54823664R00221